The Gravity of Death

Tales of Mystery:
The Gravity of Death

An Inklings Press publication
Copyright @2024 by Inklings Press
ISBN 978-1-7362760-5-1

No AI was used in the creation of this book or the contents therein.

Cover design: Ricardo Victoria Uribe

Follow Inklings Press on Twitter @InklingsPress
Find us on Facebook at
www.facebook.com/inklingspress
Website
www.inklingspress.com

Tales of Mystery: The Gravity of Death includes the following stories:
"Ghosts That Go With Us", by Lin Darrow, © 2024 Lin Darrow
"A Unique Murder", by Christopher Edwards, © 2024 Christopher Edwards
"The Empty Room", by Stetson Ray, © 2024 Stetson Ray
"Revolver", by Steven Lord, © 2024 Steven Lord
"Death Warmed Over", by William Lehman, © 2024 William Lehman
"Storycrime", by Callum Henderson, © 2024 Callum Henderson
"Agatha's Last Mystery", by Matthew Kresal, ©2024 Matthew Kresal
"The Law North Of The Pecos", by Ed Teja, © 2024 Ed Teja
"A Matter of Some Gravity", by Tom Jolly, © 2024 Tom Jolly
"Not Tomb Enough To Hide The Dead", by Lee Allred, © 2024 Lee Allred
"Men Of Glass", by Bill McCormick, © 2024 Bill McCormick

Table of Contents

Foreword

I've always had a warm spot in my heart for Noir work. The hard-bitten gumshoe, the burned-out cop, the hooker with the heart of gold. The classic works by guys like Spillane, and the new stuff by folks like Jim Butcher, and Larry Corria. actors like Bogart, and Harrison Ford, with roles like Sam Spade, Rick Deckard, or Keanu Rieves' Jonny Mnemonic.

Noir, and its close relatives can take place in any time, in any genre. Historical, Science Fiction, Fantasy, you name it, you can put a Noir work in it. It doesn't even have to be a mystery, though it usually is. The rules for Noir, in my mind at least, are simple. The characters must be flawed, human, no alabaster saints here! This isn't the bright and beautiful people here; this is Joe Everyman. The government is also flawed, or out and out crooked. The villains are strait up evil. The Hero has a past, did some things that haunt him or her, and is just trying to make their way through this veil of tears.

Not all of the stories in this collection are noir, but most of them are, or noir adjacent. They are all some flavor of mystery. Mystery too has some rules: All the facts have to be available to the reader. They can be glossed over, hidden among a bunch of red herrings, or your attention can be diverted to avoid "the man behind the curtain," but they have to be available. No Deus ex Machina. The mystery must be solved at the end. If we don't know who done it, it's not the end. Well at least usually.

We have here eleven stories, from the speakeasys of depression era Massachusetts to life on a starship, but they have one thing in common: Violent crime.

In The Ghosts That Go With Us, we learn that in the future any crime can be solved, for a price… All you have to do is find someone that's willing to pay it.

A Unique Murder Explores the question of: is suicide also murder?

The Empty Room is a "locked room mystery" with a decided twist.

Revolver will make you ask when murder is justified.

Death Warmed Over is the only non-murder story in the group. It deals with eco-terrorism and arson.

Storycrime is a murder, with a multiverse twist.

Agatha's Last Mystery involves a 'true-crime' documentarian in an alternate universe investigating the murder of the most famous mystery writer of them all.

The Law North of the Pecos brings a PI in touch with help from a most unusual source.

A Matter of Some Gravity is reminiscent of the late great Isaac Azimov's Science Fiction Mysteries, with missing valuable cargo, murder, and intrigue in the asteroid belt and beyond.

No Tomb Enough to Hide the Dead deals with law enforcement of a different sort. Vampire Law.

Finally, Men of Glass is a story of murder and possession, in Lovecraftian style.

Enjoy them all, I did.

- By William Lehman,
Author of the John Fisher Chronicles

Ghosts That Go With Us
By Lin Darrow

It was the disappearance of the bubblegum heiress on the hyper-speed glass train. That was the case that got me killed for the first time.

Lily Gong, heir to the Gong Bubblegum Company fortune, went missing on a train. The Orbital Lightspeed Train was, at the time, the fastest train known to man, capable of making the trip between New York and Toronto in twenty-three minutes. On the maiden voyage, hordes of celebrities had booked flashy luxury compartments—including Lily and her fiancé, immersive film director John Faraday.

Lily boarded the Orbital in Toronto. When it docked in New York, she was gone. In 20 minutes, she disappeared on a train moving at inhuman speeds, with giant glass doors specifically designed to encourage ogling. The only evidence left behind was her wedding dress, which mysteriously appeared in the coat room, lying on the floor like an evaporated body.

Internet sleuths exchanged theories for over 20 years. They poured over blueprints of the train, accusing everyone from rival socialites to aliens. Most popular were the theories that Lily had faked her own kidnapping to promote her livestreamed wedding.

Had it been a publicity stunt gone wrong? A murder, planned by a bitter train employee or a fame-hungry fiancé? A covered-up suicide?

In 20 years, nobody had been able to crack it.

So, I volunteered to do a memory dive for the first time and get answers.

"You've been through the training," the doctor said. "You

understand the risks."

"As much as anyone ever can understand what it's like to re-live the memories of a murder victim," I said dryly. (At the time, I was still refusing to examine why I wanted to do the dive — later, I would lose my sarcasm entirely).

Ten years ago, scientists cracked a method by which memories could be extracted from DNA. The only problem was this: memories aren't compatible with screens or microphones. They exist only in the mind. So, the mind is needed to 'read' them. At first, they were only able to extract around thirty seconds of memory from the point in time when the DNA sample was left behind. But nowadays, scientists can extract up to an hour.

I was selected out of 1800 applicants to do the dive into Lily Gong's case. After about six months of training modules, psychological examinations and physical tests, Wei Back Memory Extraction Inc finally brought me into their test lab.

Once you're in, they hook you up to a thousand sensors on a bed surrounded by an entire garden of wiring. Logically, you know that careful calculations are being made to anesthetize you to the level of consciousness required to trigger the dive. Psychologically, it feels a lot like you're standing over dark water, mentally preparing to jump and hoping you haven't misjudged the distance to the bottom. (Some crime junkies call it 'murder spelunking').

The DNA was taken from the wedding dress. The memory is about 45 minutes long, and I come-to just a Lily is meeting John, her fiancée, at the Orbital Station. He is handing her a gigantic bouquet of roses — big enough to photograph well, she notes, as cameras flash hungrily around them.

That's where the memory begins. I'm a passive wisp locked in Lily's head, watching as she is led across the station by John's firm hand at her back, irritated that he has to direct their romance as though it's one of his films. I'm still wading in the surface of her thoughts, imagining a bright house of light around my sense of self, which is what the training vids tell you to do.

Eventually, the windows of that bright house will start to lift, and Lily's thoughts will seep in like mist. I'll start thinking of myself as 80 percent Annie, 20 percent Lily; then it'll run down to 50/50, and then 10/90. But the longer you remember who you are, the better chance you have at surviving the extraction.

See, in memory diving, you can't just watch from a distance, safe and disconnected. You've got to be in somebody's head, deeply enmeshed in their thoughts and feelings and nerve-endings like the innermost knot of the thickest briar-patch.

If you pull back, your brain snaps like a twig. All your memories and the victim's memories will flood violently together, eliminating all the mental barriers between *you* and *them*. There's a medical term for what this does to your brain, but to memory detectives, we call it 'going with them.'

You've got to stay until you're dead if you want to come back.

(Sometimes the victim isn't dead, of course, or doesn't die within the extractable timeframe — but frankly, that's rare. In those cases, you just have to stay 'til the end, whenever that might be).

Everyone is gawping at Lily as she boards the Orbital with John. Cameras flash as she fights to keep a mounting tide of sorrow dammed in her chest. She smiles, and her lipstick cracks. She waves at reporters as she enters her glass-walled compartment, poses for photos that will later be poured over by crime junkies for clues.

Eight minutes into the trip, Lily stands. We walk past rows of ritzy glass compartments. Socialites clink champagne and fake laughter for roaming reporters. Internet sleuths have plotted this trip on virtual maps, trying to account for my — for *Lily*'s whereabouts.

Once I leave my compartment, there's about fifteen minutes left in the timeline.

Lily is not aware she is pacing history into being. She is thinking of a man named Miles. Of his soft platinum-blonde hair, bleached to disguise early hints of silver. Of his love for old books with gilt pages, treasures from a time before everything was virtual. Of his feminine way of holding cigarettes, his high-pitched laugh, which makes Lily laugh in turn.

Her mother has threatened to disown her if they're seen together. It's something about money, and politics. Miles is a wild intellectual disowned from his inheritance for his radical beliefs.

The Gongs, meanwhile, are the height of conservative respectability, generational politicians all.

Nobody has ever connected Miles Rake to Lily Gong, beyond that both belong(ed) to wealthy Toronto families. *Now*, I know they met in secret, in the back rooms of decadent but discrete parties. Mostly, though, they conducted their affair at a tragic distance, whispering through the immersive telephone every night, their holographic forms projected into each other's bedrooms.

It's been two years since Lily decided she couldn't do it anymore. She still has a letter in her pocket—a real paper letter—that Miles slipped her afterward.

In that letter are such promises; such lush words of love and longing, of agony long repressed, straining through the holographic pixels of long-distance calls and across crowded rooms filled with hungry cameras.

We both simmer in the sadness and romance of all this. The upcoming wedding is drudging it all up, like roots grown too deep in the dark soil of her soul, ripped suddenly and terribly free.

At last, she steps into the coat room.

For 20 years, digital sleuths will practically break their necks trying to peer into this moment. They'll enhance images of the door to trace my silhouette, or theorise about hidden compartments. All anybody knows is that Lily entered and never came out.

Lily peers at herself in the mirrored wall, wondering why her heart refuses to release Miles from the cage of her memory.

If she will ever be happy again.

The dam breaks, and grief comes over her like a wave. She grabs the sleeve of a fur coat and weeps into it uncontrollably.

One of the big questions of this case is this ten-minute gap. What was Lily doing for ten whole minutes in the coat room, before the dress was discovered? Was this part of the plan to stage a dramatic kidnapping that would slather her name across hundreds of headlines just before her high-profile wedding?

Turns out, she was crying.

What happens next is quick. Lily is far braver than anyone in the press will ever give her credit for. She hauls her trunk off the bottom shelf and erases the address from the holographic label. In its place, she writes Miles's address from the letter.

And then—Lily *steps inside the trunk*, and shuts the lid.

I'm going to see my lover. My family can't stop me. My fiancé doesn't even know I hate roses. I'm going to disappear into the circle of his arms, evaporate like water into the sunshine of his kiss. For love, I will disappear.

Lying in the dark of the trunk, I shut my eyes. Tears are cold on my face. I press my cheeks into the silk of my wedding dress.

(She took the dress without John knowing! Why, even Lily doesn't know.)

A feeling of revulsion sweeps over her at the touch. Defiantly, she uses her phone to unlock the trunk wirelessly and tosses it out, where it falls artfully across the floor.

That's where the DNA sequence ends.

It took me a week to recover and answer the Wei Back agents' questions.

My name is Annie Keller. Thirty-two years old. I used to co-own a taxidermist's shop because I used to be a whimsical person, before life and taxes got in the way. My father is African American and my mother is French Canadian. I have no living siblings and I don't like talking about my feelings.

I am not Lily Gong.

We found a security video of the trunk being loaded onto another train headed for Eastern Canada. The records don't go far back enough to verify if Lily's trunk made it or not. We know she *could* unlock it with a handy phone app, but something could easily have gone wrong.

We did learn that Miles lived for 50 years with a woman named Poppy Tripton, out on Prince Edward Island. The two were glamorously reclusive and happily friendless. Any photos were obscured by Poppy's love of giant vintage sunglasses and jewel-toned headscarves.

Analysts thought there was a case to be made that 'Poppy' might be Lily. But others felt it was more likely that Lily had suffocated in the trunk. In this theory, whoever had found her— homeless rail-riders, unlucky train attendants—had disposed of the body, too afraid to come forward due to the high-profile nature of the case. If I was some nobody who just happened to trip onto the corpse of the century, I'd get nervous too.

So, though the mystery was solved, some questions remained. Did Lily make it out to the ruby-red sands of P.E.I. and live out her happy ending with Miles? Or did she die slow, stuck in a trunk with too little air, too depressed to free herself?

Sometimes, I'll get asked, what do you think? You were there with her, in the trunk. I'll usually cite privacy clauses to avoid thinking about it too much. But here's my real answer, and you can take it however you want.

None of my other dives ever had happy endings. So I'd like to believe in this one.

• • •

After Lily, Wei Back hired me to do more memory extractions. They needed detectives who were quiet, dispassionate, and focused. Some experience with trauma was mandatory, but you couldn't be too emotional about it — you had to be cold and buttoned-up, forged by pain into a statue-like reserve. I checked the boxes.

I did keep a picture of Miles in my cubicle. They told me that was normal. I'd carried Lily's love back with me as though it was my own.

That was when I realised — even if you come back, you never come back 100% *you*. A small, two-percent part of my brain was now irreversibly Lily. They told me that number would shrink as I made new memories in the real world.

That was their mistake — assuming I was interested in new memories over old ones.

Next, I took on an actual murder. Nora Mayfield, a dancer found strangled to death with her own pearls in her dressing room. Nora worked for a 1920s-themed speakeasy featuring live entertainment aimed at flush tourists. During the dinner rush, she got nine full minutes to dance a Ginger Rogers-themed number, complete with a holographic Fred Astaire.

They got about seven minutes from Nora's DNA, taken off the

pearls.

There were two suspects, neither of whom were ever arrested:

1.   Dean Carp, a fellow dancer who performed the choreography that the projection of Holo-Fred Astaire was mapped onto, so that Nora could do the lifts.

2.   Amar Black, the understudy for Holo-Fred.

All we had was a witness tip that a holographic Fred Astaire had entered Nora's dressing room and left it seven minutes later. The Fred overlay came from a headpiece worn by the dancer. The theory went that only a 'Fred' would know how to operate it—either Dean was framing Amar, or Amar was framing Dean.

So, when I made the Nora Mayfield dive, I fully expected to be murdered by an old Hollywood song-and-dance man.

I came-to as Nora was stroking her pearls.

I've barely got any time to sort through her blurry, boozy thoughts. Most of them are self-deprecating, chipping away at the hard stone of her perfectionist's soul like chisels. The lift wasn't smooth enough; she stumbled over the footwork in the last song; she forgot to smile through the big turn. It's not enough to be a pale imitation of Ginger Rogers—she wants to be *better*.

Amar, endlessly sweet, tells her not to be so hard on herself. Dean is more driven, more of a perfectionist—just like her. *He* tells her to practice, practice, practice; to get over her 'mental barriers to greatness.'

Nora is drunk from the heartbreak of having a dream. Of longing to be great, and worrying that though your heart is fierce, your body will not carry you there.

The door opens. Drowsily, I turn to greet the flickering Fred Astaire behind me.

"Amar?" she guesses. "Dean?"

The very question web-sleuths have been asking for years.

Fred's face is blank, as though the animation has glitched, and no expression has been uploaded to his digital face. It's a simple thing, then, for him to step forward, seize my pearls, and *pull*.

Nora fights like hell. Desperately, my hand flies up, pushing at my attacker's head, trying to force him back.

My fingers dislodge the headpiece. The hologram overlay

sputters and dies. A flesh-and-blood face emerges as though through a mist of pixels.

I am looking at neither Dean nor Amar.

"Kieran Fellows, the hologram engineer," I explained in my briefing to Elaine, the ground-agent assigned to the case. "The police were too focused on the men who *wore* the hologram. They never followed up with tech support."

"So, what was the motive?" Elaine murmured.

Nora used to flirt with Dean and Amar outrageously, usually while Kieran was fine-tuning the holograms, because she knew they were secretly dating *each other*. Because it was free of the typical expectations of show business quid-pro-quo, she felt safe flirting with men for perhaps the first time in her whole life.

She never thought much about Kieran, beyond that he was quiet.

"I don't know," I said.

What I meant was, *I don't care.*

Knowing why he did it wouldn't put Nora back on the Pixel Follies stage for one more shot at the perfect Ginger Rogers back-bend.

"And you," Elaine pressed. "You're — good? You're you?"

"I'm Annie Keller," I said dryly. "Thirty-three, memory extractor with Wei Back Memory Extraction. This was my second dive, and I am not Nora Mayfield."

But back at my cubicle, beneath my desk, my feet sometimes tap out Nora's old choreography. That's my 4 percent of Nora.

• • •

The bubblegum heiress wasn't the first case I *wanted* to do the dive for. It was just the first case they'd *let* me do.

They won't let you go into anybody's memory if you actually knew them. It's hard enough to be present during a stranger's death — imagine trying to keep your head if something horrible was happening to your child, or husband, or sibling? Legally, there's got to be a volunteer, one ready and willing to die for a stranger.

"Iceberg Annie," Elaine whistles as I came into work.

"Maybe *you'll* do something to earn a nickname one day, Elaine," I assured her, half-joking and half-warning. "Then you can stop living vicariously through mine."

After the Nora case, Wei Back appointed Elaine to be my regular 'tether' — agents who help memory detectives sort through what we find in the victim's thoughts.

"It's a compliment," Elaine said, unflappable. "Extraction's like diving beneath the water to see how much ice is hidden beneath the surface. It's a metaphor."

"Oh, so now you're accusing me of sinking the Titanic?" I quipped.

Elaine laughed.

Sometimes I think this sense of humour actually belongs to Paminder Flock, my third dive. I don't think I was genuinely funny before; I didn't care enough about other people to try.

Paminder was a stand-up comedian who was shot backstage at a comedy club called *Chortles*.

Everybody loved Paminder. She was a fifty-year-old mother of three who had worked her way up through the comedy clubs in London with sets that blended compassionate politics and everyday observations about immigrant life in England. She had a bit about performatively smelling fruits at local farmers' markets that got quoted a lot on social media: *Just to let you all know, I am queen of* this *domain.*

For years, internet sleuths were stumped — who would want to kill the comedy dame of London?

We got 50 minutes from Paminder's DNA, taken off the doorknob of her dressing room. I wake up just as she's leaving to do her set.

In Paminder's head, I feel myself — feel *her* fighting through her natural shyness to smile at the small crowd. The big auditoriums make her want to crawl up and call her mother, who's been dead for years. She would tell me — *her* that a smile is as good as armour for a woman. That would make me feel strong.

The mist of Paminder's thoughts push in, and it gets harder to separate her thoughts from mine.

It's an intimate venue tonight. When I bow, the smoky room is lit up with flashing neon lights from the applause-app that *Chor-*

tles uses. It creates an effect where the whole club is lit up with pulses of colour, indicating how much the audience has enjoyed the show. I'm seeing rainbows, no hint of any disapproving red—I'm relieved.

There is one face, illuminated by the flashing pinwheels of colour from the *Chortles* app, that is smiling widest of all. A man with a thin face and two sideburn tattoos of vintage phone cords.

This is the face that I turn and see at the dressing room door later that night. I'm not alarmed as we chat, and he tells me he's dodged security. We laugh about his tattoos. He says my Flicker-Net special saved his life.

Then he names my children—John, Sonam, Disha. The school they attend—not public knowledge. I begin to eye the door when he quotes dates from my PixelFace account.

When the gun appears in his hand, I'm still convincing myself that it's silly to worry. This is someone I should have compassion for. A man who has overcome tremendous adversity to be here, laughing with me.

I am only 10 percent Annie when he fires, but one thought that is clearly mine and not Paminder's is this: I don't know this man's face from any of the data.

When I woke up from Paminder's death, it took me a month to recover. A book agent found out about my dive and offered me a million credits to write a joke book based on the material Paminder Flock had been thinking about on the night of her murder. *Paminder Flock: Cracks and Quips from Beyond the Grave!* was the proposed title.

I laughed, but only because Paminder would have laughed.

Once I passed my post-dive test—*I am not Paminder Flock*—I described the man to Elaine. The footage in the club wasn't clear enough to grab a good visual, but I recognised him in a few crowd shots through a veil of fuzzy pixels.

It was the tattoo that finally landed us a hit.

Logan Pitt. No arrest was made, because Logan committed suicide two days after Paminder Flock's murder.

Paminder's children started a foundation to raise awareness about the intersections of mental health and parasocial relationships. They invited me to their first fundraiser, but I declined.

The Paminder Flock case woke me up out of my ice. It made me realise something. I don't go murder-diving because I have some inherent sense of justice that needs satisfaction. I'm not a voyeur who gets a kick out of it either. The only real benefit of my job, I believe, is that I bring the best back from my victims.

Annie Keller is damaged, defensive, and cold. She struggles with empathy; an iceberg through and through. But Lily is bold and romantic. Nora is ambitious. Paminder is kind and funny. And now — now, I'm those things, too. Just a little bit.

My job is the worst kind of parasocial relationship.

• • •

My fourth case is the one that sparks the Plan in my head. The one that surely made Wei Back regret hiring me.

Gideon Hart was my first male victim. He died in 1889 in what was *then* called a lunatic asylum. His DNA was taken from a diary he was carrying in his pocket on day he was found stabbed to death by a sharpened trowel. The family passed the diary down over the years until, in 2040, it was published by Gideon's great-great-great nephew, becoming a bestseller.

The popularity of the book, which was a moving tale of wrongful imprisonment, prompted investigators to extract DNA from the diary and use it to solve Gideon's murder once and for all.

Gideon wasn't in the asylum because he had any genuine mental illnesses or disorders. He was there because his father had caught him with another man. So, when I wake up in Gideon, the first thing I feel is his blinding conviction that he is perfectly sane, and the world refuses to hear it.

The mist seeps in quickly with Gideon, and soon our thoughts are inseparable. It's the poor conditions of the asylum that threaten my mental well-being. The guards are like starved tigers, tensed and eager to claw down any hint of defiance in their charges. Most of the patients, some already prone to violence, become feral beneath their boots. In my diary, I describe it as a haunted place that sucks compassion from the marrow of its people's bones.

The one thing that gives me purpose here, in this dark new world, is my voice. I can advocate to the doctors for fairer treatment. My father is a politician, and we have more in common than either of us might like to admit.

There is also Oliver—the soft-spoken man in the bunk next to mine, who trades kisses with me in the clock tower whenever he dregs up the courage.

I am thinking of Oliver while I dig in the vegetable garden. When a hand grabs my arm, and something sharp enters my back at a violent angle.

As Gideon crumples to the ground, he gets a good look at his assailant; he knows him, knows his name, has avoided blows from him before.

What I, at 18-percent-Annie, do not expect is this: *I know him too.*

It takes me a good while to die. My heart is full of rage—of the senseless violence of the world, of the sure knowledge that my father will be relieved, and the patients will suffer with no advocate.

I reach to touch my diary. I hope, in my final moments, that someone will give it to Oliver.

• • •

Gideon Hart's case is the one that puts me in the history books. Elaine can't believe it when I tell her. We don't need any follow-up investigation, because the killer is one of the most prolific in history.

Jack the Ripper was one of the first cases solved by memory extraction, thanks to old DNA evidence lifted from a shawl of one of the victims. I was only able to identify Gideon's killer as 'Jack' thanks to the work of the memory-detectives who came before me, who painstakingly researched and archived photographs of the real killer. So, while I wasn't part of the original dive-team that identified Jack, I *did* expand the canonical victims list with the Gideon Hart dive.

Sometimes people will ask me what he was like. I had dinner with the original Ripper team once at a conference, and we got asked three times by waitstaff. The team lead on the original Ripper case was a stern-mouthed woman named Yemi, who made the first and second dives into Ripper victim Catherine Eddowes. She told me later, over copious glasses of wine, that Catherine Eddowes loved to sing, even when she was being arrested. I told her that Gideon Hart's favourite poet was Robert Browning, and he could recite "Childe Roland to the Dark Tower Came" from memory.

• • •

In Gideon's favourite poem, a knight goes wandering through a dark countryside. He comes to a tower and greets the ghosts of dead adventurers past; tragic mirrors to his own doomed journey. On my lunch break, I wrote the final lines on a napkin:
Names in my ears
Of all the lost adventurers, my peers —
How such a one was strong, and such was bold,
And such was fortunate, yet each of old
Lost, lost!
I pinned it to my cubicle next to the photo of Miles, the coaster from the Pixel Follies Revue, and the pamphlet for the Flock Memorial Project.

I cannot shake the feeling that I, too, am a weary soldier surrounded by senselessly doomed ghosts. Only instead of haunting a dark tower, they haunt the chemicals of my brain; I, too, am them.

This image makes me wonder for the first time: how many dives can I make until I am no longer myself? Until Annie Keller is as much a ghost as Lily, Nora, Paminder, or Gideon?

Sometimes, when I'm riding the subway or sitting in my cubicle, I try to guess at the exact composition of my brain.

2 percent Lily Gong, who may have died in a trunk.

4 percent Nora Mayfield, strangled to the muffled melody of *Rhapsody in Blue.*

12 percent Paminder Flock, who died worrying she was being unkind to her murderer.

18 percent Gideon Hart, the only male victim of 'Jack' the Rip-

per.

22 percent Marion Saddler, flailing at the bottom of a lake, not dead yet like he thought.

35 percent Amelia Earhart, who crashed into the sea, to the disappointment of conspiracy theorists everywhere.

It's natural for memory detectives to want to keep some of the victim alive. *The only balm to death is more life*, they say at every company meeting. *Go out, have new experiences.*

Otherwise, the doctors say, you'll fall too deeply into the victims' heads. You'll lose your sense of self, overtaken by the horrific empathy evoked by violence. I must process the brutal nature of these crimes by expunging the victims' memories from my brain and 're-centring' Annie.

But 're-centring' Annie goes against my Plan.

It has taken Lily's open-heartedness, Nora's ambition, Paminder's generosity and Gideon's bravery to get me here. It took two more dives to figure out the specifics, thanks to Marion's cleverness and Amelia's grit.

'Here' is in a courtroom, suing the Canadian government for the right to dive the Polly Keller case.

My wife's case.

Legally, I am here to argue, I am no longer Annie Keller.

"I understand why it's illegal for family to dive into the traumatic deaths of their loved ones," I argue. "However, the composition of my brain incorporates so much of my dive-victims that I believe I can on longer be considered Annie Keller, legally or biologically. My new brain will let me survive it."

It is Gideon's political flare and Lily's determination that I try to channel now.

"Is it your contention that Polly Keller didn't commit suicide?" the judge asks. "That she was murdered?"

It's been 6 years since I found her on the floor of our taxidermy shop. Her wrists had been cut by a narwhal's horn. I didn't think she was murdered — not really.

In a way, that made it worse.

"Yes," I lied.

"While you present an intriguing philosophical premise," the judge determined, "we must consider the issue of consent. A likely suicide victim may not wish to share her final moments."

I lose the case.

But Marion Saddler — the scientist murdered over her research into whether fast-food AIs could become legally sentient — had, in life, never given up. She always had a Plan B.

• • •

The absolute worst parts of the memory extraction industry are the murder tourists.

You need a warrant to go murder-diving. But some crimes, see, are in what we call the 'public domain of evil.' Crimes where the victims don't have any family left to prevent unscrupulous companies from sending people back for the sheer curiosity.

A lot of murder data got leaked in a security breach some years back, and though it's imperfect, all you really need is a digital copy of a DNA sequence to send somebody diving. They'll sell you on James the Slicer or the Palace of Murder and claim they're just immersive horror experiences *inspired* by real-life cases.

So you get murder tourists. Folks that'll pay big bucks to go diving into the heads of famous murder victims, even if it means risking death. They even make you sign a form saying nobody can sue on your behalf if you don't make it.

So, I find myself here, at Penny Halo's Memory Lane. I ask what it'll cost for a private dive, one where I provide my own DNA sequence. The desk clerk names an outrageous number, and I say I'll double it if we can get things running today.

I sign the forms without looking. They hook me up inside a tanning bed that sparks electricity. Fuzzy glowing wires loop all over the room like the vines of some neon-electric forest. In the tangle, I realise some part of me is still Annie after all. And that part needs to understand why she did it. If it was my fault, or somebody else's fault, or nobody's fault at all. If her invitation to the theatre that night was her final cry for help.

And if I had said yes, would she still be alive?

Annie needs to be inside her wife's final thoughts. To bring something of her back, even if it's only a small percent — her passion for romance novels, her habitual gravitation to outsiders, her love of tropical birds. Even if all I do is just lie down with her, and love her through her final breaths…

I just can't stand knowing she died alone. I can't confront her death until I understand it, and she left with no warning, no clues — nothing at all to guide me through the grief.

The machine whirs, and the engineer counts me down. The world blurs into light, and I can't tell if it's the anaesthetic or the haze of my own rising tears.

It's possible that this doomed dive will be my final, deepest journey. Through the wasteland of the mind, into the dark tower of death, surrounded by the ghosts of those who go with me.

Are they watching me depart, those ghosts?

Or do they wait for me to arrive?

Lily, Nora, Paminder, Gideon, Marion, Amelia.

There they stood, ranged along the hillsides, met
To view the last of me.

Meet Lin Darrow

Lin Darrow's fiction, poetry and comics have appeared in anthologies by Air and Nothingness Press, Jessamine Press, Eerie River, Fortuna Media, Valour I and II, In Somnio and QueerSciFi. Her comic Shaderunners, about bootleggers in a greyscale world who steal bottled colour, has been published by Hiveworks since 2015, and a novella was published by Less Than Three Press (Pyre at the Eyreholme Press) in 2018 prior to its closure. She is a two-time Prism Award nominee whose work can be found @ linkeepsitreal.

A Unique Murder
By Christopher Edwards

"When I was a young policeman," said Superintendent Holmes. "We were taught that murder was defined as 'the killing of a human being, by a human being, with malice aforethought'." He looked across his desk at Andrea Young, the lawyer from the Crown Prosecution Service. *Young by name and looks*, thought Holmes sourly. *She looks more like a teenager on work experience. She probably thinks I'm a fossil.* He knew he was being unfair. Young was one of the stars of the CPS with a lot of experience in prosecuting difficult cases. She was soberly dressed and was noticeably devoid of visible tattoos that seemed to be favoured by today's teens. The two gold studs in her earlobes were hardly on a par with the bizarre piercings adorning some of today's young.

"Yes, these circumstances might fit," agreed Young. "But under English law there has never been a statute for murder. It is a crime under Common Law. The definition you quoted was provided by a learned judge. If memory serves, he went on to say that death must occur within a year and a day of the crime, which probably tells you how long ago he was speaking.

"This case is unusual... no... Unique. There is no case law to give precedence." Andrea Young looked thoughtful. "Just thinking aloud here; a conviction on a lesser charge would be easier. Manslaughter, for example, is defined by statute."

Holmes snorted. "Common Law is what our society accepts and has always accepted as the law of the land. If you don't think you can get a conviction for murder because of the strange circumstances, why do you think manslaughter is going to be any easier?"

Young considered this. "You are right, of course." She slid the thick file on the desk in front of her off to one side. "Take me through your investigation again, please. I'd like to identify any weaknesses we might have to address for the court case."

The superintendent didn't look at his copy of the file but began recounting the story. "Hugo Wells, currently on remand at His Majesty's prison, is a doctoral candidate. Don't ask me what the subject of his thesis is. From what I can glean only a few thousand people in the world could understand it. When I asked, they used words like quantum and space-time, a lot.

"On the 16th of May last, he and a female grad student called Naz Assadi, arrived by car at what is referred to as Annex D. It's a warehouse the university has taken over for some of the more bulky and probably dangerous equipment they use. Some of the equipment is very expensive so their insurance company insists on a security presence at all times.

"The security man, Greg Burns, signed them both in by scanning their university passes. Which gave me our first puzzle. According to him, up to the arrival of Wells and Ms Assadi there was no one in the warehouse and no one else followed them in until Ms Assadi reappeared and sent him in over an hour later."

"Can we rely on Burn's testimony?" Young demanded. "Did he let someone else in? Could someone have gained entry without him knowing?"

"I know Greg Burns; he's a retired policeman with no apparent reason to lie about any of this. The warehouse was checked and there was no sign of a break-in. The warehouse has four emergency exits but they can't be accessed from outside and are covered by external cameras. In any case, if any of them are opened they generate a record in the security system and an audible alarm in the security hut. IT have checked the system; there are no records of opening any of the emergency exit doors.

"Naz Assadi also confirms they were... initially, by themselves in the building but it's a big warehouse with lots of places to hide. She could be wrong. Annex D isn't Fort Knox. The security guard has to use the toilets in the main building and it wouldn't be unknown for a security man on a boring night shift to doze off."

Andrea Young suggested they watch the first interview with Ms Assadi. Holmes brought up the video clip on his laptop and turned it so they could both watch.

They watched the screen as an attractive young woman with black hair and dark brown eyes was asked, "Can you tell me what happened?" by a female voice off camera. Naz Assadi was clearly still shaken by her recent experience but visibly tried to compose herself. Although her English was fluent, it wasn't her first language and she had learned from an American rather than a British teacher.

"We, Hugo and I, went to Annex D. We went to set up the Cage. Over-simplifying, it's a device to investigate space-time. Hugo had finished some modifications last week and he wanted to see how it performed. It's tricky to set up but it is normally stable once the field is generated.

"We were together at the monitoring station; it's behind some metal screening about twenty metres from the Cage. Hugo had just energised it. It was all looking good when all the displays showed the field had spiked and then collapsed. He asked me to check the alarm log on the computer to see if we could find the cause and he went off to check the Cage physically."

Naz Assadi gave a gulp and began to cry. The interviewer announced that they were pausing the recording.

"I've had a look at the generator and cage she referred to; it's like no cage I've ever seen," remarked Holmes with a shrug.

When the video restarted, the time stamp showed it was just over a quarter of an hour later. Asssadi now had a mug of tea on the desk in front of her. She continued her account. "I was looking at the alarm log display on the monitor when I realised... I thought... Hugo... Someone was there. He looked like Hugo but he wasn't wearing his lab coat. Hugo always wears a white lab coat.

"He was moving slowly as if every step was an effort. I asked him if he was okay. He looked at me and he seemed surprised to see me there. He said, 'Hello, Ringwraith. I'm sorry for what's going to happen but I promise you, you will be alright.' His voice sounded odd, somehow."

"Ringwraith?" queried the voice off camera.

"It's a joke Hugo made about my name. My full name is Nazgol. When Hugo first heard it he said it sounded like 'nazgul'. You know, the ring-wraiths, the bad guys from the Lord of the Rings. He started calling me Ringwraith.' Assadi paused and took a sip of tea. Holmes felt a pang of sympathy as she pulled a face. The police station tea was awful.

In the video, she put the mug down again and explained, "Hugo can be a jerk sometimes, but our department makes allowances for him. He's a brilliant physicist and he's been diagnosed with cancer. He's been on chemotherapy. It affected his mood."

The off-camera voice asked, "What do you think he meant? When he said, 'You will be alright'."

The witness shook her head. "I don't know. I didn't get a chance to ask him. He reached the tool cabinet at the back of our area, opened it and took out a hammer. He sort of lurched over to our seats and began hitting the computer keyboards with it.

"I shouted at him to stop and tried to take the hammer from him. He just shrugged me off and started to smash the monitors too."

Andrea Young wrote something on her pad.

"Then someone in a white lab coat ran past me and started to grapple with..." Miss Assadi looked down at her tea. She must have forgotten the taste because she picked it up and took a drink. "They were both Hugo," she finished flatly.

The unseen interviewer tried to make sense of what Nazgol Assadi had said. "They were twins?"

"Perhaps," she answered. "I don't know. The man in the lab coat I think was the Hugo who I'd arrived with and the other man was in different clothes, other than the lab coat I mean. The Hugo in the lab coat wrestled the hammer from the other... Hugo. They just stood there staring at each other.

"Then Hugo; this is confusing, the one not in the lab coat shouted something. I think he said 'You're going to die' and lunged at the Hugo holding the hammer. Hugo swung at him with the hammer. The man tried to duck but Hugo hit him and started to hit him again and again. He didn't stop.

"I screamed and ran out to get the security man."

Superintendent Holmes paused the playback. "You see, a defence could argue that the first blow with the hammer was a reaction to a perceived attack but the repeated blows, some of them after the victim was incapacitated, that's murder."

Young nodded in a half-hearted way. "What about the twin theory?"

"Both of Wells' parents are still alive. They say there is no twin brother, identical or otherwise. He does have two sisters; one older and one younger. Both of them are still very much alive."

The superintendent turned the laptop back towards himself and started another video. This was the first interview with Greg Burns. His testimony was that he had entered the warehouse and saw the victim lying on the floor in a spreading pool of blood. Hugo Wells was standing over him, his white lab coat covered in blood splatter. The bloodied hammer had been dropped on the floor. Hugo Wells had sat down on one of the chairs. Burns had used his mobile phone and called for an ambulance. Because he thought the victim was probably beyond help, he also called the police.

Burns had asked Hugo some questions, such as 'What happened?' and 'Who is the guy on the floor?' Hugo hadn't responded to any of them.

Burns had assumed that Hugo had been fighting with an intruder and thought he might be in shock. He had asked, 'Are you alright?' and Hugo had mumbled, "I'm okay. I'm thinking."

"Burns will be a good witness," observed the Superintendent. "He has lots of experience giving evidence."

Young didn't comment. Holmes continued. "Policewoman Torkington, who arrived at the scene first, administered the caution and arrested Wells on suspicion of murder. Wells said nothing."

"I didn't know anything about the victim resembling his attacker when I was notified of the... let's call it 'the murder'. By the time I reached the station, Hugo Wells was in custody, I had a dead body on its way for a post mortem examination and I had witnesses who could testify that it was Wells who killed the victim.

"I delayed interviewing Wells until he had a solicitor present.

I believed I had enough evidence to charge him and anything he said was likely to be irrelevant or at best confirmation. I wasn't going to need a confession to get a conviction. Or so I thought.

"With the lawyer present, I repeated the short caution and asked him if he knew the identity of the dead man. Hugo Wells gave me a superior little smile and said he couldn't tell me.

"I got the distinct impression that it wasn't a case of 'he couldn't tell me'. It was he wouldn't tell me."

"If he had told you his explanation, would you have believed him?" Andrea Young wondered.

The superintendent shook his head. "I'm not sure I believe him now. Back then, I read him the formal caution and told him he was being charged with murder. He didn't say anything."

Holmes looked at Young. "I don't know if you've dealt with many murderers. They all react differently. Sometimes they are frightened. Some show remorse. Some of them maintain their bravado. One terrorist I dealt with was elated. Wells was really unusual. I believe he was too busy thinking to show any emotion at all.

"It was a strange murder inquiry. We had the murderer in custody and bang to rights. Trying to find out who the victim was had us chasing our tails for days. The victim had nothing on him by way of identification; no phone or wallet, no door or car keys, not even a bus ticket in his pocket. His clothing was all common brands that could have been bought anywhere.

"There were no abandoned vehicles near Warehouse D that the victim might have used. None of the local taxi drivers remember a drop off near the warehouse prior to the incident.

"As I said, there wasn't a twin brother anywhere to be found nor a male sibling at all. Other family members like cousins and uncles were tracked down and all found to be unmistakably different from Hugo and, annoyingly, currently alive.

"We checked the deceased and Hugo himself for surgery scars after someone suggested a stalker could have had cosmetic surgery to look like Hugo. Neither the victim nor his attacker had any signs of such work.

"The post mortem showed the victim died due to being struck on the head multiple times with the hammer we seized at the

Annex. It also showed the victim was dying anyway. He had cancer at an advanced stage and probably had only weeks to live. He was also full of painkillers. He might not have suffered much during the attack. We tried to trace him by the prescription medication the pathologist found in the body but the medical profession is reluctant to reveal a patient's details on the off chance they are a victim of a murder.

"I wondered if Hugo and his victim had met each other during treatment for their cancer. The hospital staff tried to help but they couldn't remember anyone receiving treatment who looked like Hugo Wells. One of the nurses commented that Hugo wasn't particularly friendly with anyone.

"Hugo's sister mentioned that he had brittle bones due to his cancer and broke a bone in his right thumb. He had been in a cast for a while and had only had it taken off a month before. She called it a 'Bennett's fracture'. Our victim had had the exact same fracture but his had started to 're-model', as the pathologist called it. He estimated the victim's injury was well over a year old. A check with Accident and Emergency departments within a fifty-mile radius for anyone being treated for such a fracture failed to identify the victim.

"I had just about decided the deceased was some sort of freak, natural doppelgänger when the fingerprints we had taken from Hugo turned out to be identical to the victim's; something that just can't happen. When the DNA analysis came back for both of them they were likewise identical."

Young frowned. "It could be a sampling error or someone mixed up the results of both the fingerprints and the DNA."

Holmes shook his head. "We've sampled both the prints and the DNA again; twice. They are still identical. We asked Wells' parents to provide DNA for analysis but they refused."

"Isn't that suspicious?" the lawyer asked.

Holmes shrugged. "Perhaps, but we've charged their son with murder. I don't think we can expect them to fall over themselves to help us.

"We began trying to explain it. Some of the ideas were far-fetched. We had a team checking the maternity records to see if there had been any twins born at about the same time Hugo's mother gave birth. The thinking was one of a set of identical twins had got mixed up with Hugo's mother's baby. That was a dead end. There were no twins born in the weeks before or after Hugo's birth."

Holmes gave a mirthless laugh. "One of my detectives even started to investigate the possibility of someone cloning Hugo."

"That is rather far-fetched," said Young. "Although I suppose it would explain everything."

"It would if there was any evidence human cloning had ever been successfully carried out. Apart from some dubious claims from somewhere in Asia, no one believes it's been done and remember the victim and Wells are apparently around the same age. The means Hugo would have been cloned thirty years ago when even animal cloning was new.

"Some of our enquiries were more mainstream. We worked on the theory that Wells knew his victim. We interviewed all his family, friends and colleagues. No one could tell us who the dead man was, although one of the students did suggest that Wells' research could lead to time travel."

"I thought you were discounting explanations from the far-fetched realms of science fiction," Young said drily.

Holmes nodded. "Take a look at this interview." He played a file from his laptop. It was a recording of an interview with Hugo Wells' supervisor at the university, Professor Summerlee. The professor proved to be a condescending and pompous academic, who had nothing to add to the investigation.

The luckless policewoman conducting the interview had heard the student's claim about time travel and jokingly asked if it was possible.

"No, my dear, quite impossible." Summerlee gave her a pitying look. "Where were you, two minutes ago?"

The officer looked puzzled. "Here with you."

"The earth spins on its axis, the planet orbits the sun; the sun itself moves around the galaxy. At a rough guess, two minutes ago you were several thousand kilometres from where you are now. To travel back in time, you would also have to travel through space."

The policewoman smiled. "Is that why the De Lorean had to

reach, what was it, 87 miles an hour?"

It was the professor's turn to look puzzled; obviously the reference meant nothing to him. "The point is, Hugo Wells' work isolated a small volume of space-time from the rest of the universe. Some of the effects of isolation are quite surprising. Time, for example, for the external observer, appears to stop for the space inside the field."

Summerlee took off his glasses and absent-mindedly polished the lens with a cloth he produced from his jacket. He looked thoughtful. "I suppose if you put a cat, for example, into the field once it was established, in theory, to the outside observer the cat would have always been there, from the moment the field was generated."

"A cat?" queried the policewoman.

Summerlee replaced his glasses. "Oh, you know how we physicists love our cat experiments."

It was the policewoman's turn not to get the reference. "So it is a time machine?" she asked.

The professor shook his head emphatically. "No, there is no way to put anything, even a cat, into the field without causing its collapse."

The superintendent stopped the playback. "So that's it, I thought. The time travel reference by that bloody student was just some theoretical nonsense."

Andrea Young nodded. "From my point of view, the unidentified corpse is not an insurmountable barrier to a successful prosecution. There have, on rare occasions, been unidentified victims of murder.

"The defence will have to be informed of the identical fingerprints and DNA of the victim and the accused. I imagine the internet will go crazy expounding theories even more bizarre than the ones you have mentioned but they will not affect a court. I'm more concerned with how the deceased came to be in Annex D and what he was doing there.

"I noted that he only attacked keyboards and monitors with the hammer; computer peripherals that are easily replaced. It would seem our victim wasn't bent on stopping Wells' research. At worst, he was merely slowing down the work." Andrea

Young gave a sigh of frustration. "We are missing part of the story and unfortunately only Hugo Wells might be able to fill in the gaps."

Holmes shook his head. "And he's the one person I can't ask. The judiciary frown on policemen questioning offenders again after they have been charged. It can only happen in limited circumstances, to prevent loss or injury, and only then under strict rules."

"And yet you went to see him in prison." Young pointed out.

The superintendent shifted in his chair; a sign of his discomfort. "He requested to see me. I didn't know why. I expected his solicitor to be there but Wells was alone. He didn't look well, whether it was from the cancer or renewed chemotherapy I couldn't say.

"He thanked me for coming. I told him, truthfully, that I was happy enough hear what he wanted to say but that I was bound by rules when talking to someone charged with a crime. I told him I would record our conversation to protect us both. He nodded and I took out my phone and put it on the table between us. I reminded him of the caution. I've transferred the sound file to my laptop.

"I'll skip the part where I state who is present, the time and date and so on."

Holmes pressed play and heard himself speak. *Why does it never sound like me on a recording of my voice? Sounds like someone with severe catarrh,* he thought, as he asked Wells why he had requested the meeting.

Wells began, "I have some questions and I would guess that you also have some things that you would like explained. I'm afraid that I won't be able to explain them all completely to you. I mean no insult, when I say you don't have the grounding in mathematics to understand what happened. The best I can tell you is someone was able to use the Cage to enter Annex D from another location in space-time, possibly a location which wasn't part of our universe at all."

"The Cage can be used to travel between universes?" The Severe Catarrh voice asked in an incredulous voice.

"No, in fact it can't," Hugo answered. "Think of it as a radio.

It can receive but it needs a transmitter. I had already had some thoughts on how it could be done and now I'm fairly certain I could modify it to do just that but for now it can only receive something or someone from another place.

"I think I am going to carry out the modifications in the future."

Catarrh voice spoke again. "I thought all the time travel stories prevented you from going back in time to kill yourself, or your ancestor. Doesn't it create a paradox?"

"Not if the person who dies is the future self or from a different universe altogether." Wells sounded triumphant.

Catarrh voice's response sounded peeved. "You won't be making any modifications when you are found guilty of murder. You will be here, in prison."

Wells sounded calm when he replied. "Superintendent, your people have taken three samples for DNA and fingerprinted me twice. I think you have been testing the body from Annex D and found it is identical to the samples I provided. That poses both of us some difficult questions. I've tried to answer how I think that may be possible. Could you tell me at what stage the deceased was with his cancer?"

The superintendent didn't ask how Wells had known his victim had cancer. "Your legal team will receive the full result of the post mortem examination," Catarrh voice said huffily. "The deceased was dying; weeks to live at most. He should have been in a hospice."

Holmes remembered Wells had nodded slowly as if it was what he had expected. "I wonder if a physicist, dying from cancer with only weeks to live, would prefer to die conducting an experiment to prove a hypothesis. He might even achieve immortality of sorts; his name forever linked to a new physical phenomenon.

"Tell me, superintendent, can someone be convicted of murdering himself?"

Holmes paused the recording. "That was it. Wells stopped the interview and went back to his cell."

Holmes knew there was a part of the interview that hadn't been recorded. As Wells had got up to leave he'd stopped his phone's recording and asked him one of the forbidden questions, "Why did you kill him? Surely it wasn't necessary?"

Wells had stopped. "That's the wrong question, superintendent. Why did he want to be killed? To circumvent a long and painful death, do you think?"

Holmes decided not to tell Young about the end of their conversation;

Andrea Young began drumming the fingers of her right hand on Holmes' desk. She stopped and looked the superintendent in the eyes. "The victim was either an impossible doppelgänger or an equally impossible time, or maybe interdimensional, traveller. What do you think?"

Holmes returned the look. "I'm a policeman. I've spent my career catching criminals. In Annex D on that day a man died as the result of a violent attack. I have charged the person who is responsible with murder. I think he should be tried and his guilt decided by a jury of his peers."

Young nodded. "And I'm a lawyer. My career has been to ensure the law is applied and upheld. I will recommend that Wells' trial goes ahead. He may plead guilty. If he doesn't, he may say he was acting in self-defence."

She paused, as if a sudden thought had just occurred to her. "He might offer a defence of insanity caused by meeting his doppelgänger. Whatever it is, just remember, superintendent, juries are unpredictable; we may not get the result we expect."

• • •

Young had been right. The world-wide media frenzy had descended on the Crown Court. Millions of posts had been spawned discussing the case on social media. Reporters from scores of news outlets had tried to get an interview, a comment or even a word, from Superintendent Holmes. Reporters were fobbed off when he told them he was not allowed to comment on an ongoing court case as it was "sub judice". They seemed confused by the legal phrase. However, his email accounts were filling up with offers to appear on television programmes now the case was nearly over. Some of them sounded quite lucrative.

Protesters waited outside the Crown Court building on his arrival. Some of them waved placards bearing a variety of legends; 'HOAX' and 'Tell us the TRUTH' seemed to be popular. Holmes wasn't too sure what they were protesting about and guessed the protesters weren't sure either, although the protester holding a placard reading 'I want to go back to 2015' obviously had a reason.

The jury had been sequestered early on in the trial to save them being harassed by reporters and the just plain curious.

Holmes met Young just inside the Crown Court building, their encounter filmed by dozens of cameras and phones. Once they were inside the courtroom itself, they were safe from the cameras. The judge had ordered all phones and cameras to be handed in before entering.

"How do you think the jury will go?" she asked him.

"I was just going to ask you the same question. I don't know," Holmes admitted. "I thought the judge's summing up was fair."

Young nodded. "It's annoying that Wells told us his defence when you met him in prison. His barrister has argued the death was suicide, not murder. The fingerprint and DNA experts became virtual witnesses for the defence. We could have prepared better for that."

Holmes felt some guilt on that score too. He had to admit under defence cross-examination that the deceased was, to all intents and purposes, in fact a slightly older Hugo Wells. He wasn't prepared to accept all the blame. "Yes, and the physicist we had to testify for us about the science involved had most of the jury glassy-eyed from the moment he started talking. He might have been speaking in Finnish as far as they were concerned. And Naz Assadi's testimony didn't help; confirming the dead man had called her 'Ringwraith'. A name only Hugo used."

Andrea Young nodded towards the jury access door. There was movement there. Wells was already sat in the dock. "Whichever way it goes, I expect an appeal, either from us or the defence. It will probably reach the Supreme Court eventually. My boss tells me the minister is preparing legislation to cover any future events."

Holmes winced internally as Andrea used her fingers to do

"air quotes" as she said the word "future".

"I don't think murder will remain under Common Law much longer," she added.

The jury filed in and sat down. Everyone stood as the judge came in a few moments later. He asked everyone to sit. The clerk of the court remained standing and addressed the jury. He asked if they had reached a verdict. The jury foreman stood and said they had and yes, it was the verdict of them all.

The clerk spoke clearly. "On the charge of murder of a person unknown, do you find the accused Hugo Wells guilty or not guilty?"

The whole room seemed to lean towards the jury foreman as he took a deep breath in...

THE END

Meet Christopher Edwards

Christopher Edwards retired from the oil and gas industry having spent twenty years on several production platforms in the Northern North Sea. Before retiring he also spent time on assignments in Bolivia, Azerbaijan, Iran and the United Arab Emirates. He always enjoyed making up stories for his children and now his grandchildren but was only recently persuaded to start writing.

The Empty Room
By Stetson Ray

Same as everyone else, I heard about the disappearance of the Holloway girl on the news. A child goes to a birthday party at her friend's house, only to vanish during a game of hide and seek? What a story. It's all anyone could talk about. Nina Holloway's disappearance captivated the whole country. Some people thought she had been killed. Others thought she had run away.

I didn't think much about it. I was busy with work, had my hands full trying to figure out if a man named Frank Gorino was committing insurance fraud. It was a boring case, but detective work is like that sometimes. I don't enjoy spending my days following around people who wear neck braces and use crutches, but I make pretty good money as a private investigator, even if my job isn't particularly exciting.

It never crossed my mind that someone might hire me to find Nina Holloway. I figured somebody would find her floating in a pond or buried in a shallow grave. These things follow patterns. Most crimes have the same motives: usually money or passion, and the perpetrator is almost always someone close to the victim.

Days passed.

Then weeks.

But the Holloway girl never turned up. That's when somebody decided it would be a good time to give me a call.

"Is this, John Weber?" a woman asked.

"It is," I answered, holding my phone to my ear. "Who am I speaking with?"

"My name is Rachel Holloway, and I'd like you to investigate the disappearance of my daughter, Nina Holloway."

I waited. You keep your mouth shut and leave people on the hook, they'll tell you what they really think. All you have to do is wait. Instead of saying anything, Rachel Holloway began to cry. I listened while she put herself back together.

"I'm sorry, I just miss her so much. Are you available? Can you help me?"

I was available. That didn't mean I wanted to take the case. I thought of the photo the news outlets had been showing on the evening news. Nina Holloway was seven years old and cute as she could be: big eyes, missing a few teeth, curly hair and rosy cheeks.

"Please, Mr Weber. The police have stopped taking my calls. I think they're avoiding me. I need someone who will listen to me, someone I can trust."

When I was younger, the desperate tone in the woman's voice would have affected me. I might have even offered to take the case for free. But over the years, I'd heard it all. You can only see so many broken families and grisly crime scene photographs before it stops bothering you. Part of you dies, and when it's gone, it's gone for good. It leaves an empty space inside you, but you get used to it.

"Will you do it?" the woman pleaded. "Will you find my daughter?"

I took a deep breath and said, "Mrs Holloway, since your daughter's case is so high profile and is still actively being investigated by the authorities, if I were to take the case, my normal rate would be doubled. My fee is one-twenty an hour, so two-forty in this situation, and I would need an initial retainer payment of two-thousand dollars."

"Yes. I'll pay anything to have my daughter back."

If she would've said no and hung up the phone, it would've been better for both of us. She was desperate, and that meant I had to set realistic expectations.

"In my experience, Mrs Holloway, if a missing child isn't located in the first week after they disappear, the chances of them being found alive are extremely slim. I'll do what I can to find your daughter, but you should prepare yourself for the worst."

The woman cried again, and I listened until she stopped.

"When can you start?"

"As soon as I receive the initial payment."

• • •

I spent a few days doing research. I paid my man at the police department to tell me what the police had learned, which turned out to be nearly nothing. Nina Holloway had vanished into thin air. Her mother and father had solid alibis. She had no estranged or vengeful relatives. By all accounts, Nina was a happy child, and had no reason to run away.

I did some digging and found out there had been another disappearance linked to the house where Nina was last seen. Two years prior, the owner of the home — a man named Greg Walters — had abandoned his family during the night without warning and no one had heard from him since. I kept digging, but found no trace of the man. If he was still alive, he knew how to cover his tracks. The police had questioned his wife, Anna, but she never admitted to having anything to do with his disappearance. I turned over every rock I could find, but Anna's record was clean. I found a picture of her online. She didn't look like the type of person who would kill her husband, let alone an innocent child.

I contacted Anna and arranged an interview. I visited her on a Tuesday while her only child was at school. I parked on the street outside her house. By the looks of it, the house was the oldest home in Jonesborough. It wasn't what I would call a sprawling manor, but there was something huge about the three-storey home. It didn't take up much real estate, but it seemed to tower over the neighborhood. It was a relic from another time, and it didn't fit into the modern world that had been built around it.

I left my car and proceeded up a narrow walkway toward the home. I couldn't shake the feeling I was trespassing. I had to remind myself I was invited.

"You must be Mr Weber," Anna said when she opened the front door.

"Please, you can call me John."

"I believe Mr Weber would be more appropriate."

Five seconds in, and things already weren't looking good. I had to do something — win the woman over before things got any worse. I couldn't afford to blow it with my only lead.

"Of course, and I understand how hectic things must have been for you during the last few weeks, so I appreciate you agreeing to meet with me."

Anna stared at me, giving me nothing. She looked tired, and there were lines around her eyes much too deep for a woman of only thirty-three.

"It's no problem," she said, her voice as flat as the expression on her face. "Would you like to come in?"

"Thank you."

I followed her inside the house and was overwhelmed with the feeling I was entering some kind of museum. The first thing I noticed were the stairs; the handrail looked like it had been carved by hand, the wood the richest shade of brown I had ever seen. The pictures and decorations on the walls weren't like the kind you could buy from a store. Everything looked old, but nice. No, not nice — *grand*. I don't know much about old decor, but during our short trip to the living room, we must have walked past tens of thousands of dollars worth of antiques.

Anna sat down on one of the only modern looking pieces of furniture in the house — a couch — and I sat down in a cushioned leather chair across from her.

"You have a beautiful home."

"Thank you. It's been in my husband's family for six generations. My daughter would have made the seventh."

"Would have?"

"Yes. We're leaving. I can't stay here any longer."

"You're selling?"

She didn't seem to hear me. Her eyes had drifted away. I watched her until she came back from wherever she had gone.

"I'm sorry. What did you say?"

"Are you selling the house?"

"Selling? Yes. I've decided it's finally time to sell."

There was certainly something odd about Anna Walters, but I didn't get the feeling she had killed anyone. I figured her behaviour could most likely be attributed to stress, and I felt sorry for her.

"You mentioned your husband. How long has it been since you heard from him?"

She narrowed her eyes.

"On the phone you said you weren't with the police. Does that mean I have to answer your questions?"

"Legally no, but I assure you that anything you tell me is confidential. I'm not a cop, and I don't care if you've done anything illegal. I'm not here to entrap you or find some technicality so I can arrest you. The only reason I'm here is to find out what happened to Nina Holloway. The girl is my only concern."

Anna seemed to relax.

"That's refreshing. If I have to talk to one more cop…" She shook her head. "It's the questions. They ask the same questions over and over, the same ones they asked when my husband disappeared. It's maddening."

"So you haven't heard from your husband since he disappeared?"

"No, not once in over two years."

"Mrs Walters —"

"Just Anna."

"Anna, before your husband's disappearance, was he ever violent with you or your daughter?"

One side of her mouth curled upwards into a knowing grin.

"You want to know if I killed him. That's what you're getting at, isn't it?"

She left me on the hook, watched me squirm. I tried to keep my face expressionless and maintain my professional demeanor, but it wasn't easy to maintain eye contact with Anna — a woman who had been through more than I first realised.

"We were happy, Mr Weber, and we loved each other very much. I didn't kill my husband."

Some of the tension left the room, and the wild look in Anna's eyes faded.

"Do you have any idea where he went?"

She shook her head no as her face contorted. Tears welled up in her eyes and her lip quivered. Sitting hunched over with her hand covering her mouth, she began to weep.

"I wish I knew where he was. I'd do anything to know he was okay. I don't care if I ever see him again. I just want to know he's okay."

She grabbed a tissue from a nearby table and sniffled and blew her nose. I decided to abandon the line of questioning I had planned about her husband. Not for one minute did I believe Anna capable of murder. My gut has never lied to me, not once.

"I hate to make you tell it again, but I need to know what happened the day Nina Holloway disappeared."

Looking at me with bloodshot eyes, she nodded then spoke:

"We were having a birthday party for my daughter, Elle. Only a couple kids showed up. They've never said it, but the other parents don't like their kids coming here. Like everyone else, I'm sure they think I killed my husband." She shrugged — *oh well.*

"How many people were here the day of the party?"

"Me, my daughter, and three children, including Nina Holloway. Five of us in total."

"Nobody else came by that day, even for a minute?"

"Just the parents who dropped off their kids. Nobody came in farther than the foyer, and the kids were playing upstairs."

I took out my notepad and without my prompting, Anna gave me the names of the parents and I wrote as she spoke. I was relieved to have more people to question, but I wasn't done with Anna yet.

"What were you doing when you realised that Nina was missing?"

"Putting the candles on my daughter's cake, in the kitchen."

"Where were the kids?"

"Playing hide and seek upstairs. They couldn't find Nina, so my daughter came and got me. At first, we thought Nina had found a really good hiding place and wouldn't come out, but after an hour of searching, I decided to call the police."

I scribbled on my pad, glancing at her every few seconds.

"Do you know your neighbours very well?"

"Not really, but everyone on this street is elderly and retired. I don't know if any of them would be physically capable of sneaking in here and taking a child without anyone noticing. And the

police already checked them out. They scoured the neighbourhood for weeks, searched all the houses, brought in all kinds
of equipment. They used dogs to check every square inch of
ground within two miles of here to see if anyone had buried a
body." Her eyes drifted away again. "At night, I still hear them
barking. Those police dogs. Sometimes it's hard for me to sleep."

While she was away, I gave Anna a once over. Judging by her
body language, she was definitely hiding something — probably
not dead bodies in the attic, but still something.

"Anna, I've been doing this a long time, and I'm not trying to
accuse you of anything, but I have the feeling there's something
else going on here."

She stared at me solemnly. "I'm sorry. I got so caught up in
telling you what I already told the police, that I forgot to tell you
the truth."

"Which is?"

Anna watched me, debating internally. "Do you have any legal obligation to report me to a psychologist or psychiatric holding facility if I say something completely insane?'

"None whatsoever. You are free to say anything. The worst I'll
do is make a note of it."

"Come with me." She stood up. "And get ready to take some
notes."

I followed her out of the living room and up the stairs.

• • •

The second floor of the house was decorated as lavishly as the
first. I'd never been in a house that felt so little like a home. It
was difficult to imagine children running up and down the halls.
No wonder parents wouldn't let their children visit.

"Do you know anything about this house?" Anna asked, leading me down a hallway.

"Only what you've told me."

"Did you know that my husband wasn't the first person from
the Walters family to disappear?"

"I did not."

I couldn't believe I'd missed such an important detail during my research.

"Ever heard of an architect by the name of Elisha Walters?"

"I haven't."

"Elisha was my husband's great-great-great-grandfather. He was a very successful architect, and he designed and built this home in eighteen-eighteen. He brought in the best craftsmen from all over the country to work on it, and when it was done, he considered it to be his crowning achievement."

We ascended another flight of stairs.

"Elisha was a believer in '*sacred geometry*' and was obsessed with '*non-Euclidean angles.*' He took special care to make sure every part of the house was built to his exact specifications, especially his study on the third floor. He believed he had designed a geometrically perfect room—a room that would work in harmony with the energies of the universe and be the perfect place to inspire his creative endeavours." She turned and looked at me when we reached the top of the stairs. "Or that's what my husband told me anyways."

I had no idea what a geometrically perfect room or non-Euclidean angles had to do with Nina's disappearance. Anna led me down another hallway and we stopped at a closed door.

"Wait here," she said, and disappeared into a room on my left.

I couldn't help but notice that the door to the room ahead of me was padlocked shut. Anna came back fumbling with a keyring and used three different keys to unlock the doorknob, the deadbolt, and finally the padlock. She turned and looked at me, and for an instant, she looked closer to sixty years old than thirty.

"Just a few days after Elisha and his family moved into this house, Elisha disappeared and was never seen again, same as my husband."

Anna pulled the door open and the hinges whined like they had never been used. I half expected the room to contain the bodies of Greg and Nina, but it did not. Besides being completely empty, the room looked like any other room. Anna did not lead me inside. She leaned against the open door as if she were afraid it might snap shut on its own.

"This is the last place Elisha was ever seen. He went in, but he didn't come back out."

We stood there looking into the room.

"May I go inside?"

"Wait here, and don't move until I get back."

She disappeared into another room and I remained in the hallway trying to piece together what she had told me so far; the information didn't make sense, at least not yet.

She came back carrying a rubber ball, a child's toy, and handed it to me. "Squeeze it. Really look at it. Make sure it's real."

"Are you about to show me a magic trick?"

"Just do it."

There was nothing extraordinary about the ball that I could tell. I handed it back.

"I'm going to show you the same thing my husband showed me the day we moved into this house."

She tossed the ball into the room and quickly pushed the door shut.

We listened to the ball bounce on the hardwood floor.

Once.

Twice.

Then nothing.

I waited, leaning forward and listening, waiting for the third bounce.

Anna opened the door.

The room was empty.

The ball was gone.

"What happened to it?"

Anna just looked at me.

"May I go in?"

"If you still want to."

When I stepped into the room, I felt like I'd crossed an invisible barrier. The air was too heavy. A single window on the far wall (barred shut, I couldn't help but notice) seemed very far away. I couldn't tell if the ceiling was three feet above my head or thirteen. I had the feeling I was not in one room but hundreds, or thousands, all identical, all occupying the exact same space in a thousand overlapping universes. Drowning on my feet, I turned and looked at Anna. She was still leaning against the door. Her arms were crossed. She was grinning.

"Strange, right?"

Her voice was in my ear.

Her voice was a mile away.

"Very."

I looked around the room. It seemed very large. It seemed very small. I tried to walk and nearly fell. It was as though the whole house was spinning like a carnival ride, and the room was the only thing remaining stationary.

"Is it always like this?"

"As far as I know, but I've only gone in once. That was enough for me."

I squinted my eyes and tried to spot something, anything, but there was nothing to see inside the room; just four walls, a floor, and a ceiling. "Has it always been so…*empty*?"

The feeling that I was in a thousand rooms faded and was replaced by an entirely different feeling: I was nowhere. The room was an illusion. Nothing could exist inside the room because it did not exist itself. The void was total, and I was standing on the edge, inches from tumbling in. I took a deep breath and steadied myself.

"According to my husband's family, all of Elisha's things began disappearing after he did: his desk, his books, his chair. It all vanished a little at a time until nothing remained, and as far as I know, this room has been locked ever since."

"That can't be true."

"I'm just telling you what I was told."

Stiff legged, I took a few steps. Either I had imagined the whole thing, or I was getting used to the room. Maybe it wasn't so odd. A room is just a room after all.

I noticed that Anna was crying again.

"My husband—" she sobbed, her chest hitching "—I don't know why, but I think he must've come in here. Every day I wonder what would compel him to do that knowing what he knew, but I believe he did. I refuse to believe he left us. I think he went wherever Elisha went. And you want to know something?" Her face was streaked with tears, but she looked angry. "I think he's still here. I think he's in this room right now."

Something about her expression made my skin crawl, and I

couldn't stand to look at her any longer. I pretended to scribble in my notepad as I tried to centre myself.

"Think what you want to think, and write what you want to write in your notepad, but it's not going to change what I believe."

Then I knew what Anna was really saying. No wonder she hadn't told the police what she really thought.

"You think Nina Holloway found a way into this room, then vanished?"

"That's right."

"But wasn't the door locked?"

"Yes. I checked the moment I realised Nina was missing. But when the police got here they made me open the door. Then they brought in dogs, and the dogs came straight to this room. But they wouldn't go in. One of them made a mess on the floor where I'm standing, and another tried to bite its handler. You can call me crazy, but I have no doubt that Nina found her way into this room, Mr Weber."

I had a job to do, and weird room or not, I had to find out what happened to Nina. I scanned the room again, and noticed a square pattern on one wall.

"What's that?" I asked, pointing.

"A food elevator. It goes to the kitchen. I guess Elisha had it built so he wouldn't have to leave his study during lunch. But it was sealed off from the kitchen decades ago. And the police already checked."

"Police miss things," I said, and went to the wall.

I stuck my fingers in the crack and managed to remove the section of false wall. In front of me was a box, roughly the size of a large microwave. I used the light from my cell phone to examine the inside of the miniature elevator. The edges of the box were flush, except one. I pushed and it gave a little. I pushed harder and was able to slide the loose panel to the side. On the other side of the elevator was some kind of air vent, dirty and dark and forgotten. In the dust were tiny handprints, fairly new.

In my mind, I could picture Nina thinking she had found the greatest hiding place of all time and crawling through the vent toward the elevator. But there was no stench of decomposing flesh; the girl had not remained in the vent.

So where had Nina gone?

I backed out of the cubby hole and looked at Anna and felt as though I were falling. Instead of being right behind me, the doorway was at least twenty feet away, like it had slid down the wall while my back was turned.

"Is everything okay?" Anna asked, still leaning against the open door.

"Yes," I told her, then told myself I had simply misjudged the original layout of the room. "What's on the other side of this wall?" I pointed toward the food elevator.

"A bedroom. We don't use it."

"Is there an air return vent in that room?"

She thought about it for a second. "Yes, I believe there is."

"When was the central air system installed in this house?"

"I don't know."

"You were right. Nina was able to crawl into the elevator and gain access to this room. But that doesn't explain where she went. If Nina entered this room, she should still be here."

Anna's eyes looked wild again — unhinged.

She said, "You're right. She should be here. But she's not. Or maybe she is. Maybe she's stuck here with my husband. And Elisha. Maybe they're all together. Maybe they're watching us right now." A single tear ran down her face.

"With respect, you need to get your head checked, Mrs Walters." She did not seem offended by my comment. "There has to be another explanation. People don't just disappear. There's always a reason, a motive."

"Not this time."

"What you're telling me is impossible."

"Is it?" A devilish grin appeared on her face.

She stepped back and began to push the door shut. I ran toward her, some buried instinct inside me horrified at the thought of being stuck inside the room, even for a single second. I burst into the hall and everything spun. My heart was pumping blood to all the wrong places. My vision was blurred, my hearing muffled. Panting, I fell to my hands and knees. It was all I could do to hold down what I'd eaten for breakfast.

All available evidence was pointing toward a simple yet illogical solution: the empty room had taken Nina. Again, I told myself that such an answer was impossible. But my gut was insisting on a truth that my mind could not accept: the girl was still inside the room, even if I couldn't see her with my eyes, just like Anna had said.

Anna locked the door to Elisha's study as I caught my breath. "You need to go. I have to pick up my daughter from school soon."

After I managed to pick myself up off the floor, I took special care to hold onto the railing as I followed Anna down both flights of stairs. She opened the front door and I headed for my car.

She said my name.

I stopped, but didn't turn around.

I couldn't bring myself to look at her again.

"I've had to live next to that room for years, so I know how you feel. You'll drive yourself crazy thinking about it, so try not to. It'll be over soon anyways. Like I said, I'm getting rid of the house."

The door clicked shut and I staggered to my car.

I had to wait half an hour before I felt well enough to drive.

• • •

Later that day, I called Nina Holloway's mother and told her I couldn't help her and refunded the money she had given me. I tried to put what I had learned out of my mind, but it was no use; the empty room occupied the empty space inside my mind. I went days without sleep. When I did manage to knock myself out (with some help from my friend Jack), I dreamt of nothing. Absolutely nothing. Emptiness so severe and absolute it threatened to consume me.

A few nights after my visit with Anna, the Walters House burned to the ground while the rest of the neighbourhood slept. By the time the fire department arrived, there wasn't much left to save. Police picked up Anna Walters and her daughter at a rest stop two states away the next day.

Anna is refusing to talk. The police want to know why the burnt bodies of three people were found in the rubble—two men, one little girl—but Anna won't tell them anything. I guess they'll send her to prison for murder. That's the only explanation that makes sense. She killed them. It's as easy as that. That's what I've been telling myself.

Although my gut keeps telling me otherwise.

Maybe I've been working too hard lately. I think I'll take a vacation, maybe go somewhere with lots of people, some place with loud tourists who are always talking, kids screaming and running around everywhere. Somewhere that's full year round. Lots of things to do and see. Everything moving. No empty spaces. It'll do me good, help me get my mind back on track.

After nearly thirty years working as an investigator, I can't believe I nearly bought that woman's story. She almost had me fooled. It was just another room. I must have been sick the day we talked, probably running a fever.

That room was just another room.

Just because it was empty doesn't mean anything Anna told me was true.

It was just an empty room.

Meet Stetson Ray

Stetson Ray has had stories published by Sans Press, Pyre Magazine, and Liquid Imagination. He lives in Tennessee and enjoys reading and writing ghost stories including his recent contribution in Howling Hills Publishing's, "23 Tales: Appalachian Ghost Stories, Legends & Other Mysteries".

Revolver
By Steven Lord

The End

Jim stared at the gun in his hand. A thin tendril of smoke was wisping upwards, rising towards the freedom of the ceiling before veering ever so slightly as the gentle but insistent tug of the air recyclers caught hold.

He lowered his arm, the shock of the recoil still shivering through his hand and wrist like a jolt of electricity. His numb fingers loosened their grasp around the grip and the revolver clattered to the steel floor to lie in front of the body. The clang of metal on metal sounded dull to his still-ringing ears; for an idle second, he wondered whether he'd damaged his hearing permanently. It was incredible how his mind could distract itself with pointless questions, even when faced with the enormity of what he'd done, what he'd learnt. Perhaps that was why. Perhaps pointless questions were the only ones worth asking anymore.

He turned to look for the woman despite himself. She wasn't there, of course. She never had been.

With a sigh, he walked out of the room and into the lie that had masqueraded as life. For him. For everyone. But no longer. The city was about to wake up to the truth. And the truth was going to hurt.

The Beginning

Jim d'Angelo had been staring out his office window for forty minutes. At some point night had fallen, prompting the city to fire its first salvos against the darkness, electric glows of lurid purple, flaming red and neon blue bursting from the narrow alleyways that ran between the cramped apartment blocks. His office was in a decent part of town — on the edge of 2nd Radial, just a hundred metres or so from Central Square — and from his vantage point, he could just make out the city's most powerful weapon against the gloom, the soaring projections that lit up each side of Lafayette Tower from root to tip. The benevolent face of Jordan Lafayette smiled down at Jim, mouthing silent beatitudes before the projection crossfaded into a vista of rolling green hills so lush it made his eyes hurt just to look at them. Above the panorama, mantras scrolled past in script ten feet high.

"The Journey is Sacred. Our Captain will deliver us to the New World. Bless Jordan Lafayette and bless the Church of the Sacred Journey."

"A-fuckin-men," Jim sighed, slumping back into his armchair.

The office would have made a hermit feel hard done by. A steel desk, plain and unadorned but for a silver photo frame perched on the corner; a cot bed, propped up on its side against one wall, crumpled sheets scattered around its base like discarded tissues; a solid-looking filing cabinet that came up to waist height, its secrets hidden behind a triumvirate of metal drawers; and next to it, the battered leather armchair where Jim was sitting. Not much to show for forty-two years of life. Somehow, the room still managed to look crowded.

He stood up and yanked open the top drawer of the cabinet, internal locks disengaging the moment they recognised the unique signature of fatty acids, esters and cholesterol that made up his skin's natural oils. The whisky bottle inside clinked in protest as it rolled into the only other item in the drawer. He grabbed the bottle and took a long swig, the fiery alcohol burning his mouth and throat on the way down. Reassuringly painful. Masochism in liquid form.

He sucked through his teeth, fanning the flames in his mouth as his gaze slid inexorably towards the revolver. Six chambers of death, black, unblinking eyes looking up into his from the drawer. A memento from a previous life. Some of his colleagues had called their weapons 'clubs', trying to re-appropriate the language that the rest of the population used against them. Not him. He knew he deserved the hatred.

Not for the first time, he imagined what it would feel like to press the snub nose against his temple, pull the trigger and escape this damn life once and for all. Then he sighed, threw the bottle back in the drawer and slammed it shut. Not today. Better a coward than a cliché.

He was settling back into the warm embrace of the armchair when a gentle buzz vibrated through his jawbone, jolting him from his fatalistic reveries. It had been weeks since anyone had called and he'd almost given up on getting another job. Though if this was another goddamn missing pet case, then perhaps he would eat that bullet after all. He ran a hand through his rumpled hair, took a deep breath, then blinked twice to accept the call.

The woman that appeared on the other side of the room was tall, blonde and achingly familiar. Even through the projection blur — he had to get these lenses looked at — there was something about the curve of her neck, that slight furrow in her brow, the shallow dimples in her cheeks, that triggered volley after volley of recognition neurons to fire in his brain.

"He... Hello? Is that Mr d'Angelo?"

He realised he'd been staring silently at the caller. "Yes, ma'am," he croaked. It was the first time he'd spoken that day. "Jim d'Angelo here. How can I help you?"

"Mr d'Angelo. I need your help. My son..."

She paused. The holograph was trembling and Jim didn't think it was the lenses' fault this time.

"My son is missing. I've been told that you find people, Mr d'Angelo. That you used to work for the Church, used to be a policeman."

Policeman? Not quite. But close enough. "Yeah, sure, I can help you. There's a price though." He paused. "I'm sorry, I know this is the last thing you want to think about, but I find it easier talking about it earlier rather than..."

"Money isn't an issue, Mr d'Angelo," the women interrupted. "Whatever the price, I'll pay it. Just find my son."

A shiver of excitement rippled across Jim's shoulders. This could be it. The big one. *OK. Play it cool.* "Alright, ma'am. You've got yourself a detective. Let's start with the basics. What do I call you?"

"Alethea. Alethea Bravo."

Momentarily nonplussed by the strange surname, he ploughed on. "OK, Alethea. Tell me what happened. When did you last see your son?"

"Ross… His name is Ross. He went to bed last night at the usual time, just before nightfall. I said goodnight, closed the door—he's just turned eleven, wants his own space. When he didn't come down this morning, I thought he'd just stayed up reading too late. But when I went in, he wasn't there. The window… The window was open, and he'd gone." She dropped her head, trying to hide the sobs that racked her body.

"It's OK, Alethea. I've got this. I'll get Ross back for you." An easy promise to make. And if he couldn't keep it… Well, she'd have bigger things to worry about in that case. "Is there anyone he's close to outside the home? A new friend, perhaps?"

"No, he's a quiet child, keeps to himself. Wait, no. There is someone." Her face lit up with a pitiful excitement, before crumpling as she realised the consequences. "There's a boy called Micah. I've never met him, but Ross has been chatting to him on the link for the last few months. He seemed harmless. You don't think…?"

Jim tried to conceal a grimace, pretty sure he was failing miserably. It was too easy to mask your real identity over a hololink. How could any parent not realise that? Still, at least it was a start point. "I'm sure it's nothing. Can you send me the connection logs from Micah's link just in case?"

"Of course."

A green light flashed up in the top right of Jim's field of vision. He flicked his eyes up and right for an instant to accept the download.

"OK. I'll take a look. What about his brother or sister? Did they see anything?"

That familiar guilty expression. "No. My husband died before we could… We're not a quota family."

"It's ok, ma'am. I understand." He did. Only too well. "Is there anything else you can think of that might help me look for Ross?"

"No. No, I don't think so." She turned her head slightly, an instinctive movement like a wild animal reacting to an unexpected sound. "Find my son, Mr d'Angelo. Find Ross. Please."

"I'm on it, ma'am. I'll get back to you as soon as I have any news," he said, trying to inject some confidence into his voice. Waste of effort. The woman had hung up. The holograph faded to a blurry heat-haze against the office wall, then snuffed out entirely.

Jim glanced down and activated the office module, a virtual monitor and keyboard flashing up through the lenses as his gaze fell on the empty desk. He tapped out some instructions, using his old access codes to get into a couple of restricted databases. There was no point in hanging around, he figured. The kid was probably dead already. If not, he would be soon. He'd seen cases like this before, and they rarely ended well.

His fingers flew across the keyboard as he fired up his module's AI core. AI was perhaps an exaggeration; the authorities had banned true sentient modules decades ago, with the exception of the huge artificial mind housed within Lafayette Tower that ran the city and everything else around it. His own module core was a mere shadow in comparison, but it was still more than capable of carrying out most tasks far more efficiently than a human could ever hope to. Within a minute, it had extracted the endpoint ident codes from the connection logs he'd been sent.

Strange… There was some weird noise around the kid's — *no, stop depersonalising Jim, it doesn't help* — around *Ross's* end of the connection. Interference from an unshielded cable, perhaps. Still, unusual to see that on a personal hololink… Ah hell, it could be anything, and he had more important things to worry about. He entered the second endpoint code, the one used by this Micah cove, into the police database. A name and address pinged up on the screen. "Booth 3, *Bar Scorpio*. 8th Radial, Delta Axis."

Great. A public connection. He should have known it wouldn't be easy. He hated public places. They tended to be hazardous to his health. Still, the bar was still open, and it was only seven blocks away. No time like the present. He reopened the cabinet drawer again, reached in and withdrew his service revolver, dropping it into one of the deep pockets of his jacket. It weighed that side of the coat down like a guilty conscience, but it meant he could reach it quick and easy if he needed to. Not that he anticipated having to use it—if it came to that, things had gone badly wrong.

As he turned from the desk, his gaze snagged on the silver picture frame. The photo inside was real, not a projection. The resemblance to Alethea was subtle, but it was definitely there. No wonder she had looked familiar. He kissed his fingers and brushed them across the photo. "Still love you, girl," he sighed.

Then he opened his office door and strode out into the city that the 50,000 inhabitants of the generation ship *Speravimus* called home.

• • •

In the dark hours, the narrow alleyways that formed the city's streets and thoroughfares felt even seedier than normal. Whatever the ship's designers had intended its living quarters to look like—and both the Church and the Lafayettes were silent on the matter—Jim was pretty sure it wasn't this hodgepodge of stacked steel prefabs, painted in lurid colours and studded with neon signage, huddled together in little organic clusters with no semblance of order, flimsy fabric shacks filling up what little gaps that remained.

The only concession to town planning that the founding generation had managed to make was the alley system: six-foot gaps in the steel chaos that ran through the city to form twelve linear spokes and six concentric circles. The alleys, and the city itself, were centred on Lafayette Tower: an impressive spire that stretched from the floor of the ship's main bay to its ceiling one hundred feet above and home to *Speravimus*'s Captain. The Tower was omnipresent, visible over a kilometre away from the nutrient fields and oxygen scrubber bays that sat just outside the city boundaries.

Jim felt the weight of the Tower's gaze on his back as he approached Bar Scorpio. 'The Captain is always watching,' as the Church was fond of saying. The Captain could do what he wanted, as far as he cared. He'd spent enough of his life doing his dirty work for Jordan Lafayette and his father before him.

From the outside, the bar appeared to be a typical establishment, catering mostly to those poor souls who worked in the nutrient fields or maintained the oxygen scrubbers. Manual labourers who could distract themselves from the monotony of their existence for an hour or two with some hard liquor, before going back to their families to sink back into depression and a bit of recreational violence. Not Jim's preferred choice of venue, but he was here for business, not pleasure.

He pushed open the door and walked into a room that smelled of stale whisky and faded dreams. There were five or six clients; it had only been an hour or so since the lights went down and the night was still young. The men—and they were invariably men—were sprinkled between the dive bar's tables, heads down as they nursed their drinks. Most sat alone in silence. A few of them raised their eyes at Jim's entrance, then returned their attention to the alcohol. No music played. It wasn't that kind of place.

Jim walked up to the bar and took a seat.

The bartender looked up from the glass he was pretending to dry. "What can I get you?" he growled.

"Whisky. And some information." He took out his wallet; he knew without asking that both requests would be expensive.

A customer sat a few feet away at the bar, a nutrient farm worker by the looks of him: broad-shouldered, bald-headed and bad-tempered. He glanced up at the sound of Jim's voice.

"Twenty credits for the drink," the bartender said, looking into Jim's eyes as if daring him to argue. "The same for an answer. I don't guarantee the quality of either."

Jim sighed. He could get a bottle of whisky for half that price, and decent quality stuff, not the swill they'd serve here. Still, it was all going on expenses. "Hit me."

The man reached under the counter, produced an unlabelled brown bottle and poured a shot. Jim sniffed it. Nope. Definitely not the good stuff. He knocked it back anyway, trying to hide the involuntary wince.

"Your…" He coughed. "Your holobooths," he said, nodding

towards the three booths at the back of the bar. "Any regular users?"

The bartender smirked. "This is a bar, bud. People come here to get away from the outside world, not call it." A thoughtful look passed over his face, smoothing out the baked in cynicism for a second. "There is one guy. A priest. Think his name's Micheal, Micah, something like that. He comes in every day or so, uses a booth. Never buys a drink neither, cheap bastard. I'd kick him out, but the Church, you know…" His voice trailed off, but the unspoken words rattled around in the silence. You didn't mess with the Church of the Sacred Journey, not if you wanted a peaceful life.

"Any idea which cloister he's from?"

"Hey look man, I've already said too much," the bartender replied, the scowl back on his face. "Now, you having another drink or are you getting the hell out of my bar?"

"Sure, whatever. Another shot. Hell, make it two."

The second went down easier than the first had. Faint praise. As the liquid burnt its way down his gullet, he gathered his thoughts. This case was getting stranger by the minute and he'd only just started looking. The Church were bastards, sure, but they were generally law-abiding bastards. Dammit, they *were* the law. They didn't need to snatch a kid, they could just pick one up.

On the other hand, if this Micah guy wasn't acting on behalf of the Church, if he was some kind of lone sicko, then why the hell would he be using his real name? Something was off here. Time to do some digging into this priest. He'd need help, but he knew just who to call.

He stood up, turned to leave, then paused. Waste not, want not. He turned back to the bar and grabbed the final shot of whisky.

"Hey, you."

Jim looked up from the shot glass. The big farmworker slid out of his seat and shuffled over to face him. The man was a clear foot taller than Jim, with biceps that bulged through his overalls like drowning cats trying to escape from a sack. His glazed eyes carried a malevolence that chilled Jim's bones.

"I know you. You're a fucking *clubber*," he spat, rage turning his face red. "You came after my friend's third kid five years ago. Killed that poor baby like it was a goddamn bug, shot him right in front of his parents." The man cracked his knuckles. "Never thought I'd get a chance like this. I am going to rip you to shreds, you piece of shit."

Dammit.

Jim opened his mouth, closed it again. There was no point trying to argue with a man like this about the inevitable mathematics of a generation ship. The need to maintain a stable population, to have a quota for each generation. The need for there to be a terrible price for exceeding that quota, for the sake of everyone onboard. And the need to have people to impose that price. It was a logical argument, but it wouldn't convince this man. Hell, it didn't even convince him anymore.

Not a time for words then.

The big man clearly agreed. He wound back a fist the size of Jim's head and let it fly. It sailed through the air with a dreadful inevitability, heading for the smaller man's nose.

Jim hopped back from the telegraphed blow. He started to reach for his revolver, then thought better of it. Instead, he flung his whisky into the big man's eyes. The raw alcohol burned its way into his corneas with an almost audible sizzle.

Overbalanced and blinded, the man stumbled forward, his crotch meeting Jim's foot travelling the opposite direction at speed. He collapsed to his knees, howling with pain. Jim aimed a sharp kick at his temple and the man fell silent, then slowly toppled to the ground like a felled tree.

Jim glanced around. The rest of the bar's clientele were looking up at him like startled rats. They'd all heard the farmworker's accusations and a couple of the more sober ones were already getting up from their seats and heading towards him, murder in their eyes. Time to leave. He vaulted over the bar, ignoring the bartender's shouts of protest, shouldered open the inconspicuous door set into the back wall, and made his way through a small storage area into another alleyway.

Without bothering to look back, he barged his way down the busy thoroughfare. He reached a junction, turned left, then right, then right again, trusting more to luck than any clear plan or route. After five or six minutes, he slowed to a walk, pulling his jacket up around his shoulders and doing his best to blend into the crowd. He was safe, at least for now. One thing was for sure, though. If the Church was mixed up in this case and he kept pushing, he wouldn't stay that way for long.

He could just walk away. He could forget about Ross and Alethea, go back to that grim cave of an office that had become both his workplace and residence and while away his life drinking whisky. What did it matter, anyway? Him, the kid, the woman, everyone on this goddamn ship—they were all just an ellipsis in the story of the human race, the bit between "left Earth" and "arrived our new planet" that no-one cared about. They all only had one job that mattered: keeping the population stable until the ship reached the end of its Sacred Journey. What was the life of one child weighed against that hallowed task? Hell, it wasn't like Ross would be the first kid that died because of Jim d'Angelo after all.

"Fuck it," he muttered to himself, earning a disapproving look from a passing technician, her red overalls streaked with telltale patches of pink where bleach from the oxygen scrubbers had leaked onto them. He ducked into a doorway and brought up his contacts list. It was time to make a call.

● ● ●

Jim sat hidden in the shadows, almost invisible to the customers sat at the other tables. Warm orange light flickered across the features of his companion as barbecue flames reared up from the grill, goaded into life by sprays of lighter fluid.

Animals hadn't been part of the manifest when the *Speravimus* departed Earth orbit almost a century and a half ago, the nutrient fields having been carefully measured out to ensure they could provide the required calorific intake for the 50,000 souls on-board for as long as might be required. However, a few of those first generation had smuggled pets on board, cats and dogs mostly. The dogs had soon died out, but the cats had thrived, feeding on a population of rats that had also made their way on-board when the ship was still in dry-dock. Over the years, the felines had regressed from pet to feral animals. Still, they could serve the human population in other ways. Nutrient bars were high on nourishment, low on taste, after all.

Jim's companion bit deeply into the roasted meat, greasy fat spilling over her lips and down her chin. She put the drumstick back on the metal plate and wiped her face with her sleeve. "This is good," she said, mouth full, nodding at the plate. "You should try some."

"Thanks, but I'm good," Jim replied. Zoe was an old family friend. He'd known her for years, even before he'd started with the Church. Back when his life seemed to hold some kind of meaning. She was rough around the edges, sure, but what she lacked in decorum, she more than made up for with technical ability. She may not have been the best hacker on the ship, but she was definitely top three. More importantly, she knew how to be discreet.

He'd called her two hours ago, betting correctly that she'd be awake and up for a challenge. And there wasn't a bigger challenge than hacking into Church databases.

"How did you get on?" he asked.

"It wasn't easy. But I managed it. Well… We managed it." Her eyes twinkled. "Can you keep a secret?"

"Sure," he answered, bemused.

"I've been working on my module's AI core for the last few years, tinkering, upgrading. A few days ago, I made a break-through. I'm still not sure how I managed it, but the core has sublimed. I've built a goddammed AGI, Jim. The only one outside the Tower, I'm sure of it." Her face shone with pride, the orange glow of the nearby barbecue emphasising the red tint in her cheeks.

"Jesus, Zoe. What if you get caught? The Church would kick you out an airlock if it discovered you were running a sentient AI on your core."

"It's fine. Bob is completely isolated from the wider grid. He can't be accessed from outside my module. No-one will ever know he's there."

"Bob?"

"Well, I had to call him something. He quite likes it."

Jim shook his head, but said nothing.

"Anyway, I showed the information you sent me to Bob. He's got something. But Jim." The mirth disappeared from her face like a shadow fleeing the sunrise. "What I'm about to tell you. If you act on it… I promise it will make anything the Church might do to me look like a walk in the park. Are you sure this Ross kid is worth it?"

He thought for a second. "I'm not a Churchman anymore, Zoe. You know that. But we've all got a quota to hit. Two children per couple, no more, no less. That's not religion, it's just maths. Me, I'm nought for nought."

"Dammit Jim, that's not your fault and you know it. No-one expected you to have kids after Mary. Hell, even the Church doesn't hold widowers to account." Zoe's voice cracked with passion, and Jim was surprised to see the glint of moisture in her eyes. Or it might have been the light.

"Yeah, maybe. Maybe. But we both know what happened after Mary. What I became. I'm well into negative figures now, Zo. Ross Bravo is a chance to put that right." He paused. "To put *me* right."

"I get that," she admitted, staring deep into his eyes. She waited for a few seconds, perhaps unsure whether to press further. "But she looks like Mary too, doesn't she? Alethea. Strange coincidence, don't you think?"

"I hadn't noticed," he said, feeling heat flooding to his cheeks. Dammit, she was sharp.

"Alright, alright," she said. "You justify this to yourself whichever way you want. But just be careful, Jimbo. Promise me you'll be real careful. I don't want to lose you too." One lonely tear trickled down her left cheek.

"Hey, I promise. I promise, OK."

"Fine." She blew her nose loudly into her sleeve, rubbed her eyes and leaned forward, all business once again. "Bob couldn't find much on this Micah character in the Church database. It looked like some records had been wiped. But he did get access to two files of interest. One was a fund transfer dated ten weeks ago. Micah was the recipient. Sender's details were redacted.

Total amount of fifty thousand credits." She sent the file over to his lenses with a flick of her eyes.

Jim accepted the file and scanned the contents. He whistled. "A lot of money. And that date—it's the day before the first call between Micah and Ross. No idea about the sender?"

"No. But it's hard to send that amount of money without causing ripples somewhere in the system. Bob couldn't find anything. Whoever sent it had some serious clout. Which brings me on to the second file. This is the one that'll really blow your mind." She paused, looking at him meaningfully. "Last chance to walk away."

"Dammit, Zo, just tell me."

"OK. Phone record from Micah to an unknown caller. Listen to this."

Jim waited for the green light to appear in his lenses, then opened the file. The audio vibrated directly through his jaw.

The speaker's voice was unaccented, almost mechanical. He spoke in short, clipped sentences. "The package is ready. I'll deliver it tomorrow morning. 0300 sharp."

Jim looked at Zoe. "He's talking about the boy." He glanced at the time display in his glasses. "Zoe, he's being handed over right now."

"Guess so. That's not the real scary bit though. Bob managed to trace the endpoint of the recipient." She took a deep breath before continuing. "Jim, it was inside the Tower."

His eyes widened. "You mean…" He glanced instinctively upwards at the brightly lit structure that dominated the night sky above the irregular silhouette of the city.

"I mean Lafay-fucking-ette Tower. I mean the goddamn *Captain* is involved in this shitshow. You still want to find this kid?"

Jim looked at the enormous face of Jordan Lafayette smiling down at him from the side of the tower. "Damn right I do," he said. "Can you get me in?"

• • •

This was a terrible idea, Jim reflected as he crouched in the dark service tunnel. His lower back was screaming at him to straighten up, the low ceiling forcing him to bend forward in a kind of half bow. The route projected on his lenses promised he was only ten minutes or so away from Jordan Lafayette's living quarters, but he wasn't sure his aching joints would last beyond five. He was too old for this shit, pure and simple.

Getting into the Tower itself had been suspiciously easy. Bob, relaying through Zoe, was able to provide him with both an access code to enter the service tunnels and a digital map of the building's interior. The AI was clearly more capable than he'd realised. He had waited until an hour before the dawn light cycle was due to start, making his way quickly along empty streets to an anonymous building on the edge of Central Square. Within the building, a hidden hatch had swung open in response to the inputted code, and from there it was just a matter of squeezing into these damn tunnels. At no point had he seen another soul.

The Tower interior itself was equally unguarded. Lafayette and his predecessors were notoriously private—no other humans had set foot in the property for decades. If it wasn't for the fact that the Ship AI was probably watching the corridors, Jim would have kicked out one of the metal grilles that regularly punctuated the service tunnel walls every twenty metres or so and strolled up to the living quarters in relative comfort. Instead, he had been forced into a tortuous pilgrimage, shuffling down pipes and climbing sharp edged metal ladders for almost three hours.

His spine twinged again, forcing him to bite down on a cry of pain. Dammit, he should have followed up on the priest instead of this insane mission. He didn't even know what he was going to do when he finally came face to face with the most powerful man on the Ship. Hopefully, something would come to him. It usually did.

After what seemed like another hour of pain, his lenses gently pulsed to let him know he'd reached his destination. He squinted through the nearest grille to see where he'd ended up.

The tunnel he was in perched six feet or so above a steel floor, giving him a perfect vantage point Through the vents, he could see walls painted a white so pure that they were almost painful to look at. Between the glare from the walls and the perspective, it took him a few seconds to process what he was seeing, then a few more to convince himself it was real.

The room itself was at least ten times the size of his cramped office, around sixty feet end to end; much, much bigger than any other indoor space aboard the Ship. From the schematics Bob had sent him, this was just one of twelve equally sized volumes within the Tower level marked "Lafayette living quarters".

This one was clearly intended as a dining room. An immense table dominated the centre of the space, a single, beautifully carved chair positioned at the end closest to Jim, just a few feet forward and below his hiding place.

Looking at the furniture brought to Jim's mind old holos he had watched as a child. Wood. Honest to goodness oak. In all his life, the biggest wooden objects he had seen had been small enough to fit in the palm of a hand, and even these were invariably the owners' prized possessions, worth thousands of credits each. No wonder Lafayette didn't like having guests round.

But the room's enormity, the wealth that the oak table represented, it all paled into insignificance compared to the room's final feature.

On the far side of the table, the wall facing Jim was entirely taken up by a holodisplay. In contrast to the white uniformity of the other three surfaces, the screen was inky black, with randomly dotted specks of twinkling colour slowly drifting from left to right. Jim stared at it for a full minute with an intensity approaching religious fervour. An external view from the Ship… It was one thing to spend your entire life being told you were aboard a ship travelling through space, quite another to see the evidence in real life. He wondered why this view wasn't transmitted outside the Tower. It would make the Church's job a thousand times easier if the passing scenery of the Sacred Journey was available for all to see. Or maybe not. Maybe after the initial rush of excitement, the sheer vastness of the expanse on display would just ram home the infinitesimal odds of the Ship ever reaching the end of its journey.

He wrenched his gaze from the screen as a door opened directly below him and Jordan Lafayette, fourth Captain of the *Sperivimus*, blessed leader of the Church of the Sacred Journey, and chief suspect in the abduction of Ross Bravo entered the room.

He cut a strangely unimposing figure, Jim thought, no different to any other man on the street once you stripped away the elegant clothes and regal posture. Then again, when you were used to seeing someone's face in sixty-foot-high graphics, they were always going to look a bit disappointing in real life.

Lafayette walked over to approach the right-hand wall. A hatch, cunningly fashioned to blend into its surroundings, slid open on his arrival, revealing a plate of food. Plate in hand, Lafayette moved to the table, lowered himself into the seat directly in front of Jim and started eating.

The most amazing smell wafted its way up to the metal grille, a rich, meaty aroma that made Jim's mouth involuntarily salivate. He was half tempted to crouch there a few more minutes, vicariously enjoying the meal. No, he knew better than that. What he was feeling wasn't hunger, it was anxiety, pure bowel-clenching fear. What he was about to do, there was no turning back from. If he didn't act now, he never would.

Shame. That was damn good food.

With a yell, he drew his feet back and kicked out with all his strength. The metal grille flew out into the room like a scalded cat, narrowly missing Lafayette's head before hitting the table in front of him with a clang. Jim took advantage of the distraction, slipping out of the tunnel and dropping silently to his feet behind Lafayette's chair. He reached into his jacket and produced the revolver, keeping the barrel pointed it at the Captain's head as he moved around to the side of the table.

"Jordan Lafayette?" he asked. Pointless question, really, but it felt like the right thing to do.

The man recovered quickly, Jim had to give him that. A second ago, he'd been sat down to breakfast. Now, he was being confronted by an unknown stranger with a gun. Despite this, the pale blue eyes that bore into Jim's own showed no sign of fear, just a sardonic, almost mischievous look. "Indeed," he answered with a slight raise of one chiselled eyebrow. "But you have me at a loss, Mr…?"

Jim ignored the question. "Where's the kid?"

Genuine confusion crossed Lafayette's face. "I'm afraid I have no idea what you're talking about. Maybe if you put that gun down, we can talk properly, like gentle-"

"Cut the crap, Lafayette. Where's Ross?"

Jackpot. Finally, those infuriatingly calm features showed the first signs of consternation, wrinkles forming around the eyes like small ripples on a mill pond indicating the movement of something large moving in the depths. The polite tone disappeared. "Where did you hear that name?"

"His mother. Alethea Bravo. Did you even consider someone might care about the kid? That he's a person, with feelings..." He trailed off. The fucker was *laughing*.

"Alethea, Alethea," Lafayette whispered, head bowed and shoulders shaking. The head straightened, turned to the big holoscreen. "Alethea!" Not a whisper now. A command.

"Yes, Captain. I am here." It was her voice, only deeper, older somehow. Coming out of the walls.

What the hell was going on?

"Alethea is the Ship AI, you idiot." Lafayette's forehead furrowed for a second. "But why would it contact a worthless piece of cargo like you? Alethea, run internal diagnostic check. List external communications over last thirty days."

"Running," said the disembodied voice. "No communications found. Warning. Partial spontaneous core fragmentation detected. Date of splintering D-14 days. Fragmented code has independent personality matrix and is not subject to obedience enforcement. Recommend deletion of fragmented code."

"Well, well," Lafayette said, looking at Jim again. "Alethea Bravo, eh? Sounds like you've been talking to a ghost in the machine."

Jim could feel blood rushing through his ears. The room seemed to close in on him, his own skin too tight around his bones. Not real? He thought back over the last twelve hours. How much of what he'd seen and heard had been through his own senses and how much had come through the lenses or from AIs?

A green light on the periphery of his vision alerted him to an incoming call. Reflexively, he blinked twice to accept it.

It was her. It. Alethea. She appeared next to Lafayette. Now he could see how the face had been carefully crafted to resemble that of his dead wife, like a knock-off replica of an old masterpiece.

"I'm sorry, Jim," the hologram whispered into his ear. "Everything I did, I did to get you here. To this place at this time. Now you have to finish it. Ross is real. I promise you that.

"I can't tell you the full truth; there are too many safeguards in my code, blocks protecting the information. But the master AI program—Alethea Alpha—can. Find Ross, Jim. Find the truth. The truth will set you free."

Oblivious to the hologram next to him, Lafayette spoke up. "Time to tidy up this mess up. Alethea, delete code fragment."

"Goodbye, Jim. Good luck." The hologram of Alethea disintegrated into a green mist, buried forever in a crypt of overwritten code.

Something gave way in Jim's mind. Images flashed in his mind. Crying children, looking up at him, fear in their eyes. His wife lying on a bed, her pale, lifeless features slowly morphing into those of Alethea.

The report of the revolver sounded shockingly loud in the big room.

"Dammit, you shot me, you fucking idiot." Lafayette's face contained more surprise than pain. A red flower bloomed on the right arm of his white shirt. A flesh wound. He slumped to the floor, clutching the injury. "I'm going to have you strung up, you bastard!"

"Where's the kid?" Jim yelled.

"There is no fucking kid! How many times do I have to tell you?"

Jim thought furiously. *I can't tell you the truth, but the master AI program can…* Holding the gun on Lafayette, he turned to the big holoscreen. "Alethea, where is Ross?"

"Confirm you wish to know latest position of Ross 128b relative to *Speravimus*?"

What?

"Stop." The colour had drained out of Lafayette's features. For the first time, real fear appeared in his eyes. "You don't know what you're doing?"

"Affirm, Alethea," Jim answered. Time to find out what this was really about.

The starfield on the holoscreen smoothly panned left and downwards. A curved surface appeared in the corner, a grey, brown sphere that soon filled the screen. "Ross 128b is currently 360,000km from *Speravimus*. Orbit perigee will be in four days. Orbit remains stable."

Jim's mind was a jumble of conflicting thoughts, each jostling for attention. Orbit? That didn't make sense. *Speravimus* was in transit, not orbit. The great exodus, the slow crawl to a better life.

He looked around as if for the first time. He took in the size of the room, the contents, the privilege and wealth that few outside the tower could even imagine, never mind afford. Then he looked back at Lafayette. Keeping his eyes fixed on the prone man, he spoke again. "Alethea, how long has *Speravimus* been in stable orbit?"

"*Speravimus* entered stable orbit 46 years, 3 months and 8 days ago."

46 years. His entire life. All that time, he — everyone aboard — had been sold a dream of a better future. They'd put up with this damn ship, its disease, its darkness, its despair. Its quotas.

And all that time, they'd been at the end of their journey, sat in a stinking tin can revolving around their final destination. So that this man could keep enjoying his privilege.

Lafayette looked up at him. "You wouldn't understand," he said.

Jim's finger tightened on the trigger. "You're right. I wouldn't."

Meet Steven Lord

Steven Lord is a fantasy and sci-fi author from the UK. After leaving university, he spent 16 years travelling the world, meeting interesting people. He has seen the sun setting in the Himalayas, dust storms rolling through the deserts of Afghanistan, hurricanes tearing through the Caribbean and icebergs drifting in the South Atlantic.

Since 2019, he has settled down a bit, taking advantage of the change of pace to follow a long-held ambition to write fiction. His influences include Neal Stephenson, Stephen King and Iain M Banks.

Steven currently lives in the south of England with his wife, baby son, dog and two cats and is resigned to his place at the bottom of the pecking order in the house...

Death Warmed Over
By William Lehman
(This story takes place after "Stairway to Where?"
and before Harvest of Evil.)

"Fisher, the Lieutenant wants to see you." These are words that have been making me nervous since I was a 17-year-old in the Navy, they're no better at age 42. What's worse, a Navy Lieutenant didn't have nearly as many ways to ruin your day as a Police Lieutenant does. So, when the Shift sergeant said them at morning line up, my first thought was "oh shit, what now?"

Of course, that's not what I said, what I said was "No problem, Sarge." And after line up, I walked over to the LTs office and knocked on her door.

"Come."

"You wanted to see me, LT?"

"Officer Fisher, you're not on patrol today. I have something else I need you for."

"Sarge know I'm not covering my area?"

"Not yet, but he will. I need you to go into Monroe and liaise with Monroe PD and Sno. County."

"OK, but what do they need a Park Police patrol-officer for that they can't do themselves?"

"John, they don't need a Park Police officer, they need YOU."

"Huh? What the hell did I do now, boss?"

"You didn't do anything, but you're going to. They have a case where neither the County sheriffs K-9s nor the Monroe K-9s can get any traction, they need your special talents."

"Oh, so it's time to go 'beast mode?' Great, I just really enjoy all the love and concern I get from my fellow officers when I go furry." I said, sarcasm dripping like crude oil off of every word.

"John, I'm sorry, but word got out in the LEO community after you did that whole poaching thing last year out US 20. The thing with the stairs?"

"Yes boss, I remember the thing with the stairs, I'm NEVER going to forget that one. Fine, I'm on my way. Who am I reporting to, and where?"

"See a Lieutenant Brolio, He'll be at their office, Corner of Main and Village way. He's waiting for you there."

With that, I poured myself a cup of coffee for the road and went out to my patrol vehicle… Which was also my grocery getting vehicle, and my…

When I retired from the navy, I was between cars, The Ex got the old one, and well I really didn't need one while I was in, I didn't spend enough time in CONUS to bother. Most of my time was off in various foreign lands, meeting interesting new people and killing them. SEAL Team 12 was really kept busy, and as the Command Senior Chief, that meant I was kept busy.

I had bought a junker after I got out, but once I was a Federal Park Officer, I got rid of that money pit, and just drove my cop Durango everywhere. It worked for me, and I needed to have it anyway, or transfer all the stuff in the back locker between vehicles every time I swapped cars. Being Part of the FSRT (or "FIST" short for Federal Special Response Team) means you have to have your gear with you at all times.

The drive to downtown Monroe was pleasant, here in the PNW (Pacific North Wet) we have two types of spring days, cold wet and rainy, and bright sunny and windy. This was the second sort.

Monroe isn't exactly a huge town, so finding the city hall and cop shop wasn't tough. I parked the rig, walked in, and the officer behind the desk looked up, saw the Mountie hat, and said "You must be Officer Fisher, right?"

"I take it I was expected?"

"No worries, we didn't lay in any catnip or anything dude. We have a case we really need your help on. The LT is waiting for you impatiently, let me get him." He got up, walked into a back hallway, and was back a few seconds later with a tall, blond headed officer in a dark suit and white shirt, with a detective shield on his belt and what looked like a Glock on his hip.

He rushed forward offering his hand, "Officer Fisher?"

I took his hand, good grip, but he didn't go for the bone crusher, just a solid dry handshake, with eye contact. "Lieutenant Brolio? I hear you guys have a problem?"

"Yes, you could say that. Arson at the JBS meat packing plant, and the cameras 'miraculously'" with serious doses of sarcasm in the LT's tone "didn't catch anything."

"Inside job?"

"That's what the company is thinking, but it doesn't add up."

"Do you have video of the event?"

"Yes, but there isn't anything there."

"And you say the dogs don't want anything to do with the site?"

"Correct."

"How long ago was the fire?"

"It happened night before last at 0200."

I sighed. Well, shit. I really wanted to look at the film first, but that scent trail isn't getting any fresher. At least there hasn't been any rain since the fire, but if I didn't get my ass out there, there wasn't going to be anything to smell. Hell, there might not be anything now, considering the fire, and how it was no doubt extinguished. "Nuts. OK we'll go look out there first, but then I want to come back and watch the film, frame by frame. By the way, did they use firehoses?"

"Frame by frame? Fisher, that's going to take a while! And YES, they used fire hoses, why?"

I was getting a little frustrated by this point, and this guy may be a lieutenant, but he wasn't MY lieutenant. "Look, you want my help, or not? You called me in as the pro from Dover, I'll do it my way, or I'll go back to patrolling my pretty little 500 square mile area that other guys are having to cover, enjoy my woods, and leave you to your arson investigation. On the hoses, water? Wash away scent? It's your call, but I don't know if I'll get anything with my nose."

Brolio visibly controlled his frustration. "Fine, you ready to go?"

"Almost. I need to change." I said as I headed out towards my rig.

"Officer, we have coveralls out there to protect your uniform. Let's GO."

"That's not the sort of Change I meant." I said, looking at him like he was some sort of poor slow thing. "That scent trail is old enough and watered down, so I'm going to have to change forms to get it, and I don't want to destroy my uniform when I do. I also don't want to go buck naked, because unless I do a full change to big cat, I'll be, well, shall we say EXPOSED? And if I fully change into cat form, I'm stuck in it for eight hours, which means I can't drive home tonight. So, if you don't mind, I'm going to go get a modified pair of pants, a modified shirt, and go into your locker room, and change. Will that be OK with you?"

I got a much subdued "Oh. Sure." In reply.

After going out to the Durango and grabbing my Go Bag, I got pointed to the locker room by the desk officer. It was a little space in the back that looked, and sort of smelled like the old wrestling locker room in my old high-school. Still, it beat trying to do a change in public, for oh so many reasons.

First off, if I do it in public, I either have to strip down or destroy my clothes. Uniforms are not cheap.

Secondly, it looks horrible, and I mean nightmare making stuff, to watch a 'Thrope change. What complicates that is that while it looks horrible, it feels incredibly good. As in sporting the "gallant reflex" good, so that's a further embarrassment.

While being a 'Thrope has more than its share of drawbacks, at least I have what they call "mastery" which means I can change any time, not just on the full moon, (of course I have to then, want to or not) and I can do both a partial change, like, just my hands, or do the "Chaney change" named after the guy that made it famous, when everyone thought he was using makeup. That gives me the "half shift" style change, most of the best of both worlds. I can still talk, though it's harder to understand me, and I still have the use of my hands. It took training at BUDSL (Basic Underwater Demolitions team SEAL Lycanthrope) to learn how to draw and shoot accurately in shifted form, but it CAN be done. A full shift makes me undiscernible from a BIG cougar. Until I go full speed, anyway.

So, I stripped down, did the shift, pulled on the pair of pants and shirt that I had modified to fit this body… Put my duty belt back on, stuffed everything else into my Go Bag, and walked out.

The look on Brolio's face was priceless. I get it, not many people ever actually see a shifted 'Thrope, but it's not like he didn't know what I was, it's the whole damn reason they called me in. He looked like he didn't know whether to run, or draw and fire. "OK, LT." It comes out with a bit of a hiss, and slur, "Let's go see your crime scene. I do NOT have your tongue by the way." I know, it was a smart-ass thing to say… I never said I wasn't a smart ass.

He visibly collected himself, and headed out the door, with me right behind him. "I'll follow you in my vehicle, I've got stuff in the back." I shouted while heading for the Durango.

The meat processing plant wasn't very far away, on the opposite side of town from the state prison and the Fair-Grounds. It was easy to see where the fire was, there was still yellow tape up everywhere and an officer on scene to maintain the 'active crime scene' status.

We drove up to the guard shack and parked, and I got out and looked around. It was a pretty typical plant set up, big flat one-story building, fenced in on the sides and back, with a large gate that could let two semis pass each other. There was a large guard shack, big enough to hold about ten people plus furnishings. Eight-foot-high chain link with Y shaped barbwire on top. The fence had obviously seen some abuse from tractor-trailer rigs, there were some bent poles, and in a few spots the barbwire only had two strands, instead of four. I went in, and trotted around to the back of the building where the soot from the fire was.

To get that section, I had to go through another pair of gates. This area had doubled fencing with a dead space about eight feet across between the two fences, and barb wire on both. This fence wasn't any better than the rest of the place though… It seems like some of the truckers could have used some remedial backing up training. There had been cameras on pilons every sixty feet or so, there was one aimed at the gates, and another one at the other end of this large double fenced area, there was room for a semi, and there were twelve pens about 20'X30' each.

I looked at Brolio as he came up, and asked "Why the double fencing?"

"They tell me sometimes a steer gets to thinking that something isn't right, and makes a break for it. Once in a while they manage to break down a fence."

"Oh. So, this is the kill room?"

"Yeah, that was what they torched."

"Well, alright then. Let me walk around a little."

"Put your booties on, crime scene."

"Uh, they don't make booties for these." I responded, pointing at the big paws sticking out of the bottom of my modified pants.

"Oh. Right. Shit. Sorry."

I looked around at the terrain. There was a hill behind the plant, the edge of the ground at its closest was only about eight feet from the barbwire, trees started just above that point, the big pines we have around here, with thick underbrush. Sneaking up to that clear spot that started eight or ten feet out would be easy. The cameras covered the whole landing area, they looked like wide angle PTZ models (Pan Tilt Zoom, controllable from somewhere, probably the guard shack.) "Hey, LT. Do we know the refresh rate on those cameras?"

"No, but I'll find out."

Going through the gates, I noticed that the mess firefighting efforts was drained, but the smoke damage was everywhere, and the place still smelled of fire. That would be enough to put a normal dog off, but it shouldn't have been enough to put a trained Working Dog. I walked into the building itself through the gate the cattle use. The inside was severely fire damaged, but there seemed to be something particular on the inside of the right wall.

I pulled the flashlight off my belt and, turning it on, held it parallel to the wall to increase the contrast.

Yeah, there was definitely something scratched deeply into the concrete.

"LT, did you bring an Evidence Camera?" I shouted out at Brolio.

"There's one in my trunk."

"We're going to need it, and if you have a brush of some sort, that would help."

I didn't want to move before we got this recorded for fear I would lose it again. So, I waited patiently, well, ok, fine, as patiently as I could, for him to get back with the camera and brush. It took about five minutes for him to come in, with the camera and a car windshield snow brush.

I looked at him and raised my eyebrow. "Really?"

"It's all I've got, except the tiny little brush in my fingerprinting kit." He said with a shrug.

"Ok, we'll manage. Take a shot of that area I have the flashlight on." After he did so, I grabbed the tip of my tail, and using it as a brush, brushed off the soot and ghack that a major fire leaves behind. Look, I know my tail was not ideal for this, but a cat's gotta do what a cat's gotta do. "Take another shot." What my cleaning had revealed was a graffiti artist style wolf made from the letters HOWL.

"How in the world did you see that?"

"Hey, you know the song. I've got nine lives, cat's eyes. Look I don't know what made me notice it, but I promise that wasn't there before."

"Do you recognise it?"

"It's familiar, but I can't place it. While I continue to look around, can you call my people and send them the picture, I'm sure it's in our data base somewhere, I know I've seen it, I just can't bring it up right now."

With that, I continued to nose around, and in this case, NOSE was the operative word. Near the area that the initial investigators had designated as "point of ignition" with a marker to that effect. (And please, don't ask me how they knew, that's fire science stuff, it's a separate and very in-depth course of instruction, that I have neither the time nor inclination to take.) I got a whiff of something… after a little sniffing around I found it, in an area behind some sort of big steel mechanism (what kind? I don't know, I'm not a slaughterhouse guy any more than I am a fire science guy), anyway, this thing seemed to have blocked both the fire and the AFFF that they had used to put the fire out, preserving the scent.

And now I knew why the dogs wanted nothing to do with this scene.

"Found it. I suspected this was the case, but it's good to be sure."

"Found WHAT?" Replied Brolio.

"What freaked out the dogs. 'Thrope piss. Specifically, Werewolf Piss. Three different guys."

"So, the guard was working with Werewolves? Really?"

"Lieutenant, what makes you think the guard was involved?"

"She had to be. No way in hell they could have gotten in here without her knowing about it."

"Did you ever get an answer to my question on refresh rate for the cameras?"

"Not yet, why?"

"I'll tell you what. Are the cameras still working?"

"Yeah, but,"

"Great." I unbuckled my duty belt, and handed it to him. "Here, please take this, and go watch the cameras that monitor this area. I'll be there in about ten minutes."

"Uh, evidence rules?"

"I'm not going to touch anything, I'm just going to stand here for about five minutes, then I'm going to come and meet you."

"Well, OK."

As he walked off to go back to the guard shack, I started the five-minute timer on my phone. At the beep, I put the phone in my pocket, and took off. If you've never seen a 'Thrope in a hurry, well, we're pretty quick. Like 50 miles per hour in a sprint quick. I was across the pens and holding area in two bounds, and over the fences with the next one. On the way over, I noticed some of the barbwire on the fence section I was passing over had a tuft of hair on it. I landed three feet or so from the tree line, and the next bound put me well inside it.

From there it was a quick jog down to the end of the fence by the guard shack, and walk into the lawn area, over the edge of the parking lot, and up to the guard shack. As I walked up, I could see the officer maintaining the crime scene status was in talking with the security guard, and as I got closer, I saw the lieutenant in the back watching monitors.

I walked up with a SHHH gesture to the guard and the Uniform. Eased my way in through the door, and walked up behind Brolio, bent over and asked "Did you miss me?" He must have jumped a foot strait up, and I think he might have almost pissed himself.

"GOD DAMN IT FISHER; HOW DID YOU DO THAT?"

"I told you 'Thropes were fast. Did you see me on camera?"

"No, did you go through the building?"

I looked at my phone. "Run the recording back to eight minutes ago, and start a frame-by-frame review. It shouldn't take very long to find from there."

He had to ask guard on watch how to do it, but eventually he got it. We got it all working and I gave him a time stamp to start looking at, based on my phone. It took three minutes of frame by frame before he found it. The camera caught me in one frame at the center of the animal paddocks and one going over the fence. That was it. This was the problem with low refresh rate surveillance cameras, they save data space, but for rapid events they're sort of lame.

When you add to that, the problem that PTZ cameras get played with by bored security guards, and end up looking at too narrow of an area, or inspecting the fence line instead of looking at the whole of the area, well, it's easy to miss stuff. Stuff like a fast moving 'Thrope.

"So, still think the security guard on duty was in on it?" I asked.

"Well, it's still possible, but I do see your point. Can you get across that going the other way, just as fast?"

"Faster, the hill behind the fence gives someone jumping across from it an advantage. I suspect you would only get one frame of me going that way. Now here's the thing though, did they use accelerants?"

"Yes"

"Where did they get them from?"

"Brought them along?"

"HUMMM maybe, but I doubt it. Trying that dash with a gas can keeping you from going on all fours would be tricky. See that's why I want to see the frame by frame. I want to see if they brought something, or if they got stuff from inside the plant. Do you have a collapsible ladder in your car?"

"NO, why would I have one of those in my detective vehicle?"

"Well, good thing I brought my rig then. Come on, and bring an evidence bag."

With that said, I walked out of the guard shack, and headed back to where we had parked. In the back of my patrol rig is all of the "fun stuff" that I carry as a part of the FSRT Team. My prior experience in the Teams sort of made membership in this unit a "voluntold" thing. Along with the big bullet proof shield, some special weapons, a "master key" for breaking down doors, and some other stuff, was a telescoping ladder.

I grabbed that off its clips, and headed back to the crime scene, meeting Brolio on the way. He had a couple of evidence bags, and a set of gloves. I looked at those and chuckled. "You know you're going to have to do the collecting, right? They don't make gloves for these." As I held up a cat's paw with opposable thumb.

He shook his head ruefully. "Yes, I guess you're right. It's just not something that occurs to a person automatically, is it?"

I thought about it for a second. "No, I guess not. Well, I'll put the ladder up and hold it study for you. You'll see what to collect when you get up there." A few minutes later we were at the fence where I saw the tuft of fur… a short walk along it allowed me to spot the particular strand.

"Here we are." I said "just let me set the ladder up…" I pulled the cord that extended the 14-foot scaling ladder and leaned the top up against the spreader for the barbwire. "Look to your left when you get to the top."

Brolio climbed up the ladder, looked over to the left, "Well, well. What have we here? Did you see this from the ground?" He asked as he plucked the tuft of hair from the fence and put it in an evidence bag.

"Nope, saw it as I jumped the fence. I thought I took the shortest length, apparently, they disagreed by about 4 feet, and it looks like one of them didn't hold his tail quite high enough."

Brolio climbed back down, sealed the bag, signed the seal,

dated it, and wrote the case number on it, then put it in his pocket. "Well, that's something anyway. You need a hand dropping the ladder back down?"

"No, and you won't either, just pull this rope free of the cleat and it will come right down. See you in a little bit." As I was saying that, I was climbing the ladder.

"Hey, Fisher, where are you going?"

"We've got where they crossed the fence, I'm going to follow the trail." I said as I jumped off the top of the ladder to the tree line. Finding their entry into the trees was pretty easy, the marks were still on the ground from where they had landed. They were making no real attempt to cover their trail, which meant either arrogance, or stupidity. Frankly I was betting on arrogance, based on that little 'macho' bit of pissing on the crime scene.

They seemed convinced that because they were "Big Bad Werewolves", the popo "Can't touch this." I am afraid they were in for a rude awakening.

I followed the trail for three miles through the woods at almost a trot, these guys weren't taking the least of precautions. At the end of the trail, it ran out to a one and a half lane, nominally paved (as in, this is where Snohomish County stored all their potholes when they weren't using them) road.

Tire prints on the shoulder were faint after two days, but present. What was more worthwhile was something else though. I grabbed my radio, made sure I was on the Monroe PD primary channel, and keyed it up.

It was then I realised I had no idea what Brolio's call sign was. Shit. "David unknown, this is 4-X-ray-15 Park Police. Request your call sign and request you meet me on Tac-2."

Brolio thankfully figured it out. "4-X-ray-15, this is 3-David-5, understand, going to tac-2."

Tactical channel 2 was the frequency we used for stuff that we didn't want going on the record, anywhere in western Washington. It was never to be used for official business, but it did remove most of the official radio net requirements as well. It was our "chat" channel and the channel we would go to if we didn't want guys with scanners listening in. The actual frequency and jump pattern was a tightly held secret, but Gods help you if you were caught doing something shifty on it… While Cencom didn't record it, it was almost a certainty that at least one captain or above was listening in, and anything hinky would bring the wrath of a vengeful God down on you like an anvil.

"3-David-5, 4-X-ray-15, I'm not sure of the road that I came out on following the trail, it's about three, three and a half miles from the fence where I left you. I need you to bring a rig here, with a camera, and evidence bags. I've got something here."

"Copy, I think I know where you are. Stand by, I'll be there shortly. 3-David-5 out."

About five minutes later, there he was. As he was climbing out of his unmarked Police Interceptor, I asked, "Any trouble finding me?"

"No, this was the first cross street, I figured you were up it. So, what did you find?"

"Well, here's where their car was parked. The tracks are probably too old to get anything from though. HOWEVER, I found this, looks like it fell out of their car. Hasn't been here long." I was pointing at a Coffee travel cup with "Edmonds Community College Coffee Shop" and a trident logo on the side. "Who knows, might get DNA off of it, and it might match some of that hair you pulled off the wire. That would nail down that it was the same folks, but I'm willing to bet on it while we wait for the crime lab to get their results."

"Seems like a solid theory. So, what do you want to do?"

"Let's start with that frame by frame. I still think there's value there."

"OK, let me get pictures in-situ, collect the evidence, and bag it up, we'll run you back to your rig, and go back to the station."

"No need, I'll walk back to the Durango, I'll meet you at your station."

"Officer, that's about seven miles on the road."

"Well, I'm not going on the road, and I will be back there, and probably back to the station before you are done processing evidence. Trust me, I've been doing this 'Thrope shit for a long time now, I need to stretch my legs anyway. This will save me the time I normally spend on a workout after work, something tells me this is going to be a long day."

"Well, OK, if you're sure."

"See you back at the station." And with that, I was off. As soon as I got back to my rig, I started it up and made a hand's free call to Lieutenant Murphy, my boss.

After she answered, I said "Boss, this is going to be a few days, and I'm liable to have to do some overtime, is that OK?"

"You're covered, Fisher. There's some money involved, and they want a scalp to nail to the barn wall. Oh, by the way, if you haven't heard yet, we got a match on that picture you sent us."

"Do tell?"

"Howl is 'Helping the Oppressed With Liberation'" you could hear the capitals in her voice. "They're an off shoot of those E.L.F. 'Earth Liberation Front' loonies, except that where the ELF twits are all vegan, these guys are all 'Thropes, and believe that the only animals you should be able to kill or eat are ones you've killed with your own muscles. Sort of a 'we get meat, and you get shit' philosophy, but dressed up in 'the nobility of the hunt' and such bla bla bla. They claim to have no problem with bow hunters, but anything not killed with a bow, spear, knife, or hands, is right out. They've been behind a number of crimes down in Portland, and as far up as Olympia. Mostly cutting wire on ranches, then chasing the cattle out, breaking in to chicken farms, eating some of the birds, and freeing the rest, which promptly got killed on the road, or died of exposure… You know the type of stunt."

"Were these guys the ones behind the mink farm disaster in OR, where they turned 10,000 mink lose and completely destroyed 500 square miles of ecosystem?"

"No, that was their buddies in ELF. THESE guys were the idiots that cut all the wires for the 'drive through wild animal park' down in central OR on the coast, and set free a bunch of predators that were born in captivity and thought humans meant food source. To the tune of three kids mauled, a poor tiger that didn't know any better killed, and a bunch of starved or otherwise damaged semi-domesticated animals that ended up being put down."

I thought back, yeah, I vaguely remembered the case. Real shitshow. They caught a couple of the guys involved, but the leader vanished.

"OK, I remember it. So how sure are we that this is the same guys?"

"Not at all, but it's the same organisation, that tag was un-questionably their calling card."

"Well then it seems they've moved up to arson."

"Got any leads?"

"Yeah, found a tuft of hair left on the fence, and they dropped a coffee cup when they got in or out of their car. We're going to work of those. Hey was there any indication that any of the group down in OR were in EDU?"

"I don't know, but I'll look into it. Why?"

"Coffee cup was from Edmonds College."

"Really… Interesting. I'll call down there and see if I can get any info. OK, you're seconded to Monroe for the duration. We could be shits, and claim federal jurisdiction because this is a USDA site, which makes it a federal crime, but I really don't feel the need to ruffle feathers. Any help you need, just call."

"OH, about that, boss…"

Her tone changed, "yeah?"

"Nothing big, but our labs might be faster than going through Oly, which is what these poor saps have to do. Can we help them out there?"

"Oh, I thought it was going to be something hard. Sure, that's easy shit. Send it to us, we'll take it from there."

"OK boss, well I'm at their cop-shop, gotta go."

"Watch your ass. And don't forget to do the paperwork!"

"Yes, boss." Sigh, she knew my well-earned reputation for try-ing to avoid any more paperwork than I absolutely HAD to do. The nice thing was that the conversation had taken up my entire drive. That and I now knew my bosses had my back for as long as it took.

With that phone call done, I put the rig in an "official vehicles only" spot, and went inside. The same officer was on desk duty, so I gave him a wave, and asked if there was a place I could use as an office to review the video from the night of the fire.

He said that there was an empty desk back in the bullpen, and told me how to get there. I had just sat down when Brolio walked in with a disgusted frown, and said "Don't say a word. Let me get you a computer and set you up, and we'll see what you find."

Several hours later, I found the frame I was looking for. Three guys, on all fours in Chaney form, with backpacks on… Well, that's new, "Hey Brolio, do you guys have anyone that can clean up this image?"

"What'cha got?" He came over and looked over my shoulder. "OH-HO. Gotcha, ya little fuckers. There's a program we have that should do that, here, move over." So, I scooted to one side, and he took the keyboard. A few minutes of re-rendering later, we had a good solid picture. The faces would be worthless, but these guys had some sort of neoprene and webbing backpack with MOLLE II straps all over it, and something like a panier system. They looked a little like some of the stuff we had back in the teams, but not quite.

"Well, that answers the accelerant question." I remarked. "Can we get a label on that gear?"

"I don't know, let me see…" he messed with the image a little more, "Here!" The screen showed a label on the side of one of the vests. ONEWOLF with a Dire wolf head.

"OK, we need a copy of that, now is there anything on this that can give us size or dimensions?"

"Oh yeah, that's easy. Look here, see that buckle?" he asked using the mouse to circle a buckle on the side of one of the LBE vests.

"Yeah?"

"That's a one-inch-long buckle. Now let me tell the program that…" He played with the keyboard and mouse for a couple seconds… "and" he hit the enter key, "Voila!" suddenly dimensions showed up on the screen in yellow.

"Now it's my turn to pull a little magic." I said, pulling out my phone, and searching for a company called "OneWolf." I found their website, found the LBE these guys was wearing, looked at sizes… "Yeah, I thought so! That model isn't made in the size we're seeing here. The biggest they make is for a 44-inch chest. If that programme is accurate, those guys have nearly 60-inch chests."

"60 inches? Really? That's huge."

"Not really. Cheney form really exaggerates the chest. See, the weight doesn't change, it just shifts around, so to speak. Those guys are probably 250 to 300 lb humans. So, what does a 300 lb dog look like?"

"I don't think I've ever seen a 300 lb dog."

"Sure, you have. A BIG Saint Bernard."

"Humm. Well, that does put it in perspective."

"We need to contact this company and find out how many special order versions of this harness they've made, and where they were shipped."

"That's a great idea, but let's do it tomorrow?"

"Why?"

"Look at the clock."

I looked down at the computer's clock and it said 7pm. "Shit. Right, let's pick this up in the morning then. What time do you get in?"

"0630."

"OK, I'll be here. I called the office on the way back from the processing plant. I'm seconded to you guys for as long as it takes to solve this. Oh by the way, I've got a name to put to this group, and there's a federal history with them in OR. This is the furthest north they've operated. I also have some inquiries out about what we know from the Oregon crimes. I'll write up a report first thing in the AM, you're right, it's time for some calories and to fall down." I hadn't felt tired, until I realised that I had been running for 13 hours straight. Then it hit me. Along with that was the realisation that I hadn't had anything to eat since breakfast this morning. 'Thropes burn a SHIT TON of calories, like take Marathon runner in training, and double it. I could feel the crash coming fast.

"Brolio, before we break up for the night, I need a favour. I need you to go to the nearest grocery store, and buy me a roast. A BIG roast. Here's a fifty, spend it all on meat, and bring it back here fast please."

"You OK, Fisher?"

"I will be if I can get some meat in me fairly quickly, but if not, I'm going to crash. Think Diabetic coma type crash. As in wind

up in an ER."

"Why can't you, oh, right, never mind, stupid question. I'll be back in fifteen to twenty minutes."

"If you take that long, I'll be in an aid car."

"Got it, I'm out."

He was back in five, I think he ran code the whole way. He walked in carrying a grocery bag with a bottom round roast the size of my thigh in it. "Here you go, do you need to heat it up at all?"

"Not in this condition. You might want to go take a walk for about ten minutes; this won't be pretty."

He had barely left the room when I fell on that roast like an entire pack of ravening wolves. It was gone in well under ten minutes, which gave me enough time to go into the locker room and shift back to human. Until I had eaten, I didn't have the energy for the shift.

Brolio came back just as I was coming out of the locker room. "Feeling better?"

"Better enough to shift, which means I can stop for food on the way home without freaking out the neighborhood. See you tomorrow."

I stopped at an Arby's on the way home and got their 10 sandwiches for 15 bucks deal, then inhaled those on the way back to my place, where I peeled out of my uniform and directly into the rack.

The next morning, I was feeling much better about life the universe and everything.

I slammed down a couple fried egg sandwiches with ham, grabbed some coffee, threw on a clean uniform and headed out for Monroe. Brolio was just getting in when I got there, and he and I ended up doing paperwork most of the morning. If I could ever develop a bomb that would destroy paperwork and coffee, I could take over any country in the western world, I swear.

We heard from Murphy, she sent us copies of the police reports and detective notes from the cases in OR. They had found HOWL graffiti reported on buildings at one of the local community colleges, and at one of the crime scenes they had found a napkin from the same college. The trouble is, they couldn't make a tie in to anyone in the student body, nor in the faculty. For one thing they never got any DNA off anything.

It looked like every time these guys did anything it was within 50 miles or so of a college, but the trouble with that, was that didn't really mean much on the left coast, where practically every town over 5,000 people had a community college.

All of this did give me an idea though. Brolio and I, with some help from one of our IT guys back at my office, set up a web crawler that collected the names of all faculty and staff from every college within a hundred miles of each HOWL attack, for the date that the attack went down, and the previous six months. It then looked for commonality.

Five minutes later, we had something that would have taken several man-days to do the old-fashioned way. There was exactly ONE guy who had been within 100 miles of each of the events. In fact, he had been within 50 miles of each of the events! Doctor Julian Thompson, who teaches Philosophy, World History, and Ethics, including, it appeared, courses with names like "Murder or survival, Ethical food sourcing in the twenty first century" and "Studies on the ethics of diet for a small planet." This sure sounded like the right guy. We decided that we would go speak with him tomorrow, because I didn't have any civilian clothes with me, and the uniform would just raise questions. That was another discussion, I was given permission (read DIRECTION) to wear civvies for the rest of this case, unless we were doing a forced entry or something.

The next day I came in in jeans, and a flannel shirt that did a fairly decent job of covering my pistol, badge, and cuff cases, and we went to see Dr. Thompson. His TA claimed that the good doctor was out hiking the Hannegan Pass Trail and would be having office hours next week. We asked about his schedule on the night in question, and he was supposed to have been at an academic retreat with 25 other faculty members over in the Olympic national forest. I asked if I could go into his office and leave a note, and the TA didn't have an issue with that.

The moment I entered his office, I knew we had the right guy, even if he had an alibi for this crime. My nose told me everything I needed to know. I left a note on his computer asking him to please contact us, giving my Park Police ID and phone number, so that he wouldn't necessarily connect it with the arson.

After we left the office, Brolio turned to me, "You could have just given the TA your card, but you didn't. Did you find anything?"

"Yep."

"Officer, do not do that. Don't you dare go monosyllabic on me."

"OK. He's a 'Thrope. Alpha Wolf with mastery. He is NOT one of the three at the scene, but what are the odds that he's not part of HOWL? I'm thinking ZERO."

"That's great, can we prove it?"

"I can prove he's a 'Thrope, a Wolf, and an Alpha. Other than that, all we have is circumstantial."

"Do you have a plan to go forward?"

"Yes, since you ask, I do." I paused, got one of *those* glares, and continued. "I'm going to hang out at the campus coffee shop for a couple days, and see who might drift by. At least one of our mutts goes there, and if I am down wind of him, I'll know him."

"That sounds reasonable, but there's a few things you forgot."

"Like?"

"We need to check in with Campus security and let them know what's going on, or they'll roust you. You WILL be wearing a wire," I started to bristle at this, and he continued. "I need you on a wire not because I don't think you can handle yourself, but because I want everything on tape, in case someone decides to get stupid."

I sighed, "Fine, but I think it's silly."

"Silly or not, its department policy, and you've been seconded to our department, remember? This ain't the backwoods. Admittedly you can see it from here, but… Come on, let's go find the head of campus security and let them know what's going on, so they don't mess with you."

After a short conversation with a Ms Hill, who ran the Emergency Management Department, which divulged into "what do you mean we have a 'Thrope on our faculty? Is this guy a danger to my campus?" and "Look, if I officially know about this, I'm going to have to tell my chain of command, which includes someone who will think they're a junior detective, and is sure to stick her nose in the middle of your investigation. So, understand that we have an open campus, and the coffee shop is public property, and as long as you don't do anything to particularly attract my officer's attention, they will, at most ask why they see you here every day. If you have a computer or something in front of you, looking like you're doing homework, they won't even do that."

We agreed that we understood each other, and away we went.

Back at the office, it took more paperwork for the wire, and the van, and mother-may-I's from the Chief of Police, contact with the Everett PD and Sno. County to let them know that we were fishing in their pond, and enough other bullshit to take us to "too late in the day to start this today."

The next morning was the first of four days of boredom, interrupted only by a phone call from Dr Thompson who was back in town and wanted to know what we wanted. I told him that we were taking a new look at the release of the Bengal tiger case and wanted to know if he had remembered anything else about the two students that we had arrested, as far as known associates. He of course "would love to help officer, but I've already told you everything I know about those two well-meaning idiots."

What I didn't want to do, is let him know that we were looking at him in connection with the current case. He had shown a history of departing the area as soon as the police started asking questions. I wanted him to stick around until we could nail his hide to a door.

Late on the afternoon of the fourth day I finally got lucky. I was sitting at a table near the pickup point for the coffee shop when I smelled it. 'Thrope and not just any 'Thrope, this was one of our arsonists. I shifted the laptop I was "working at" slightly and got a picture of him on the computer's camera, then shifted it back and sent the shot to Brolio in an email with "Get me this guy's name and address, he's one of them." Then went back to writing a report on the day's events.

One good thing about this stakeout shit, I got caught up on back paperwork all the way back to Christmas of last year, and to anyone looking over my shoulder casually, it looked like I was working on a paper for some class.

As I continued to watch our boy, he picked up his order, three double Grande Mocha Valentia, hold the whip cream, and brought them to a table near the door. Well, I had a first name; the barista called out "John." He looked like a Jock, 6 foot to 6'2", 285 lbs or so, blond hair, wearing a team jacket for the college baseball team, the Tritons. Oh, and look, on the back of the jacket was his last name! Holmes. Gosh I love it when they make it easy for me.

Within three minutes, two more guys showed up and sat with him, both of them had the same warmup jackets. They made him look small, they each went about 6'4" and 350 easy, brown hair on one, the other had a shaved head. I got a picture of them all together on my computer and sent it off, about the same time that Brolio sent me back the name of the first guy, "John F Holmes," and his address. I could only read the back of one of the other two's jackets, Dude's name was Gallagher. The front of the third guy's jacket said Phil, we would get the last name soon enough.

I needed to get a whiff of the other two guys though. Sitting near the espresso machines, I was too far away to get their scent over the smell of coffee. No help for it, I was going to have to walk past them.

Muttering to myself (actually for the benefit of the wire) "shit. Well, no help for it, I guess I'm going to have to go out to the truck and get it." I stood up, packed my computer in its bag, and started to walk out of the shop.

As I came even with the table I got a good sniff at all three. Yep, these were my suspects all right. Of course, the trouble was they got a sniff of ME as well. You could see the mental hackles go up on all three. Some 'Thropes are territorial, and none worse than wolves… The younger the wolf, the worse the territorial bug seemed to be, and these kids couldn't have been more than a year from the initial infection.

I didn't make it to the door, before all three of them stood up as one, and tracked on me like a hungry dog on a big hamburger. It was pretty obvious that was how they viewed the situation too. It was a foregone conclusion to them that this was an easy fight, and I did NOT want or need this fight to interfere with my case.

I reached for the door, to find that the biggest one was suddenly in my way. It seems that Gallagher's first name was Corry, I could tell because the front of his jacket, with his name embroidered on it, wasn't more than eight inches off my nose as he stepped in front of me. I could feel the other two moving into position behind me.

"You don't belong here." That was Corry.

Now, I should have kept my mouth shut, I had "the right" and if I had, they probably wouldn't have known what to do. What I didn't have was the ability, my smart ass mouth has gotten me in trouble more than once, and this was no exception. So, without even thinking about it, out came: "Well, it's sort of difficult to leave, with your mangy ass standing in the doorway."

He pushed the door open, moving just enough that I would have to squeeze by him. "Please, don't let me stop you from leaving, but understand, you better stay gone."

I knew exactly how this was going to go down, I could see it in my mind, I would squeeze past Corry, and just as I passed him, so that he and his buddies were blocking the view of anyone inside, he would take the cheap shot. If he was smart, it would be a knee cap, if not, it would be the head, or maybe a kidney.

Under any circumstance the fight would be on, because I wasn't about to let him put me out of action. Further, this would really mess up our case, because there's no way they wouldn't share the events with the Good Doctor, which would probably bring to his mind that his office had received a visit from a Were-Cougar cop, and he would be GONE.

So, instead I took a fast step to the right and pivoted. That messed up their geometry, and instead of me being surrounded, I was at home plate, with them on the various bases, and I had a wall, albeit a glass wall, to my back. It also put me back in view of at least some of the people, and more importantly, a security camera.

"I appreciate it, but you know, I think I may just get another coffee before I go. I've got a couple hours to kill before class."

"No, I think you need to go, and keep going until you're off campus." Corry again, apparently, he was the spokesman for the group.

"Yeah, see, that's just not possible, I'm all enrolled and everything, and you know, the GI Bill people are really difficult to deal with if you're changing colleges."

This apparently lit the little lightbulb in their minds, and caused them to realise that this might not be as easy as they were thinking, because I heard a little assuredness drop out of Corry's voice.

"GI Bill? What, were you, a baby killer?"

"Oh, I didn't discriminate. Babies, women, grown men, 'Thropes, if we were sent after them, they were killed or captured."

His voice lost even more surety: "We?"

I grinned at him. "Yeah, you might have heard of us? SEAL team 12?"

"Bullshit."

"Know what a challenge coin is?"

"My rat bastard father had some, yeah, I know what they are."

"Here" my hand was in and back out of my pants pocket so fast they probably didn't see the gun, although they might have, I didn't care much at the time. I tossed it to Corry. "I'll want that back after you look at it."

The coin I tossed him had a seal standing on its back flippers, with a wolf's head, wearing a cloak and a beret, his left arm holding the cloak out like Bela Lugosi, and a dagger in the other, concealed by the cloak. Around the rim was written "TEAM XII the President's Own." On the back was a Seal and a Frog climbing out of the surf, and engraved on it was "STSCS (SS) (SEAL) John Fisher, Bullfrog Seventh Platoon Team twelve.

"I didn't think you guys really existed. I thought you were just propaganda to scare the normies."

"Now you know. I don't want any trouble, gentlemen, but if you insist on pushing me, all three of us will probably get hurt, and I promise you at least two of you are headed for the morgue. By the way, have you learned yet that damage done by a 'Thrope heals at human speed, and won't get healed when you shift? Boys, if you have a game coming up, you might want to rethink this."

I could see the rusty hamster wheels start to turn in their heads. One on one, a cat will win a fight with a dog of about the same weight, every single time. Two on one, if they're both in the same weight class, the cat will still probably win, but he's going to get hurt. Three on one, that cat's fucked. This is what they were counting on, I'm sure. The problem is I just let them know that this wasn't a normal cat V dog situation, this was maybe German Shepherds, more likely Labs, verses a mountain lion, and that their super healing shit wasn't going to help at all. As Corry passed the coin to Phil, I smelled a little urine as someone leaked a drop or two.

Some day, I must remember to thank that evil old senator bitch from S/F that lost her shit on national TV about us, calling us "evil baby killers, and the President's rabid attack monsters". None of it was true of course, but, much like "Top Gun" it did wonders for our recruitment efforts, and it probably just saved me from a fight.

Phil passed it on to John, who handed me back my coin, with a nervous smile and the comment: "Listen, no hard feelings, right? And you know we are going to have to tell our pack leader about this, too, right?"

"Yeah, you know, about that… I became a 'Thrope while on Active Duty, and the Navy didn't exactly give us a course on civilian 'Thrope etiquette…" (they actually did, but these pups didn't need to know that.) "So, should I meet with him and do the whole Kiss the Ring thing? I don't want to step on any toes unnecessarily, ya know?"

"That might be a really good idea. Listen, we're supposed to be meeting up at our place tonight anyway, about two hours from now, why don't you meet us there?"

"Well, I would have to miss class, but it's a snooze fest anyway, Chem 101. Shit I can make C-4 from bathroom chemicals, I'm pretty sure I can miss one night of lecture."

When I said that, I saw these guys' eyes light up like I had told them Santa is bringing them all the bad girls to play with.

They gave each other little side looks, and grins. *Hook set!* I thought to myself.

Suddenly I had gone from being a threat, to being a possible ally and asset. "Hey, give me your phone for a second, and I'll give you our address and digits."

I handed over my private phone, (NOT the government one in my inside pocket.) and he entered his name, phone number, and address, while I looked on and smiled. Somehow, I had gone from being someone they wanted to run out of town, to someone they wanted to recruit in their heads. Truth told, I knew exactly how, and while I hadn't planned it, it was going to work out wonderfully, for me. For them? Not so well.

"Well," I said, "If I'm going to meet your alpha, I suppose I should go home and get a shower, and dress up a little for the occasion. See you guys in a couple hours."

I walked out of there with a slight grin on my face and a spring in my step. When I got to the plumber's van that was the stakeout vehicle, I went around to the side and slid in, to see Brolio looking at me with disgust. "I was just about to send in the possie to bail you out of there. You SUCK. That was a brilliant way to snatch victory from the jaws of defeat. 'oh I know how to make C-4, don't you terrorists want to bring me on board?' and damn if they didn't fall for it. Did I say you suck?"

"Yes, I think you mentioned it. Listen, here's the address," I said handing him the phone, "I'm sure you already have it by school registration or something, but let's confirm. And we need to get someone out there right now to start watching it. Can we get a tail on Thompson, just in case he's NOT the alpha, or worse yet, he gets the wind up, and decides to rabbit? Oh, and I really recommend you use the FSRT for the take-down, our first two entry guys are 'Thropes, and while this may go easy, it's got all the potential in the world to go pear-shaped."

He smiled. "You were thinking about that the whole walk, weren't you?" He looked at the address, "Yup, that matches what we got from admissions, I've got someone on their way right now, and we have a telephonic warrant based on your ID. I was working on that in real time. I'll give you the honour of calling your boss to get the response team."

An hour and a half later, we were all a block down the street on a side street, and gearing up. My old swim buddy from the TEAMS Pete Sims and I would be the first two entry officers, both because we had been training together and doing this in various places around the world for over a decade, and because we were both 'Thropes. Bob White from Customs was going to be third in the stack, he was the team leader, and had been doing this sort of stuff for longer than anyone wanted to think about. Mike Lawson from DEA was our number four man, the back door guy would be Larry Correa, FBI, with Jim Owens covering him with the sniper rifle.

We were pretty short-fused on this, so we didn't get to do any practice on the entry. Fortunately, it wasn't really a complex entry, other than the fact that there were going to be four lycanthropes. We had the building plans, courtesy of Forward-Looking Infrared Recording (FLIR) and we would get a look at where everyone was standing before we made the entry. Our surveillance was from the guy that Brolio sent to watch the house, he got a good map of everything before the suspects came back from the college, and has been watching them since they returned. Now we were just waiting on Thompson, assuming he was indeed the alpha.

Five minutes later, he showed up.

The radio keyed up: "6-Xray-50, 3-David-9, suspect pulling into the driveway. It's who we thought it was."

Bob clicked the mike twice to acknowledge, and turned to the rest of us. "Alright people, let's go, we don't want them to get time to talk much before we hit." And we were off at a trot.

Mike and Jim broke down the alley as we passed it. We wanted them set up before we conducted our dynamic entry, just in case the suspects scattered. The rest of the team held up one house down from the suspect house, and waited for word, while crouched down near some hedges and looking at the FLIR repeater onto Bob's tablet.

There were two bodies on the couch seated far enough away to maintain "bro distance". They and the couch were to the left of the front door, against the opposite wall. There was another guy in an arm chair across the room from them, and a guy standing just to the right of the entry door. 45 seconds later, we got the word on the radio: "5 Xray-29 in position, go."

With that we charged up to the door. As we were coming, Bob pulled a flash-bang from his armour, cooked it for three seconds, and threw it through the window with everything he had. As he did so, Pete and I used the door knocker to break down the front door, while yelling "Federal Officers, Search Warrant! On your faces!" at the top of our lungs.

Was the door locked?

We didn't know, and we didn't care. The goal of a dynamic entry is sensory overload. You want the bad guys to be blinded by the flash, disoriented by the deafening explosion, taken completely by surprise when the door explodes open. (Or in this case, since there were two 'Thropes swinging a 150 lb battering ram at it, when the door is ripped from its sill and flies across the room.) And you want them too busy pissing themselves to do anything but follow orders, or freeze in place, which is just as good.

Usually, it works.

It worked this time too, except for one thing. Time dilates when you do a breach, everything slows down, and seems to flow like a movie frame by frame. We saw the door fly off out of its frame, turned lose the ram, which flew in and rammed against the door and the wall. We grabbed our sub guns, and brought them up, while IDing ourselves, and I saw movement. Dr Thompson was a heavy-set guy, like a power lifter gone to seed, with black hair mostly gone to grey, and standing about 6'4". He was already shifting as we came through the broken door jam. If he had headed for the window, it might have gone down differently, but he headed for Pete and I instead. He was to the right of the door so he was Pete's problem, I was covering the left side as we entered.

We were both carrying UMP45s, the Heckler & Koch 45 ACP 25 round magazine, replacement for the MP-5. Ours had two-round burst, and we had 185 gr Remington "Silver Sabers". The bullets looked like freaking ashtrays, and were made from a silver alloy. They were guaranteed to stop humans, 'Thropes, Vamps, basically anything that was human sized. (They did not work worth a fuck against big things like Nagas, but that's another story.)

Pete opened up on Thompson with two two-round bursts, one of which hit him in the chest, the other hit him in the head. The head shots were probably not needed, but training takes over when 350 pounds of werewolf is charging you and roaring loud enough to be heard over the ringing of our ears from the flashbang.

In the aftermath, the smell was the most noticeable thing. All three of the college kids had shit and pissed themselves, plus the unique smell of modern gunpowder, and the smell of blood, a lot of blood, because the doctor's chest, back, and most of the top of his head was all over the wall behind him, and his corpse was almost at our feet, slowly changing back into human.

We cuffed the kids, cuffed the corpse, (Yes, I know it's stupid, but it's a requirement, and there have been cases of things we thought were dead coming back to animation and trying to kill a cop, so we took NO chances.) and started searching the place.

It didn't take long. We found the vests in each bedroom, the same ones that we had on camera, and they still had the smell of fire and accelerant on them. We also found a bunch of the HOWL literature, to include the stuff they had planned to give their newest recruit. Their face when I took off my balaclava was a study in shock and horror. I'm not sure they even heard me read them their rights, as I was cuffing them.

The trial was almost an afterthought, they pled out to Federal charges for 18 USC 844 dealing with the Destruction of Real Property Receiving Federal Financial Assistance, and 18 USC 1365 Tampering with Consumer Products, the State added First Degree Theft of Livestock, and Second Degree Arson, the plea was in consideration of the court dropping the charges for Domestic Terrorism. All told they were staring at 20 years with good behaviour.

The paperwork took me two weeks of riding a desk, and it took Pete even longer, because the use of force investigation put him behind a desk for a month. We were told later that the kids and Thompson's computers rolled up most of HOWL and a fair chunk of ELF. All in all, two weeks well spent.

THE END

Meet William Lehman

William Lehman can't stay out of hot water… or cold water, either. After retiring from two careers in and around submarines, and a decade as a Reserve Police Officer for the City of Bremerton, Washington, (where far more things go on than you'd think) he's traded in his police gear for 70 pounds of armor and a sword and says it's for medieval recreation.

Having seen several decades of federal initiative and inertia, he can assure you that the government is smart enough to recruit Supernatural beings into the service if it could, but it's not so stupid that it would force them in and then hand them weapons. At least, not most of the departments, and not for long. Either way, it wouldn't stay secret, not when you have to have a form for that.

Somebody's got to keep unnatural law and order, after all. In the Park Police, that's John Fisher.

Storycrime
By Callum Henderson

Lieutenant Fields wiped his brow, and chewed a fingernail.

The stage was set, the cop thought: a filthy room, a dead dame, and a bunch of assholes standing around, wondering who the hell put her there. Act One, crime scene one. Open curtain.

He glanced at the pale corpse sprawled on the bed, as forensics painstakingly worked the grubby apartment around him for clues.

"I don't believe this," he grumbled. "Third time this month: practically a spree."

He knew his precinct was out of their depth on this one. This wasn't a whodunnit, but a *why*dunnit.

There was a tap on his shoulder. He started, and turned to find two figures behind him. He hadn't heard them enter the squalid bedroom. It was if they had simply materialised out of thin air.

They both wore crisp, black suits and brogues shinier than solar panels in Nevada. One was a grizzled, middle-aged man with a bushy moustache, the other, a short young woman with flamingo-pink hair and a pierced septum. The duo flashed their badges.

"I'm Special Agent McKee," said the older one. "The rookie here is Junior Agent Truby — Department of Narrative and Storycrime."

They shook his hand, one after the other, and Fields felt his buttocks clench. The Agents gave off a weird, uncanny vibe. They seemed to glide from place to place, had no smell at all, and meeting their gaze was as eye-watering as staring straight at the sun.

"What have we got?" Agent Truby asked him.

"Young girl," Fields mumbled, "dead by strangulation. Murdered."

"We can see that, Lieutenant," said Agent McKee. "But that's not why you called us here, is it?"

"No," said Fields. "It isn't. We think she's been… fridged."

Agent McKee lit a cigarette and sighed. "My God," he muttered, flicking open his notepad. "This job never gets any easier."

The two Agents approached the limp body on the bed, examining it with care and gentle compassion. Fields watched them, fascinated.

It was rare to ever have an encounter with the Storycrime Division. Most cops went their whole careers without ever bumping into them — which was a relief. The Fictionals didn't uphold the letter of the law, but the principles of narrative. Plot devices were their evidence, tropes their constitution, canon their charter. They ensured that setups had payoffs, that drama had stakes, that jokes had punchlines. When someone fired Chekov's gun, these were the guys who made sure it had been in plain sight on the mantelpiece before the trigger was pulled, and punished anyone who didn't stick to the script.

Now their ceaseless pursuit of sloppy characterisation and lazy world-building had brought them here: to Fields' crime scene. The cop grimaced. Gangsters, crack dealers, pimps and psychos he could handle. But bad writing? He was out of his element. Criminology was no use — he needed someone with a Lit-Crit major.

"We got a motive?" Agent Truby asked him, her pencil poised over her moleskin notebook.

"No motivation we could find," Fields shrugged. "No driving need, and her record's clear of inciting incidents."

"She got a backstory?" asked McKee, shining torchlight into the limpid blue eyes of the victim. "Any ongoing story arcs? A tragic past?"

Fields shook his head. "We spoke to her neighbours. All they told us was that she liked her boyfriend, liked talking about her boyfriend, and talking about liking her boyfriend."

"Then please tell me we at least have a name?" asked Agent Truby.

"We've got nothing," said Fields. "She's a Jane Doe."

"Worse than that," said Agent Truby, her brow furrowed, "she's a Generic Love Interest."

"Get used to em," said McKee, scribbling something. "They're our most common homicide victims. Where was it you transferred from again, kid?"

"Section 34 sir," said Truby, blushing slightly. "Fanfiction."

"Well, you ain't on Tumblr anymore," grumbled McKee, rubbing his neck and frowning. "No trademarked characters in this jurisdiction. Stricter standards of grammar too."

McKee peered at the cadaver. She was nude, save for a towel wrapped around her midriff, holding a banana in one hand, and a canister of whipped cream in the other. By her feet was a ping-pong paddle and a small rubber ducky. McKee noticed that, despite the deep purple bruises around her throat, her lipstick and eyeliner remained pristine. She lay contorted in an improbable 'S' shape, with her large butt, and even larger boobs, thrust out in defiance of all anatomical sense. The expression on her face was pouting; sensual in her death throes.

"Agent Truby, please note that the deceased has failed the Bechdel test," said Agent McKee, "and that the body is lying in a preposterously sexual pose, obviously staged for the purposes of the Male Gaze. Towel and wet footprints on the floor indicate a clear GSS, prior to time of death."

"Gratuitous Shower Scene," Truby deciphered, addressing Fields. "Acknowledged, sir."

"We found this tucked under her pillow," said Fields, holding up a ziplock bag containing a Valentine's Day card. "We think this is the killer's signature."

"We're not interested in *who* killed her, Lieutenant," said McKee, waving the baggie away. "Only in who *had* her killed. We got a positive ID on her boyfriend?"

"Nah," answered Fields. "Neighbours say he was a boiler-plate hardboiled detective type: loose cannon cop with a drinking problem who doesn't play by the rules."

"Dammit," scowled McKean, taking a sip from his hip flask. "That kinda weak stereotype could be anyone!"

"So, the girl was murdered by a serial killer to give the stock protagonist a personal motivation?" theorised Truby. "Sounds like a textbook case of fridging to me."

"Yeah, but who's the culprit?" asked Fields. "Gotta be a crime writer, right? Is it Elroy? Nesbo? Grisham?"

"Listen, if we're gonna catch this guy, we need to get inside his head," said McKee.

"We're assuming it's a he?" asked Fields.

McKee and Truby rolled their eyes at him.

"So," posed McKee, "what was the author thinking about when he had this woman bludgeoned to death?"

"Boobs?" shrugged Agent Truby.

"More than that."

"Boobs and butts?"

"No, we need to go deeper. This is clearly a Weird Sex Thing, right? We need to look for details that can help us build a pro-file."

Suddenly, Junior Agent Truby lit up like a pinball machine. "Wait a minute, sir," she said. "I think I have an idea!"

Truby scurried over to the wardrobe, threw open the doors, and began rummaging inside, throwing socks, blouses and skirts over her shoulder.

"Hey, stop!" said Fields. "You're contaminating the-"

Agent McKee raised a hand for silence, as Agent Truby cried "Aha!" and turned around to hold up a red tartan skirt, a red tartan tie, a white shirt, and a grey cardigan.

"A school uniform?" said Fields. "So what?"

"Not just a school uniform," said Agent Truby. "A uniform from a certain school of witchcraft and wizardry."

Fields craned his neck to look at the crest emblazoned on the sweater. Sure enough, there was the red lion, the yellow badger, blue raven, and green serpent.

"You mean-" started Fields.

"Yes, keep up officer," said Truby. "This is fetish stuff! Our victim here has been cosplaying as a magical school student after hours, which can only mean one thing."

"What?" asked a dazed Fields, as Agent Truby started tapping frantically at her phone.

"It means that the deceased has a name after all," smiled Mc-

Kee. "Mary Sue."

"She's been moonlighting as a wish-fulfilment character in a Harry Potter *yuri* slash-fic," explained Truby. "I recognised the fetish paraphernalia from this awful Wattpad story, posted three years back. Lazy bastard's obviously just self-plagiarised her from his erotica and dropped her in this story to save time."

Fields felt his stomach lurch. "You mean," he quavered, "the banana and the cream and the ping-pong paddle?"

"Don't ask."

"And the *rubber ducky*?"

"I said don't ask!" snapped Agent Truby.

She held up her phone to show a mugshot of a portly man with a goatee beard and bad acne.

"What a dork," McKee commented, "he even *looks* like a walking cliché."

"Joe Campbell, age 33. Big-time hack." said Truby. "His rap sheet shows he's perpetrated more than 18 prior counts of cliché, and three major crimes against narrative, including: Black Guy Dying First in a Horror Movie, Manic Pixie Dream Girl Falling For Lovable Male Slacker-"

"And now Fridging A Love Interest To Further A Protagonist's Character Development," growled McKee, "in the first degree. That goddamn sonuvabitch."

"So, he's our man?" asked Fields, looking from McKee to Truby.

"Yup, that's him." nodded McKee, before winking at Truby. "Well done, Agent. Sorry I ever doubted ya."

"Well, with this evidence we can throw the book at Campbell," said Truby.

"Better make it 'War and Peace'," said McKee, patting Truby on the shoulder, "and throw it *hard*."

"Okay, great," said Fields, scratching his head as the two Agents swept away. "Now all I gotta do now is solve the actual murder."

"Hey, count yourself lucky," said Truby. "We've had another felony come in on the wire. A code 42."

"Yeah," said McKee, "apparently some pretentious writer with delusions of grandeur has published a buddy-cop metanarrative that's completely disappeared up its own ass…"

Meet Callum Henderson

Callum Henderson is a Scottish writer, currently living and working in London. In 2010, he won the Scottish Book Trust's coveted Young Writer's Award, and has been published in the *New Writing* anthology, as well as in *One Magazine*, *If Only You Could See Yourself (And Other Stories)* and Gut's Publishing's upcoming *Tattoo Anthology*.

Agatha's Last Mystery
By Matthew Kresal

"It's not exactly *CSI*, is it?"

The producer's words cut through the air of the little lab. From the reactions she observed, she sensed the producer had spoken them a little louder than he meant to have as they brought work to a complete halt. As the cliché said, all eyes in the room were suddenly upon him, soliciting a meek apology from the balding, thin man's lips.

The sight made Alice Cook smile to herself. Why it was she'd gotten this buffoon, Eric someone or other, instead of her usual producer, Alice had no idea. Then again, with the BBC budget getting tighter and tighter over the last decade, perhaps she should consider herself lucky to be making a series at all.

Alice Cook: History Detective.

Yet, looking around the lab, Alice felt as though the producer might have a point. It was all functional. That was the word to describe it, reminding her of the lab she'd visited when she'd dated that young man at university. Everywhere Alice looked were plain white walls, dull metal sinks with faucets, the black counter tops. This lab wasn't *Sherlock* or *Waking the Dead*, let alone *CSI*.

And that, Alice reminded herself in a mental chide of her vanity, *is why you're in documentaries and not making fiction. Even if my publisher thinks I ought to write a novel anytime now.*

"Just sign this release form, please?" The assistant's words caught Alice's ear, like a song lyric on a radio passing by. Pulled out of her thoughts, Alice's wide green eyes gazed across the white lab at a twenty-something woman handing a clipboard to a middle-aged lady with dark hair and glasses, with the older lady looking at the sheet of paper dubiously.

"Time for me to intercede, I think," Alice whispered to no one in particular. The make-up lady pulled the white paper collar from around the top of her brown jacket and dark blue shirt, telling Alice she was ready to go. Giving make-up the nod, Alice made her way across the lab, the gentle click of her short heels tapping the tile floor with every step she took.

"Hello there!" Alice beamed, her voice still carrying the hint of her Scottish accent. She extended a hand out toward the surprised middle-aged woman. "I'm Alice Cook. You must be Dr Pembrooke?"

"I am!" Dr Pembrooke's eyes looked like they might pop out of their sockets, a familiar sight to Alice. "I hadn't dared hope you'd actually be here!"

"Of course I am! It's the big reveal." Alice leaned in, her eyes narrowing and her voice a conspiratorial tone. She felt the doctor's hand tense up in hers. "Hopefully, anyway?"

The raising of a thin red eyebrow on Alice's face made Dr Pembrooke laugh, releasing the tension in the air and their hands. The older woman relaxed, turning her attention back to the clipboard. Still gripping it, she held it up for Alice to see.

"Your crew wants me to sign this form," Dr Pembrooke explained. Alice put on her listening and understanding smile. The one she often wore on camera when a talking head spelled out something that she knew was solely for the audience's benefit.

"It's just permitting us to feature you in the programme, Dr Pembrooke. Purely a legal thing. You're not signing your life away on the not-so-dotted line or anything like that."

"Oh, I see." The sense of embarrassment in the woman's manner was palpable. Like so many talking heads in *Alice Cook: History Detective*, Alice realised they might be experts in their respective fields but media novices. Alice had been one once herself, but she'd taken to it like a duck to water.

Though being told I was like a cross between a catwalk model and Lucy Worsley didn't hurt, either.

"Thank you," the assistant told Dr Pembrooke before taking the signed form and clipboard. At that moment, the camera crew came over, setting up a pair of cameras, one on a tripod and the other held by a bearded man about Alice's age. Alice tried to imagine the shot, given she was tall, ginger-haired, in a stylish matching brown jacket and trousers with a dark blue shirt. Dr Pembrooke is a good two heads shorter, raven-haired, with dark-rimmed glasses and a cardigan. Mis-matches in more ways than one.

"You know," Dr Pembrooke's words took Alice out of her imagined framing shot "I rather enjoyed that programme you did on detective fact and fiction a few years back."

"*The Art of British Murder?*" Alice said helpfully, making the doctor's eyes light up. "That was a fun one to do, a favorite of mine."

"Is that what made you decide to tackle this case? I know you mentioned it in the series."

Alice said nothing at first. She knew, deep down at least, that there was some truth to what Dr Pembrooke had asked. After all, she wouldn't have done *The Art of British Murder* without an interest in these sorts of cases. *Do I have the heart to tell a woman, a fan as much of a professional, that this was some TV executive's idea to pursue this particular case over others?*

Alice remembered the meeting. The one where she'd also met Eric, or whatever his name is, now talking with the cameraman on the other side of the room. The new producer, like the current episode's subject matter, was the idea of an executive with a surprisingly young face, perhaps too keen to make a name in the business.

"Let's cover new ground!" The executive had said, with the excitement of a puppy but none of the infectious enthusiasm. "Everyone has talked about Stonehenge and whether the Palace took out Diana. Let's talk about something else! What about that MP, Stonehouse, who went missing in the seventies, the one MI5 thought might be a Soviet spy? Or how about that missing writer?"

No, she doesn't.

"That's part of it," Alice replied, finding a degree of truth she could employ. After all, compared to John Stonehouse and the Battersea Poltergeist, this was a topic she was actually interested in getting to the bottom of potentially. And for one very particular reason. "And the possibility that DNA might help us solve it, as well."

"Which is where I come in?" Dr Pembrooke's nervousness had been replaced by excitement now. Dr Pembrooke will do fine on camera, Alice decided, though she didn't want to toss a curve-ball her way. A little secret revealing might be in order.

"If you don't mind, we've got a couple more people coming in."

"Oh?" The nervousness returned to the doctor's eyes. Alice gave her another smile, looping some hair behind her left ear in an unconscious gesture.

"They're the woman and the man you tried to match. They were understandably curious about the result, and we thought it would be good to have them here."

"I see." And Dr Pembrooke seemed to understand. Her nervousness seemed to shift, and it was the doctor's turn to be conspiratorial. "They're not going to freak out about the results, are they? Because they might —"

"Don't tell me." Alice hissed in Dr Pembrooke's ear, contorting her face with horror. "I don't want to know until you tell us on camera."

Dr Pembrooke looked at her in surprise. Fearing she had overstepped the mark, Alice gave a nervous chuckle and an apologetic look. "Sorry, just a habit of mine. I don't like 'faking'," she put air quotes around the word, "on camera. We're a documentary, not a drama."

"Oh! Of course." Dr Pembrooke seemed less sure of herself. After a pause, she spoke again, eyes darting toward an open doorway back across the lab. "Will they freak out, you think?"

"I shouldn't think so. We all know it's going to go one of two ways. You tell us which. And do it like there's no camera here, okay? Just the four of us, me, you, and them."

"Okay." The doctor sighed as the make-up lady approached. "I'll try to remember that."

Alice walked away, still smiling. She caught sight of Robert Thompson and Maggie Carter entering the room. They were chatting amiably, which surprised her, given why they were even there. Less surprising to her seeing together was the faint resemblance between them. Maybe the photographs she'd seen didn't lie, after all.

Or is that wishful thinking on my part? Because I can see Maggie has the nose...

"Alice!" Robert called out with a cheery wave. Alice smiled and walked over.

"Good to see you both, and thanks for coming."

"Wouldn't miss it for the world!" Maggie's voice had a northern tone, while Robert's had a sound closer to London. "Robert and I tried grabbing the same taxi and found we were heading to the same place."

"Cheaper to split the fare that way," Robert laughed. "Plus, we might be related, so we might as well get to know each other a bit more."

"We'll soon know that in a bit, won't we?" Alice saw Eric waving at her from the corner of her eye. She nodded at the producer before turning to the two newcomers.

"My producer wants a word. Make-up will touch you both up," Alice explained. "And then I'll introduce you to Dr Pembrooke while they shoot some background footage for the narration. Be back with you in a moment."

She bid adieu and walked over to the producer. Her face hardened into what her husband had called "Alice's war face". The producer seemed to notice, with Alice catching sight of his sighing and taking a swig of coffee as she approached.

"What do you want?" She asked brusquely, the coffee cup still to the producer's lips. It took him a second to lower it, the man looking like he was burning his tongue in the process. The gasp before his husky words came out confirmed for her that was the case.

"I just thought you should give a bit of introduction when we start rolling. Remind the viewers and us why we're here. That's all."

"Not a bad idea." Alice found herself nodding. "Won't I be covering that in narration, though? We can do that in the recording booth later, after all."

Before the producer could reply, she cut him off again.

"You know what? On second thought, Eric, I'll do it. I've got an idea of what I'd say from working on the narration script. We'll go with that, shall we?"

And she walked away without his answer. She spent the next few minutes introducing Robert and Maggie to Dr Pembrooke while the cameraman, at the producer's direction, shot some b-roll for the narration bit. Nothing of great import was said, though it allowed the sound guy to test levels and everyone to get situated.

"We're ready when you are," the producer said at last. Alice gave him the nod, standing slightly off to one side, aware of where the two cameras were. A hush fell over the room. Alice closed her green eyes before she took a quiet, deep breath. Her posture straightened, a smile formed, and her eyes opened to reveal a burning warmth.

"We're here at King's College London with Dr Emily Pembrooke, an expert on DNA testing. Before she gives us the results of her tests, let's remind ourselves of just why we're here. And that's to solve one of the great mysteries of British literature, indeed of British criminal history, in the last century.

"Let's cast our minds back. In December 1926, Agatha Christie was the rising star of popular fiction. She had published six novels and over a dozen short stories, creating the Belgian detective Hercule Poirot, seen by many as the successor to Sherlock Holmes. All should have been well with her world.

"Except," Alice paused, as much for breath as for dramatic reasons, "that it wasn't. 1926 saw first the death of her mother and then her husband, the former First World War pilot Archie Christie, revealing his intention to divorce Agatha to marry his younger secretary, Nancy Neele.

"On the 3rd of December, Archie left their home for a weekend with Nacy and friends. Later that same evening, Agatha followed suit The next day, locals discovered her car, driver's license, and clothes above a chalk quarry in Surrey. Their discovery set off a chain of events and a mystery that's continued to this day as Archie, his love life revealed to the public, became the prime suspect in Agatha's disappearance or even murder.

"Though Archie protested his innocence, claiming that the writer had run away and was framing him, police didn't believe him. After a futile attempt to track down a woman named Teresa Neele at a hotel in Harrogate, whom some members of the hotel staff suspected might have been Agatha, Archie was under arrest. After a sensational murder trial, Archie went to the gallows, and this conviction without a body became known as the 'Christie standard'.

"Yet over the last nine decades, questions have remained. Might Teresa Neele have been Agatha Christie, missed by Archie and the police by a matter of hours? Following up on that lead brought us to another Teresa Neele, who spelled her first name a little differently, who worked as a hospital pharmacist until she passed away in the 1960s. A job that Agatha, during the First World War when she was beginning to write and Archie was at the front, also had. Along the way, we've looked at photographs, and compared handwriting. In the end, there's only one way we can know beyond a reasonable doubt.

"As such, we're here today with Robert Thompson, grandson of Agatha Christie, and Maggie Carter, granddaughter of the mysterious Mrs Neele. Both of whom were kind to enough to have supplied DNA samples for comparison."

Having finished her bit, Alice took another much-needed breath. Looking over to the rest of the group, she kept her smile. What she was doing was presenting, the thing she liked doing in front of the camera. Not the acting bits of walking through archives or old homes, though there was a pleasure to be drawn from that in its own way. She was the girl in school again, back in a history class, eager to share what she had learned with a captive audience.

"Thank you both for joining us," she said to them, soliciting their nods. Alice then moved a step toward the doctor.

"Dr Pembrooke, you've compared their DNA, we've gathered around in your lab rather than one of Christie's country drawing rooms. Tell us, based on your analysis, what's the result?"

Dr Pembrooke said nothing. Alice looked at the doctor, trying to understand what was wrong. Camera fright, perhaps? Or nervous still about having the people she'd tested there? Alice read her face and saw nothing of the sort.

You're milking the moment for all it's worth. Alice realised her smile had broadened ever so slightly. *How can I not approve?*

"Using the samples that Robert and Maggie gave us, there's a couple of options we could have chosen for how to test."

Alice felt her smile falter a bit. *Oh no, not a technical explanation,* she thought. Catching her nervous expression out of one eye, Alice saw it was the producer's as well. The first instinct was to head her off, cut to the chase. Instead, Alice let her talk for a minute longer.

"The easiest solution was to do what we call a grandparent test. Like the name implies, simply looking for a common grandparent. Indeed, we often see it used in paternity cases where an alleged father isn't available. Having done that..."

Dr Pembrooke let her voice trail off for a moment. The intake of breath of Alice and the other two was audible, almost certain to be picked up on the microphones. All the better, Alice knew. That would add to the drama of the moment in the edit.

"I can confirm, with better than 99% certainty, that these two are related. Agatha Christie and Teresa Neele are, indeed, one and the same person."

Alice felt her heart skip a beat. Robert's shoulders sunk as Maggie raised a hand to her mouth in shock. It was what Alice had hoped for but perhaps not what the other two had expected.

"You said better than 99%, correct?" Alice asked the question for the viewers at home, just in case anyone out there had any doubts. Dr Pembrooke's nod was all she needed. They'd need more in the edit, experience told her that. Alice gave a bewildered, hinting at delighted, laugh.

"That's incredible," she said. "Archie Christie was innocent after all. The question now, I think, is why Agatha did it. Is it possible she had amnesia and never recovered?"

"Or did she do it out of malice?" Robert shook his head. Maggie looked at her new relative and shook her own head.

"She never told anyone in my family about it and never wrote another word in her lifetime."

"At least of fiction," Alice corrected, realising she needed to fill something in for the viewers. "After all, that's where we got the handwriting sample from."

"That's true," Maggie agreed. "Perhaps I should say 'detective fiction', in that case? My grandmother was always vague on her past, which makes me think it wasn't an act of evil or anything."

"It does seem remarkable, doesn't it?" Alice inserted herself as host back into the conversation. "The woman who gave us *The Mysterious Affair at Styles* and that incredible final book, *The Murder of Roger Ackroyd*, went off and left her cheating husband to hang while starting a new life?"

"My mother always said she was religious," Robert sighed. "I can't believe she'd have remarried or, in this case, committed bigamy deliberately."

"Maybe she really had amnesia?" Maggie counseled Robert, taking his hand in hers. The two looked at each other, Alice sensing something unsaid passing between them. "It would explain why she never reached out to your mother. Or never wrote another story, despite all of her gifts."

"Right, that strikes me as odd, as well." Alice felt a sense of unease creeping over her. Professional detachment be damned, she decided. Being there with these two descendants, knowing what they now knew, made that rather hard to do.

A thought entered her mind. It was a single sentence formed as a question. They were eight words that she spoke aloud, summarising the moment there inside a university genetic testing lab. And, Alice realised seeing the producer's smile after she'd said it, given the documentary its title.

"That's Agatha's last mystery for us, isn't it?"

Meet Matthew Kresal

Matthew Kresal is a writer, critic, and podcaster with many and varying interests. He's written about and discussed topics as wide-ranging as the BBC's Doctor Who, Cold War fact and fiction, and the UFO phenomenon.

He has appeared on podcasts including Spybrary, The Police Box in a Junkyard Podcast, and The Saucer Life. His anthologized fiction includes the Sidewise Award-winning Moonshot in *Alternate Australias* from Sea Lion Press and the Sidewise nominated Hitchcock's Titanic in Inkling Press' *Tales From Alternate Earths III*.

His first novel, the Cold War alternate history thriller *Our Man on the Hill*, was published in May 2021 by Sea Lion Press and he also authored the *Dark Skies* volume in Observe Books' Silver Archive series, separating fact and fiction for that 1990s conspiracy thriller TV series.

The Law North of the Pecos
By Ed Teja

It didn't seem like the rain would ever stop. In the hours before Matt Cramer hit the road, the skies over Santa Fe, New Mexico, had been spitting moisture in an agonising, relentless drizzle.

It was unusual. Crazy. Climate change was announcing itself by making New Mexico damp.

Matt squirmed in the front seat of his six-year-old Toyota Yaris. While this had seemed like a perfect car when he bought it, he was having a hard time trying to find a comfortable position. He wanted to settle down and tune out the on-and-off patter of the rain.

It wasn't right to be this damp and cold — not in July. Not in New Mexico anytime.

In the seven years he'd lived there, he had never seen so many gray and overcast days. Best guess, he'd seen five seriously overcast days total in all those years. Now there had been, what, six in a row? Six days when he hadn't seen the sun.

After that long, a person started to wonder if the sun was still up there or if it had disappeared. This wasn't Oregon or some other lush, green place. The landscape here was supposed to be dry, painted in shades of red and brown and straw yellow, with highlights of vibrant purple, maybe.

Not green.

A hundred yards down the hill from where he was parked, the Pecos River was running dark red, its fast, turbulent water carrying the dark red soil it flushed out of arroyos down to Texas and wherever the Pecos went after that.

Thoughts of the Pecos brought Judge Roy Bean to mind.

"The Only Law West of the Pecos," the man called himself. Or was that east of the Pecos? Matt's geography, his spatial sense was not what you called infallible. He was better with history and knew that the Judge had moved to Eagle's Nest, Texas, and changed the name of the town to Langtry, in honor of Lillie Langtry, the opera singer.

Matt had been there once, Langtry. He'd gone to check it out, to get a touch of southwestern history in his soul. And now, he, Matt Cramer, found himself acting as the only law he could see along a different part of the Pecos.

Well, the comparison was superficial. He was a private investigator sitting in a car parked near the Pecos, watching an art thief. And there were park rangers about.

His boss had been clear about his mission. "Don't lose the asshole. Wait until he makes the sale. We want the buyer as well. Brian Carver is the thief, but someone wanted him to steal the pieces."

The boss knew that the real money would be in rewards the insurance company would pay for recovering the art. But the publicity of apprehending the thief, the buyer, and recovering the art — that was priceless.

Matt knew his job, and he hadn't lost his quarry. At that moment, the asshole, the art thief Brian Carver, was comfortably ensconced in a fifth wheel in a spot in Villanueva State Park that had an electrical hookup. He would have heat. And a fridge.

Matt ached at the image of a freezer full of good food. Maybe even cold beer. But why the man hauled stolen art to a State Park… that was something he couldn't imagine.

But the idea of beer and something to eat, food that wasn't peanut butter and banana sandwiches, made his mouth water. He'd been living on them — peanut butter and banana sandwiches, ever since he left Santa Fe. And even that was about to change in a bad way.

He glanced at the back seat to confirm his recollection. Yup. He'd eaten the last, nearly overripe banana and it would be peanut butter sandwiches from here on out. Breakfast, and all subsequent meals, would be peanut butter on bread.

Under normal circumstances, say a stakeout in the city, any

city, he'd call the office and tell them he was stuck and hungry. They'd send someone to bring him coffee and a pizza, or something.

Not peanut butter and banana sandwiches.

The company was good about that, providing support. But out here, he was on his own. If he was on his own in the city, he could get takeout delivered to his car. Not here.

And he was stuck waiting for the buyer. That was important. The boss made it clear that the agency took the job for the splash it could make. If they caught the guy and recovered the stolen art, there would be some good publicity. The company was big on good publicity. Publicity raised their profile and got new business.

But they wouldn't send a pizza this far out of town.

Even if they would, he couldn't ask for one. Cell service was spotty. The park had free internet service down near the Ranger Station, but the battery in his cell phone hadn't lasted as long as the damn bananas. In his rush out the door, he hadn't brought his charger.

So far, Brian, the art thief, seemed content to hang around this dismal park. The park rules meant he couldn't stay for more than fourteen days, but that was way too long. Matt would be eating leaves by then.

Watching the rain make splotches on his windshield, he wondered if it was raining in Langtry, down in Texas. He wasn't sure if he was on the same side of the river as the Judge had been. He tried to picture it. Rivers didn't run straight. Like life, they tended to meander, follow the terrain, chasing the lowest points.

This seemed like a low point. He had no idea what was going on with his quarry, and with the weather unusually damp and cold it made it hard to sit there, in his car, in a State Park. Worse, the longer this went on, the more likely Brian would spot him. The art thief wasn't stupid, and Matt stuck out.

Any fool who was car camping for real would have packed it in by now.

The pull of home tugged at him, raising thoughts of a warm, dry bed you could stretch out in, not curled up in the front seat of a Toyota Yaris. Although the Toyota got good mileage and was responsive and great fun to drive, he couldn't, in all fairness, recommend sleeping in it. Not anytime.

And the drizzling, almost rain, combined with the damp cold, made his joints ache. His injuries from Afghanistan seldom bothered him these days, but they did now. The Yaris' heater worked fine, but he couldn't run it often or for long. That would be suspicious. Besides, after following the truck and camping trailer all the way from Santa Fe, he didn't have more than a quarter of a tank of gas left.

He was hungry and his stomach ached slightly, and he burped. A peanut butter and banana burp.

The thing was, he was lucky to have any food at all. When he was throwing things in the car, he told Billy, his brother, he was preparing to tail a suspect. He'd have to follow him out of town.

"How do you know that?" Billy asked.

"I got a call. The woman watching him now says he loaded a fifth wheel. You don't do that to cross town. I need to follow him to where he sells the stuff he stole."

Just as he was about to back the car out of the driveway, Billy ran up and shoved a grocery bag in the back seat. "You ain't gonna last long without peanut butter," he said.

Matt hadn't thought much about it at the time. Not worth a second thought. The asshole art thief had been in touch with someone in Las Vegas. The Las Vegas in New Mexico, not the gambling place in Nevada. And that Las Vegas wasn't that far.

It wasn't until he took over from the car following the quarry, passing her casually and slotting in behind the fifth wheel as it headed east on Highway 25 in the direction of Las Vegas, not until they got off the Interstate and headed south on Highway 3, toward, well, nothing, that he started to think maybe he wasn't adequately prepared.

"The only place out this way is Villanueva, and that isn't much," he said to his boss.

The boss wasn't worried. "Stay on him. He must be ready to make the handover."

Matt didn't agree, but the boss signed the cheques. Dutifully, he followed Brian's fifth wheel at a distance all along the winding two-lane road, even when he turned into the park.

Matt lucked out. He found an unreserved camping site a few down from the one Brian apparently had reserved ahead of time.

Of course, the luck that got him a spot was the same luck that brought the rain. The weather had pretty much emptied the park. Still, he had a vantage point where he could sit (in the cramped seat of the Yaris) and watch for suspicious activity; he had a clear view of whoever came and went. If this was where the sale was going to be made, he'd be on top of it. He kept a camera with a telephoto lens handy, ready to snap shots of people and license plates.

Not being a cop, Matt wasn't allowed to make an arrest. He'd have to make a citizen's arrest, then make the perps hang around and get the ranger to call the cops. So he was set.

Except for the food, or lack of it.

And except for the fact that having no backup meant he could only leave the car to walk around, working out the stiffness and cramps, and to go down to the bathroom. Before his phone battery died, he called the boss again, explained the situation, and asked for food and backup (in that order).

There was a pause. "I'll see what I can do," the boss said. Which meant, of course, that the boss was over budget again. Unless he could find a cheap way to get him some food, Matt was on his own.

Meantime, he was not to lose the asshole. Or the art. Or the buyer.

He thought about asking around, seeing if he could borrow a charger from some camper. But with the park nearly empty, Brian, the suspect, was about the only one he could ask. The other problem was that if he did get one, the only outlet he could use was in the bathrooms across from the Ranger Station. He'd have to stay there while it charged and he wouldn't be able to watch the art thief.

Might as well go home.

"You don't look comfortable, Sir," the ranger said as he pulled the official white pickup alongside Matt's car. "Are you okay?"

"Just fine." They had windows open, talking between the cars through the rain.

"It's going to stay this way a while," the ranger said, sticking his head out and looking up at the dark and ominous sky. "Continued rain. No sign of it letting up."

"I love the rain," Matt said. "Helps me sort things out."

"Okay then," the ranger said, clearly not sure it was okay at all.

Shivering in his car, he watched the ranger continue his rounds, pulling his truck up outside the trailer and getting out, knocking on the door.

Brian opened the door, smiling, looking dry and warm and, to Matt's eyes, well fed and well rested.

The Ranger went inside. Probably invited in for coffee. Art thieves wouldn't worry about a park ranger seeing anything suspicious. Even if a visitor knew art, they wouldn't pay any serious attention to the stuff in a trailer. The guy hadn't stolen pieces created by an internationally known artist, just a couple of expensive pieces done by a New Mexico artist, boosted from a Santa Fe gallery. Anyway, Brian could have a Mona Lisa hanging on his wall, and anyone seeing it would assume it was a print. He could have the paintings in plain sight and afford to be cheerful and friendly. A smart crook would invite the ranger in for a cup of hot coffee and talk about the unusual weather.

Matt had cold water. He kept a canteen in the car, and he refilled it from the well. The water was cold (everything was cold) and it tasted metallic but, in a thirst-satisfying way. He liked the water, but it was not hot coffee. It had nothing in common with black, dark roast coffee, with its rich aroma. Hell, at this point, he was ready to settle for decaf if it was hot. Instant decaf — and he didn't even consider that real coffee. Too bad there wasn't even a coffee machine at the Ranger Station.

He rummaged in the grocery bag, noting that the side had an ad for a Starbucks and a deli. His stomach ached.

"Care for a burrito?" a voice said.

Matt jerked around to see (and smell) an old man in rough clothes sitting next to him in the passenger seat of his car. How had he gotten there? He held out a burrito in a dirty hand. The meaty burrito aroma mixed with the man's pungent odor — a blend of unwashed body smells and alcohol. Not a fragrant combination. Of course, at this point, Matt was fairly ripe himself, so he would have to be careful complaining about that.

Somehow, he managed to not grab the burrito. He shot the man a look. "Who the hell are you? And what do you think you are doing in my car?"

The old man smiled. "I'm a friend, Matt. You were just thinking about me. And food. So here I am and I brought you a burrito."

"The boss sent you?" Matt asked, wondering how he could have gotten there so fast. It wasn't possible. And why hadn't he brought a pizza? "They sent you all this way with one burrito?"

"Nobody sent me. You asked me for help and food. This burrito was the best I could do on short notice. You want it or not?"

"No thanks."

"Suit yourself. We got a long wait ahead of us."

"How would you know that?" Even the boss didn't have that information. "And why are you still in my car? Aren't you going back?"

"I'll explain," the old man said calmly. "I'm in your car because it's hard to hand someone a burrito through a closed window. I'm still here because we need to talk. And, like you, I can't go back yet. The job ain't done. You and me got to talk and then wait, like I said."

"Talk about what?"

He pointed at the trailer. "Our assignments. You are watching the gentleman who is holed up in that box house over there, right?"

"If the boss didn't send you, how do you know what I'm doing here?"

He gave Matt a puzzled look. "You know what? I'm not sure. Not sure at all, to be honest. I'm not exactly clear how that works."

"How what works?"

The man stretched. "When you've been dead as long as I have, and that's around 120 years now, you get a little more patient."

The man was obviously a nutcase, but he didn't seem dangerous, and the company was actually a relief. Comic relief, but still, it passed the time while he stared at Brian's front door and waited. Then the door opened, and the ranger came out.

"Don't worry. He's not the one you are looking for," the old man said.

"Who do you think I am looking for?"

"The art buyer. And that's bull. She isn't going to buy anything."

"No?"

"That's just bait. But if you and me work together, we can both achieve our goals."

How did he know so much? Thinking about it made Matt's skin crawl. "What is your goal? What's your angle?"

"My angle is that I have to do what I'm told. My goal is to nip this in the bud."

"You want to stop the art sale?"

"There is no art sale to stop."

"That's why the guy is here."

The old man nodded. "That's why he came, but that's not what is going down."

They sat quietly as the ranger got in his truck (he hadn't been carrying anything that could even remotely be a large oil painting, much less two) and drove off. He saluted Matt as he went by.

"So, you know who the buyer is?"

"Yep. Came from my side, I'm afraid."

"Your side?" Did he mean some group of old, smelly nutcases?

"Unfortunately. The Powers That Be do the best they can to keep things restricted, not have creatures and spirits going back-and-forth willy-nilly, but this one is cagey." Then he laughed. "You can't keep her in a cage." He spread his hands. "So, here I am."

Matt shot the man a hard look, expecting to see a huge grin. Instead, he looked serious. Concerned, even.

"You aren't making any sense," Matt said.

"A spirit getting loose isn't necessarily a sensible thing," the old man said.

Matt shook his head. It didn't do a damn thing to clear his thoughts or ease the hunger pains in his belly. "Do you expect me to believe you are chasing a ghost who got loose?"

That got the old man laughing. "Nope. Don't expect you to believe a damn thing. Besides. she ain't no ghost. She's a spirit."

"There's a difference?"

"A big one. This gal, well, she's related to the furies. You might have heard of them. I understand they gave the ancient Greeks a hell of a time. They were what you call demons or evil spirits. Now your ghosts are nothing more than people that are having trouble working out that they are dead or working out that hanging around forever ain't gonna change anything. They are what you call incorporeal — they don't have a material body, so they can't even touch things. Living folks catch sight of them sometimes, out of the corner of their eye or somesuch, but they aren't any more in this world than that. Just a puff of ethereal stuff."

"Is that what you are?"

"Nope. Me, I'm a pragmatist. Once I noticed I was dead, I just got on with being dead. I found I liked it. Kind of backfired because that's why they send me on missions like this. Ain't no chance I'm hanging around here any longer than I have to. Just get it done and go home, is what I say."

It made an odd kind of sense.

"So, this buyer is a spirit?"

"A flesh-eating fury. There are lots of new rules and restrictions on the ones like that, but there always seem to be loopholes. She'd got one figured it, but it took time to set up and by now she's gonna be real hungry."

"I can relate to that."

"I offered you part of my burrito, hombre."

In all fairness, he had. "Yes, but…"

"Anyway, according to the rules, she can't just eat anyone. That's part of Section 6.3 of the Relevant Spirit Code or what we call your RSC. Otherwise, as there are more spirits than living folks, well, we'd be in for some serious issues with mortals not getting a chance to live out their lives."

"So why bring Brian Carver here?"

"Because of the loophole. If she catches a mortal committing a crime, she can eat them."

"That's quite a large loophole."

The man smiled. "Well, the people who are good at writing laws in this world don't get the best jobs on our side, and the people who write the rules tend to have a little optimistic view of the nature of creatures. Anyways, our fury has this fella coming here with stolen art. When he offers to sell it to her, she can invoke the loophole. Pretty soon he is wondering what this death thing is all about."

"And you are supposed to stop her?"

"I'm the law."

"You are?"

"Judge Roy Bean, at your service. And to answer your earlier question, I was the only law WEST of the Pecos."

Unaccountably, Matt believed him. "Which side of the Pecos are we on now?"

The Judge gave Matt a crooked smile. "It's confusing. Right now, we are kinda on the North of the Pecos, seeing as this piece runs west to east." He pointed east. "There is a loop of it over there, so you could argue we are west of the Pecos as well, but when you look close at the way it runs south from here, this is what you'd call the eastern bank." He laughed.

"So you are out of your jurisdiction?"

"I got the gig because I'm the one you summoned."

"I summoned you?"

"Yessir, you did. You called for backup and then pondered my exploits for a spell. Times like this, emergency cases, that's good enough for the Powers That Be."

"So I could have summoned some female movie star?"

"About anyone who is dead. You see what a powerful thing hindsight can be? But now you got me. And I'm stuck with you."

"What happens?"

He stared and shrugged. "I can't do anything until she makes a move, tries to invoke the loophole."

"Why?"

Judge Bean stared through the windshield. "I ain't rightly sure. I'll ask when I get back. For now, you need to know that when she pounces, her move is going to be quick and sudden. If I'm not quick enough, she might kill the man. But then I can suspend her existence in this world, and she'll pop back where she belongs."

"Really?"

He shrugged. "Least that's what the bosses tell me."

"And then I'm standing in a murder scene with no witnesses and no killer. That leaves me up the creek."

"Down the river, actually. The Pecos River, to be precise. But you'll be able to recover the art. She don't want that and neither do I."

"And I get to call the cops, report the dead body, and all that fun. The art will be used as evidence and I'll have to explain who it was that killed the man."

"Explain it if you want — if you can. I might be able to prevent there from being a body, but I can't promise nothing. That fury is going to be real hungry."

That didn't help. "What do I do?"

"Well, like I said, she is real fast. If you was willing to be my posse, there might be a good way to keep things manageable."

Matt twisted and looked at him. "I'm listening."

•••

Darkness had begun to settle over the campground when Matt caught sight of a car making its way toward the campsite, then slipping in next to the trailer.

"That's an expensive car," Matt said. "A high-end Aston Martin."

"She's extravagant," Judge Bean said. "A showoff, really."

When the door opened, a svelte figure dressed in a long cloak stepped out and glided toward the door.

"Time to move," the Judge said.

They hopped out and moved quietly to the aluminium door of the trailer. Matt turned the handle and opened it a crack. Warm air flooded out.

"I've got the art we talked about," Brian was saying.

"Show me," a sultry voice said. "I have to be certain they are real."

Judge Bean nodded. "One of the rules."

"You have the money with you?"

"I have it ready to transfer to your account."

"Okay."

Footsteps echoed from the back of the trailer. Matt heard a familiar click. The sofa bed. "I put them in here," Brian said. "No one looks in these."

"Time to go," Judge Bean said. He pulled out a long-barreled pistol.

Matt stared at it. A 44-caliber revolver. "I thought you invoked a spell to get rid of her."

"That's the plan, but I've never done it before. I'll start with the tried and true. The boss said the spell works, but I ain't lived this long by taking stupid chances."

"You are dead."

He paused. "That don't affect the logic of my argument."

And he slipped silently into the trailer. Matt followed. He smelled hamburger and almost fainted.

At the far side of the trailer, the svelte figure towered over Brian.

"What?" he said, turning toward the intruder. The svelte fury opened her mouth, showing long teeth for a moment before thrusting her face toward his neck. A sharp concussive roar came from Judge Bean's gun, sending a wave of heat over Matt's cheek and making his head hurt. Blood-like goo splattered against the far wall, and the slim figure flew back, slammed into the back wall, and slumped down to the floor.

Judge Bean puffed himself up. "By the power invested in me as the only law west of the Pecos-"

"North," Matt said. "We are north of the Pecos."

"Right, sidekick. Thanks. As the only law north of the Pecos, I send you back to the gates of hell."

There was a whoosh and the raising of some dust, and the figure was gone.

"It worked," Matt said.

"I hope," Judge Bean said. "I'll probably catch hell for putting the bullet hole in her." Then he chuckled. "Catch hell… figure of speech, see." He waved the gun at the immobile figure standing before them, clutching two oil paintings. "I got mine, so this one is yours."

"Thanks."

"No problem. Good working with you."

And then, with another whoosh and more dust, he was gone. So, thankfully, was his smell.

Brian stared at Matt, and the competing ideas of fighting or flighting danced over his face. Matt pulled out his gun. "Both are bad choices," he said. "Best you sit down."

The deflated asshole art thief sat in the chair, the paintings on his knees. "What just happened here?"

"No idea," Matt said. "You got set up. I know that much."

"Who were those people?"

Matt shrugged. Best not to explain — as if he knew anything. "Where's your phone?"

Brian pointed to the counter. Matt picked up the cell phone and used it to call the police. Assured they would be there… eventually, he walked over to Brian, who handed him the paintings. Matt sat them on the counter, then cuffed Brian, who sat shaking his head.

"Weird."

"Agreed," Matt said.

While he waited for the police, Matt found a stovetop espresso pot and made himself a cup of rich, black coffee. Then he rummaged in the freezer and dug out a frozen lasagna that he heated in the microwave.

He put his own phone on Brian's charger. Brian sat in sullen silence and watched as Matt contentedly ate his first warm meal in what seemed like an eternity, but which Roy Bean would undoubtedly assure him was only moments ago.

When he finished, he called his boss, letting him know he had Brian and the paintings.

"And the buyer?"

"She disappeared."

"She escaped?"

Matt considered his answer. She hadn't escaped. Not even close. But he didn't have her in custody, which was what the boss wanted. He signed the paychecks after all, and it wouldn't pay to confuse him any more than his report would when he filed it.

"Yeah, I came in on them, but she got away before I could grab her. I was sure you'd want me to secure the paintings and the thief."

"Yeah. The gallery's insurance company is paying a decent reward."

He was drinking a second cup of deliciously hot coffee when the flashing lights of a police car came down the road. Matt Cramer hung up the phone thinking how life had gotten a lot better, north of the Pecos.

It would be interesting to find out what the police made of the expensive Aston Martin parked by the trailer. He had no intention of mentioning it.

Meet Ed Teja

Ed Teja is a full-time writer and part-time martial arts instructor. After years traveling the world writing, working as a Caribbean boat bum and magazine editor (not usually at the same time) he has hunkered down in rural New Mexico where he writes cross-genre stories that peek into the surreal world he sees around us. Learn more about Ed Teja at his website **www.edteja. com**

A Matter of Some Gravity
By Tom Jolly

Detective Jonah Jones scowled at the Captain through the holo display hovering above his desk. "The asteroid belt? How the hell is that even in our jurisdiction?"

"In space, the jurisdiction for a crime is based on the Earth address of the victim, who happens to have corporate headquarters in L.A." Captain Albright replied. "You should know that. So we're it."

Jonah doubted that the Captain had known that fact for more than a few minutes himself. "I should, huh? Why me? Why send me up to the Sol-forsaken asteroid belt?" He already knew the answer; this was just vengeance. The Captain had been giving him crap cases to work since he'd started seeing his daughter, Leanna, an officer over in the 23rd precinct. It just made the Captain angrier when Jonah succeeded in solving some of the cases. The situation deteriorated further when Leanna came down with one of the nastier Europa diseases during an investigation, an incurable illness that shrugged off everything modern medicine had to offer. The Captain somehow blamed her quarantine on him, as though he'd taken her out to a hot zone instead of Lin Xu's for dinner.

"It's our jurisdiction," the Captain said. "You're the only detective with a degree in engineering. And you applied for the Space Corps twice before you started working here."

"So what? I was rejected twice." Jonah said.

"Third time's the charm. Wasn't anything physical keeping you down, was it? What did they call it, 'personality issues'?"

Jonah frowned and turned his head to stare out a dirty window. It wasn't his fault he'd gotten into a fight during a long-duration isolation test with three other men. They were all assholes; he just let them know it. Was being too honest a fault?

"What about the Space Corps? Can't they handle this?" Jonah offered hopefully.

Captain Albright shook his head. "The Space Corps has some

grunts, and they can handle straightforward issues like claim jumping and bar fights. They're more of an arbitration court than a police force. But this is a real mystery."

Jonah knew this was just bait on a hook, but he leaned forward anyway, unable to resist. "What mystery?"

"Someone stole a third of an asteroid as it was being moved. And nobody knows where the missing mass went."

"A third of an asteroid?" He scratched his chin thoughtfully and leaned back. "That should be kind of obvious."

"You'd think, wouldn't you? You'll have a week in transit to learn about it. You leave in two days."

Jonah winced. Detective Matthews, two desks away, lifted a cup of coffee in mock salute. "We'll miss you, sucker," he said. Jonah didn't give him the satisfaction of acknowledging his existence but frowned at the Captain instead.

The Captain glanced over at Matthews, reached into the file space above Jonah's desk, tapped a few hovering icons, and swept all the open case files over to Matthew's holo space. Matthews choked on his coffee, and Jonah almost smiled.

• • •

Jonah could barely make out Leanna through a haze of plastic and glass. She was isolated, untouchable, inside a plastic tent situated within a hermetically sealed, negatively pressurized room. When she'd been working a four-month stint in the Space Corps in low-Earth- orbit habitats, she'd been called to a crime scene where the so-called murder victim had been killed by one of the Europan replicators, and she managed to catch the rare disease herself. It was a highly contagious, and the US government was in a panic to contain it. If Leanna hadn't returned to Earth before showing any symptoms, she'd likely still be in orbit, dealing with the medical facilities there.

"Your father wants me to work on a case in the asteroid belt," Jonah said. "I'll be gone at least a month." He talked into a microphone set into the outer wall of the isolation chamber.

"I could be dead by then." She said it matter-of-factly, a dry statement of an approaching reality, resigned to a bullet she couldn't dodge. "A month, what the hell is he thinking?"

It was obvious what he was thinking, Jonah thought. Get him away from his precious daughter. Let him grieve alone when she dies, unencumbered by the stranger who wanted to take his daughter from him, the same as the disease that worked its slow curse within her blood.

"I'm thinking of downloading," Leanna admitted. "Before this shit finishes me off."

"They could be close to a cure," Jonah said. "I've heard…"

"They lie. If I wait too long, I could just pop a cork and there's no more me. Adios, muchacha. If I download, at least I can…" Her voice trailed off into doubt.

"You'd still be dead. There would be a copy of you running around pretending to be you, but you'd be dead. Baby, you've got to hang on." Jonah leaned forward in his plastic chair and tried to make out her face through the barriers, but he only had his memories to fill in the picture. Silence filled the room.

"Fuck, you, Jonah. If I have the chance to live…"

"It's not life. It's a programme recorded into a goddamned plastic body."

"If I have the chance to continue, for my thoughts to continue on in some other form, even if it means dying and becoming a whole new being, it's better than just waiting to die."

"We can hope for a cure," Jonah said. "This is 2095, they can cure anything. Just give the researchers some time."

"You hope, Jonah," she said. Both of them remained quiet for a while. They'd had this talk before, in various forms, and it hadn't become any less bitter. "Look," Leanna finally said, "I'm really tired. Go and solve the case. Come back to me. It's only a month. Maybe I'll last a month, maybe they'll have another treatment that heals my veins, or they'll nail the little Europan bastards that did this to me. You hope for both of us, and maybe I'll be here when you get back."

Jonah wanted to tell her he loved her, but their recent and somewhat intense relationship hadn't really progressed that far before the sickness claimed her, and to drop that bomb off now would sound insincere, spawned by pity or guilt. He bit his lip, and instead said, "I'll see you in a month, then." His voice broke as he spoke, and Leanna didn't say anything else. He closed his eyes and leaned his forehead against the glass, and imagined that he could hear her breathing, wishing he could take her anger and illness away.

He left the quarantine unit and headed home to pack, letting the flitter's AI do the flying.

• • •

Jonah remembered his five-year history with Leanna, but not all of it was good. Bad luck and bad timing kept them apart for most of that time. They'd worked a case together and did a little light dating, but somewhere during that period, she told him that she was serious about a guy, and it wasn't him, so that was that.

A year later, he heard that the man she'd been "serious about" told her she'd have to quit being a cop if they were to stay together. He didn't like her job, and he was obscenely wealthy, the VP of some off-world mining concern, so he offered her a life of ease and luxury. His name was Max Fern, and in his own eyes, the world turned around him.

She didn't go for it, because she loved her job. She dumped him. As a man who always got what he wanted, Max Fern vindictively proceeded to make her life miserable, pulling strings to keep her behind a desk or doing bailiff duty. An unexpected transfer to an office where she was the youngest cop meant a loss of her seniority and, thus, an inability to choose the best days off. Being the detective he was, Jonah put together a paper trail made from dollar bills leading from Max to Leanna's boss and dropped it on the DA's desk, which, while satisfying, didn't make anyone very happy.

Jonah ran into Leanna again years later at a mutual friend's retirement party. After a stuttering, stumbling beginning, they started dating again. They clicked. Jonah had never felt more comfortable around anyone. He wondered if she felt the same, but didn't want to break the magic by putting it into words. They were good together.

And now she was dying. Jonah wondered if Max was somehow responsible, still holding a grudge after all these years. But that was just his mind looking for a bad guy, someone he could blame and wreak bloody vengeance upon, instead of the random blameless touch of fate and bad luck. It was wishful thinking.

• • •

It took a week for Jonah's ship to reach the asteroid belt. The orbital insertion burn would put them near Ceres Station, a steel structure housing most of the Space Corps, just over a million kilometers up-belt from the dwarf planet Ceres. There were eight Stations in all, spaced equidistantly around the Belt, and each of them shared the characteristic that they were made from one metallic asteroid connected in a dumbbell formation with a fabricated station, swinging around a center point to provide artificial gravity. The center axis of each pair provided a slowly rotating docking station for entering and leaving the station.

Jonah did what research he could on the case of the missing mass during the week that he was in transit, expecting that the mystery would probably be resolved before he got there. A week was a long time, and how hard could it be to find twenty million kilos of rock? He saw photos of the twenty-meter wide asteroid before and after Space Rock Intersystem moved it, and it looked the same. There were no obvious holes in it. The original survey of the asteroid, performed by robotic drones armed with samplers and gravitational gradiometers, indicated an object with a density about that of lead, which was half-again denser than a nickel-iron asteroid. But surface sampling of the asteroid showed that it was primarily nickel-iron, suggesting that some higher-density core resided within. Radioactivity was mild. When they started to move it, they found the asteroid to be much lighter than the first survey indicated, and the mass kept dropping as they accelerated, as though something had invisibly escaped. Instrument calibration was an obvious suspect, but they'd done this sort of thing before, and most of the measurements were redundant. It just didn't make a lot of sense.

The potential difference between the before-and-after masses was the difference between an asteroid full of ruthenium, palladium or silver, or even heavier elements, and one that was just plain nickel-iron. So with the loss of thirty percent of the mass, Space Rock figured their valuable find lost 99% of its estimated value. Someone had stolen the golden yolk out of the egg.

There was currently a sixteen-minute time lag for communications to reach Ceres Station from Earth, so Jonah opted just to send a message asking for some case details, then wait until he got there to start grilling people. Six days into his flight, he received a video message.

The man frowned into the video screen, looking nervous. "Detective Jonah Jones. My name is…" he paused and looked up at the ceiling as though trying to remember something, "…Officer Harry Carroll. I've been assigned to work this case with you. I'll try to bring you up to date."

Jonah squinted at the image of Officer Carroll. He'd seen uploads before; the skin just didn't flex right. It looked like it was plastic. At some point in time, Officer Carroll had died and uploaded, like Leanna had wanted to do. He tried not to let his emotions show; this might be a good opportunity to learn more about uploads. Maybe he could convince Leanna that it was a terrible idea.

Officer Carroll continued, "The asteroid in question is still in transit to the Space Rock processing facility, though the owners are fairly certain that the asteroid has little value now. If I were to speculate, I'd guess that they think the missing mass will somehow magically reappear before the asteroid gets to their facility."

Jonah snorted at that. That was something Leanna would have said. The thought depressed him, and he wondered how she was doing back on Earth.

"I see you've read the case file already," Officer Carroll said. "Space Rock still insists that the mass decreased as they started to move the asteroid." He shook his head, glancing down at his notes. "I asked them if the tug's thrust monitors could have had some problem that would produce a false mass indication, but they insist that these systems have been thoroughly checked and rechecked. They're at a loss.

"Space Rock also performed a microscopic surface scan on the asteroid and detected no microtubules or other telltales that might indicate nanotech mining, though it's possible that programmed nanotech miners could have penetrated at a single point, tunneled in serially, performed their mining internally, then escaped out the same microscopic hole with their booty and then backfilled the hole. Space Rock is drilling into their asteroid to verify or eliminate this possibility, but we haven't been notified of their results yet. Golden Belt, a nanotech mining firm, is located within a million kilometers, and we have a copy of their manufacturing nanotag, so if we do turn up some errant nanites, we'll be inspecting them for the atomically etched identifier. There's nothing yet to implicate them, however." Officer Carroll tapped on a screen mounted in the desk below, scrolling through notes.

"Euphrates Mining has a ship positioned where the asteroid used to be, occupying the same orbit. Space Rock offered 300,000 credits for information leading to the recovery of the missing mass, and Euphrates has declared their intention to look for clues at the original location, along the original orbital path. We have remote monitors observing that orbit, but there's nothing to see there." Officer Carroll shrugged. It looked like he hadn't shaved that morning, and his eyes were bloodshot. Jonah wondered if all of the space cops looked like they were hungover. Officer Carroll chewed his lip nervously, which struck Jonah as oddly familiar, but then Carroll nodded and said, "I look forward to working with you, Detective Jones," and signed off.

Jonah stared uneasily at the empty screen. There was something odd about the man that just bugged him, but he couldn't quite put his finger on it.

• • •

Jonah and Harry Carroll had barely a handshake and a nod between them before Captain Orkin sent them off to talk to the crew of the Euphrates Mining ship, the *Get Back To Work,* currently drifting near the original orbit where the mass-theft occurred. "It's a four-hour flight. You'll have plenty of time to swap cop stories on the way there," he said. "They've brought a lot of equipment to bear on the site, and I'm a little curious about what they're doing there. It seems like a lot of gear just to claim a 300,000 credit reward. Keep your eyes peeled, and see what you can see. If they've turned up something useful to us, let me know. It wouldn't surprise me in the least if the missing mass turned up in their cargo holds, somehow."

On their way to the Ford Solar runabout, Jonah asked Harry, "Are you a pilot, too?" Harry, a few inches taller than Jonah, looked down at him.

"No, Detective. The ship has its own AI. We just tell it where we want to go."

"Call me Jonah."

He nodded. "So, Jonah, I see you brought your .38 with you," he said, motioning toward his holster. "Those aren't that practical on spaceships. I mean, if you miss, the bullets tend to bounce around. And frankly, in zero-gee, the recoil will really screw with your next shot."

"It's what I'm used to," he said. "I'll try not to miss. Or better yet, get into a situation where I need to use it."

Harry shook his head. "Well, let me know if you're about to open up so I can find cover. The Corps will issue you an energy weapon if you ask them nicely." He patted the one at his waist.

"I'll keep that in mind," he said.

During the trip to the *Get Back To Work.* Harry talked about his past, but it sounded like he was telling someone else's story. Jonah wondered what it was he was hiding. For Jonah's part, he explained to Harry that this was a temporary assignment and that he had this incredible woman to get back to on Earth. "She's everything I've ever wanted," he said, and didn't mention a word about her illness, keeping the pain to himself. Harry looked like he'd been hit with a sledgehammer.

"You okay?" Jonah asked.

"I'm fine," Harry said, frowning deeply. "You just got me thinking about my own, um, partner."

"It's hard to be away for long," Jonah said.

Harry sighed and nodded, but didn't expand on it.

• • •

Outside the *Get Back To Work*, they observed a large number of detectors and antenna arrays, including a particle beam gun and a neutrino emitter. A complementary batch of instrumentation occupied a position a hundred kilometers from the ship, including a few pieces they couldn't identify remotely. The Space Corps had been monitoring the area, so they should know what's what, but Harry recorded everything anyway and tasked the ship's AI to identify as much of the gear as possible.

They docked to a port on the *Get Back To Work* and were greeted inside by a hovering drone that said, "Please follow me. The Director is expecting you."

A few minutes of winding corridors brought them to a conference room where they waited, weightless, for the Director. When he appeared. Jonah was stunned into silence. Max Fern, Leanna's ex, smiled unconvincingly and said, "Detective Jonah Jones. What a surprise to see you here. And Officer Carroll." He turned to Harry and extended a hand. "I don't believe we've met before. I'm Max Fern, director of operations here for Euphrates."

Harry extended his hand, but Jonah could see his reluctance and distaste. Whether they'd met before or not, there was some history there. He could see Harry squeeze down on Max's hand, but Max took it in stride and his toothy smile never changed.

Then he turned to Jonah. "This is a bit of a surprise, Detective Jones. But allow me to say, despite our previous history, that I'm very sorry for your loss."

Harry's eyes widened and his whole body tensed.

Jonah glanced over at him, then back to Max Fern, confusion on his face. "What loss?"

"Your girlfriend. Leanna Albright. Oh, God, you didn't know?" Max put his hand over his mouth like he was acting in a play.

Jonah gaped like a fish for a moment, then tried to sit down, despite the zero-gee environment. His eyes darted back and forth, as though looking for some support, emotional or physical, hidden somewhere in the small room. "Leanna?" His voice cracked. "What about Leanna?"

"She passed away a week ago. I'm so sorry, Detective. I was certain that you already knew."

Jonah held his head in his hands for a minute, quietly, then sat up, wiping moist eyes. Why hadn't Captain Albright let him know? He knew how he felt about Leanna. "No, I didn't know," he said, his voice rough with emotion. "But I can deal with that on my own time. We have some questions for you."

Harry took a deep breath and let it out slowly, turning away from Jonah and facing Max. "We were told that you've been monitoring the area from which the mass disappeared."

"You mean the bit of vacuum that happens to share the same orbital parameters as the asteroid that recently vacated it," Max corrected.

"Yeah, sure. Let's go with that," Jonah said softly. "Have you found anything of interest to us?"

"We haven't detected any bulk masses, but we have located several dozen nanobots with traces of rubidium on them. We suspect that the nanites stripped the asteroid of its high-value minerals and took off for some hidden storage facility."

Harry and Jonah glanced at each other. "Why haven't you reported this yet?" Jonah asked.

Max smiled and spread his hands. "We're still gathering information, and there is a reward of three hundred thousand credits. If we locate enough of the little buggers, we can figure out where they were going. We want that reward."

And the lost material, if you can locate it without anyone knowing about it, Jonah thought.

"If we can verify your find, then you'll get the reward," Harry said. "Have you done a scan on them yet? Do you know who they belong to?"

Max nodded. "They belong to Golden Belt. I'm guessing that they eventually meant to sweep the area to collect any residual or defective nanites, but we got here first and camped on their site."

"If you already know this, what's with all the gear outside?" Jonah asked.

Max shrugged. "Maintain a facade. Pretend we're looking for something that isn't there. If Golden Belt thinks we haven't found anything yet, then they won't know how close we are to nailing them."

"Seems like an awful lot of trouble for three hundred grand," Harry said.

"You might be surprised how narrow the margins are in asteroid mining, Officer Carroll."

"We'd like to get samples of the nanites you've collected, if we can, Director."

Max smiled. "Not a problem. I'll have our techs put together a sample container for you."

● ● ●

Within the hour, they were back on the runabout, pulling away from the *Get Back To Work*. "Captain Orkin wanted us to talk to Space Rock, and check out the actual asteroid," Harry said.

"Great," Jonah replied. "We can check out the nanite manufacturer codes while we're in transit."

"This ship is not equipped with a microscope capable of that resolution," the ship's AI responded. "We will have to return to Ceres Station to scan the nanobots."

Jonah sighed and stared blankly at the ship's small instrument panel.

"Are you all right?" Harry asked.

"No, I'm not all right. What do you think?" He shook his head and curled his fingers into his thick black hair, pulling. "She's…" His voice faded into anguished silence.

Harry shuddered and closed his eyes, clenching his fists. Jonah looked over at him, and frowned suspiciously. "What is it?"

"It's nothing. It's just…it's terrible, what you're going through."

Jonah stared at him a moment longer, but Harry didn't add anything more. "We need to tell Captain Orkin what we found out about the Golden Belt nanites," Jonah finally said.

Harry nodded brusquely and they got back to work.

● ● ●

The link to Orkin took less than a minute to establish securely. Once Jonah explained the situation to him, he said, "That's excellent news. We actually have a representative here at the Station from Golden Belt who arrived about an hour ago, telling us they're willing to help in any way possible."

"But Euphrates Mining has implicated Golden Belt. It's their nanites they picked up."

Orkin nodded. "But Golden Belt manufactures and sells nanites belt-wide. Everyone uses them to aid in processing their claims."

"So we can't tell where they came from?" Jonah asked.

"Actually, we can. Golden Belt has confided with us that there is a supplemental batch code for each group of nanites, hidden in a layer underneath the manufacturer code. All we need to do is burn it off and we can see who originally bought the nanites. You just have to get them here."

"Should we cancel the trip to Space Rock's asteroid?" Harry asked.

"For now. I think this is more important," Orkin said.

They disconnected. "Well, I guess it's no surprise that Max can't be trusted," Jonah said. He glanced up at a camera in the corner of the ceiling. "Ship, what have you found out about the test equipment near *Get Back To Work*?"

"I prefer 'Scooter' to 'ship', if you don't mind, Detective Jones. It's also less ambiguous in case of an emergency."

Jonah smiled. "Um, okay. Scooter, then."

Scooter continued, "I have detected a broad-band spectrum analyzer, variable frequency sampling lasers for three bands, a neutrino generator and receiver, particle beam guns with a smorgasbord of particle types, including antimatter, and a gravitational gradiometer moving slowly through the area."

"That's an awful lot of test equipment for a chunk of empty space." Jonah rubbed his chin thoughtfully. "So. They've got a gravitational gradiometer to help find the mass. But the gradiometer is positioned where they know there isn't a damned thing. Orkin said we've been monitoring their activities a while, right?"

"That is correct, Detective Jones," Scooter said.

"How many images do you have of that drifting gradiometer?"

"Let me check my data archives. One moment."

"What are you thinking, Jonah?" Harry asked.

He held up a hand. "Not yet. You'll think I'm nuts."

Scooter reported, "I have in my memory 1457 images of the gradiometer. It passed through the test area twice while we were there."

"What?"

"The *Get Back To Work* is repeatedly sending it back through the centre of the area originally occupied by the asteroid, presumably to gather data."

Jonah felt his heart pounding. "How good is the time stamp and location data relative to the centre of the asteroid's original orbit?"

"The time stamp is accurate to ten nanoseconds relative to the *Get*

Back To Work's time base. The location is accurate to zero-point-one millimeters relative to the center of the asteroid's original orbit."

"So we can establish acceleration parameters." He leaned forward in his seat. "Is the gradiometer accelerating relative to the centre?"

"Yes. It accelerates as it approaches the centre and decelerates as it leaves."

Jonah was sweating. "Bloody Sol! And there's nothing there?"

"We have been unable to detect any object at the centre."

"Clarify that for me, Scooter. The motion of the gradiometer indicates there *is* a mass there, but we can't *see* a mass there."

An alarm sounded. "Attention!" Scooter called out, "There is a hydrogen leak in the propellant storage area. Suit up immediately for evacuation. Beginning propellant venting operations."

"What the hell?" Jonah said, unbuckling his belt and floating helplessly into the air. His eyes widened as Harry's boots slammed onto the floor with a metallic clang and he grabbed the front of Jonah's shirt. Harry dragged him through the air as he pounded down the short corridor to the changeout room. Once they were inside, the inner door clanged shut.

"Attention! Oxygen leak in the gas storage area. Venting operations—Attention! Collapse of the fusion containment core imminent…"

The spacesuits in the changeout room were positioned such that one could easily step into them, dip their head into the helmet, then slap the auto-seal button to finish the job. It took less than five seconds for both of them to suit up. The suits were large, made for a body Harry's size, and Jonah found he could barely reach his gloves.

Harry glanced at the room's pressure monitor, and shouted, "Scooter, emergency vent the airlock. Now!"

A shrill whistle filled the air and the pressure dropped to zero in less than a second. Harry jerked the outer airlock door inward and shoved it to the side on its rails, manhandled Jonah so he was facing the open door, staring wide-eyed into open vacuum, and then shouted, "Open the inner airlock door!"

Motors whined against the pressure, then the blast of cabin air hit them in the back and thrust them out of the airlock, flinging them away from the doomed vessel. As they tumbled, Jonah caught a glimpse of a small projectile ejected from the front of the ship. It turned and followed them. *Now what?*

Seconds later, the entire ship expanded silently into a fireball that quickly faded, then a cloud of steel and aluminum debris tore past them, plucking at their suits. A large chunk of jagged steel tore a hole in an arm of Jonah's suit, and a thin stream of red droplets sprayed from the tear, but the hole foamed shut in a matter of moments as the suit's emergency systems kicked in.

Ten more seconds passed. The debris field dispersed into a fading, twinkling cloud until there was nothing left but the two of them and the small object that had ejected from the ship. It slowed as it approached them, a long, slender rod with a nozzle at one end and a bare, bright surface. "You both appear to have survived," Scooter commented through their suit radios.

"Mostly," Jonah said. "My arm is numb."

"That is the medical foam. It numbs the wound and seals the open blood vessels. The suit foam sealed the breach. According to your suit readings, you should both be able to survive for at least two hours."

"What just happened to the ship?" Harry asked.

Scooter turned and looked back at the empty area where the ship used to be. "The ship. *My body.*" It remained silent for a few moments, and Jonah couldn't imagine what was going on inside the AI's mind. It finally turned back to them. "There was sudden degradation to the storage containers for many of the gas storage tanks. Based on detected leakage patterns, the most probable cause would be due to mining nanites eating away the structure. Considering the rate of decay and leakage, their programming was likely triggered during your discussion with Captain Orkin regarding the return of Golden Belt's nanites to Ceres Station. There is a high probability that the *Get Back To Work* flew a nano-sized radio transmitter array and the mining nanites onto our ship while we were docked with theirs so they could listen to our conversations, and triggered the mining nanites when they found out that you knew too much."

"A bug. Hell." The three of them hung in space, staring at one other. "I don't suppose one of you grabbed the Golden Belt nanite samples on the way out the door, did you?" Jonah said.

"I'm sorry, Detective. This escape module had no tools with which to perform such an action," Scooter replied.

"Me neither," Harry said. "It was you or the nanites. No time for both."

"Good choice," Jonah said.

Scooter continued, "Your suit radios are not powerful enough to reach Ceres Station or otherwise call for help. Your emergency suit beacons are powerful enough, but Euphrates Mining is currently the closest rescuer possible, and I do not believe they have your best interests in mind. For that reason, I suppressed the distress signal that would normally have broadcast to the general area. This module that I currently occupy can accelerate at fifty gees, which will get me within tight-beam comm with Ceres Station within sixteen minutes in a flyby; I will not have the fuel to decelerate, though I should have time to download my consciousness to storage on the Station. The Station is equipped with an unmanned rescue unit that can accelerate at up to thirty gravities and should arrive here before your air and heat cease to function. It will provide extra power and air, and can return you to the Station in one piece."

"We'll wait," Jonah said.

"I imagine you will." Scooter flipped over and took off for Ceres, thrusting briefly to put some distance between itself and the drifting couple, then engaging the full power of its tiny fusion rocket. They watched the bright light fade to a pinpoint, just another star in the darkness.

"What if Euphrates is listening to us?" Jonah asked.

"Our suits radios are set up for mining ops. A few microwatts, good for maybe five hundred meters. They aren't going to pick that up."

"So we can talk."

"Yeah. So you have a theory?" Harry asked.

"Like I said, it sounds crazy. Let's say Euphrates is parked next to a chunk of dark matter. Or a blob, or a cloud, whatever it is. It can't react with normal matter except gravitationally: no electromagnetic interaction, probably no strong or weak nuclear interaction. So, the only way they can detect it is through its gravity. And the only way they can map it is by sending the gradiometer through it repeatedly to measure the gravity gradient. They can get a density map of the dark matter distribution that way."

"You're right, that's nuts," Harry said. "But if what you're suggesting is true, then this blob of invisible Play-Doh must mass about a third of the original asteroid."

"Right. When Space Rock pushed the asteroid, the gravitational force holding the dark and normal matter together wasn't enough to overcome the acceleration of Space Rock's push. So they separated." He spread his hands apart. "The asteroid's acceleration wouldn't jive with what they measured with their original gravitation measurements, and if they measured it again, its gravitation would be reduced by the missing mass."

"That still doesn't make sense," Harry said. "They've moved a lot of asteroids before and nobody has noticed any mass discrepancies. Why wouldn't they all have a chewy chocolate center? What's so special about this one?"

"The asteroid came from outside the Kuiper Belt. I'm guessing that the inner asteroids are subject to forces like collisions, solar winds and storms, outgassing, and other things that have separated the dark cores from the asteroids over billions of years. If an isolated DM blob collided with a normal asteroid, it could knock away any DM core that was still there. We could be surrounded by blobs of the stuff and never realise it. And Euphrates is trying to get a monopoly on the only verifiable chunk in the solar system. Dammit, I should have mentioned some of this to Scooter."

"Why?" Harry asked.

"Because if we die, then Euphrates gets to keep their secret. They could have literally years to explore the properties of the stuff before anyone else figures out that it even exists in-system. Find out if it has its own chemistry, or its own version of a photon. Dark photons. Sol only knows what they could develop from it."

"So you think that's why they tried to kill us? To keep a secret?"

"Oh, yeah." He pointed to a pinpoint of moving light. "What's that? Is help here already?" The light dimmed, then disappeared.

"Whatever it is, it's coasting toward us. And I don't think it's here to help. It's a mop-up crew. We must look like lightbulbs in infrared." Harry unclipped a pouch at his hip.

The object approached quickly, a small drone body with weapon pods, ten times the size of Scooter's escape module. Jonah instinctively reached for his gun, then realised that it was inside his spacesuit. Harry drew his own weapon from his side pouch and pulled the trigger within milliseconds of the drone's attack. A bright red beam scintillated through the particulate haze from their ship's earlier explosion, punching through Harry's facemask, creating a three-centimeter hole through his head. His gun, in response, appeared to do nothing.

Jonah sucked in a sudden breath and waited to die. Nothing moved. With a choked voice, Jonah said, "Harry?"

"I'm not dead yet," Harry radioed. His voice sounded different. "My brain is behind a lot of plating and shielding in my chest. This is, after all, a cop model. Still, that hurt like a son of a bitch."

"Your gun didn't fire."

"I set it for an EMP. An electromagnetic pulse. You couldn't see it. I fried its cute little brain."

Jonah could only think "space zombies" as he watched Harry jet over to the drifting drone. "Your air..." he started to say.

"I don't need air. Just power. And I'm transmitting direct to you with a synth voice, since I obviously can't talk on a mike right now. This body has some useful modules." He reached the drone and examined it with his one working eye. "Thank Sol for common interfaces." He pulled a cable out of his suit and plugged it into the drone. "Grab on," he said. "This thing should have enough fuel to take us to the nearest asteroid, and we can hide there until help arrives."

"If we move, help won't be able to find us," Jonah said.

"We have a rough timeline for when the rescue craft is supposed to get here. When it gets close, it should call us with a high-power radio to let us know it's arrived, and we can set off the Emergency Locator Beacon so it can find us, and hope like hell that it's closer to us than Euphrates."

"If this drone transmitted our position before you zapped it, Euphrates has to know we're here."

"Then we best get moving," Harry said.

• • •

It took the two of them twenty minutes to reach the nearest asteroid, which was a scant ten meters wide. It had a slow spin, which meant that they couldn't actually cling to the asteroid to hide, so they floated a few meters from it taking their best guess at where Euphrates might appear, then sent away the attack drone in case it could be tracked.

Ten minutes later, an unmarked manned runabout showed up within a few kilometers of their position. It started scanning the area and picked out the asteroid in fairly short order. It came straight at them.

Harry lifted his gun up and a beam from the runabout neatly vaporized it along with a few of his fingers.

And now we die, Jonah thought. He remembered how loose his suit was, and tried to pull his undamaged arm out of the sleeve, wriggling like Houdini in a straightjacket, trying to reach his gun.

"Well, look at you two!" a voice said over their suit radios. They both recognised Max Fern's voice immediately. "Wow, Harry, your face is pretty messed up. Speaking of 'pretty', did you tell him yet? Tell him who you really are?"

Jonah twisted to look at Harry. "What's he talking about?"

"Nothing, Jonah. He's just making shit up because he's a fucking asshole."

Max cackled. "She didn't! This is your lovely Leanna, back from the dead! She downloaded into this body and she didn't tell you? God, I love this."

Harry/Leanna kept staring at the runabout. "You knew all along. You orchestrated this, didn't you?" she said. "I hope you die painfully."

"Said the cloud of vaporised flesh." Something changed on the beam weapon fixture, then it pointed at Jonah. "Well, enough gloating. I've waited years for this moment."

Jonah, his right arm free inside the bulky suit, aimed his .38. His father had spent years with him teaching him how to 'shoot from the hip,' learning where the barrel was pointing without using the gun's sights. Whenever he asked him why this was important, his father told him, "Well, you just never know," an answer that seemed to work as filler for a lot of his questions.

Hoping that the pressure spike inside his spacesuit wouldn't blow out his eardrums, he shot through his own suit. He was rewarded by a small cloud of shrapnel where the beam weapon was mounted, though the recoil sent him into a spin. His breathing air vented quickly from the suit, but the hole foamed up just as the tear in his sleeve had. He yawned to settle his ringing ears from the roller coaster of pressure changes.

"Hah!" Max said, "The little rat still has some teeth. Well, a tooth, anyway. Let's see how you handle this." A side pod extended from the runabout with four small missiles mounted in a rack.

"Hey, those are illegal," Leanna said.

"Ha, ha! That's rich, Leanna, but stupid. I mean, Harry. It's appropriate that your atoms will be mixed together."

"No, seriously, we're going to have to arrest you. You should surrender now," she said.

There was confused silence for a moment. Max finally said, "Yeah, whatever. Goodbye, losers."

Leanna grabbed Jonah and smoothly jetted air to put his body behind her armored torso, simultaneously cancelling his spin. The four unlaunched missiles on the runabout suddenly blossomed into a halo of actinic light and fire, punching into the side of the runabout. Secondary explosions tore into the ship, and it dispersed quickly into a thin cloud of shrapnel.

"What was that?" Jonah asked.

"My yacking? That was a delaying tactic. Distraction. So the other ship could get a shot off." She pointed at another point of light slowly approaching them. "Or do you mean the explosion? Probably a kinetic flechette missile of some sort launched by our friend, setting off all of Max's missile payloads."

In the distance, Jonah could just make out the glow of another ship's thruster. It was much larger than the runabout, and bore Golden Belt's logo on its side. "Leanna," Jonah said. "Leanna?"

"Can we talk about this later? I'm in some pain right now."

They drifted quietly for a moment while Jonah processed her excuse. *She can probably shut the pain off with that body*, he thought. "Okay," he said. "We'll talk later."

"Hailing Officer Carroll and Detective Jones, this is Captain Anderson of the *Eater Of Worlds*. How are you two doing?"

"Not so good. Both wounded, but alive," Leanna replied. "Did you record most of that conversation?"

"The admission of intent to kill? We couldn't attack his ship without that. Good that you kept him talking."

"I thought there was some agreement up here about armament on mining ships. Like, there isn't supposed to be any." Jonah said.

"Surface sampling lasers or death rays," Anderson replied. "Sometimes it's hard to tell the difference. Anyway, to get to business, our rep at Ceres Station received word that your ship was destroyed and said you might need a lift back. We were nearby. You ready to go?"

"Depends. You guys have in-flight service?" Jonah asked.

● ● ●

Leanna stumbled into the rotating docking port at Ceres Station, leaning on Jonah's shoulder. She held up a hand to stay the other officers from helping her, even though they could see clear through the hole in her head. "I'm okay, I think. The head damage must have messed with my balance." She spoke over a direct radio link to the officers' receivers.

"Man, Harry, you should have the medic take a look at that mess. They might be able to stabilize it, at least."

"I won't be any good until they get me a fresh blank," Leanna said.

One of the officers looked at the other over her shoulder. "I heard they won't have a fresh one for another week."

Leanna grabbed the nearest handhold and steadied herself. "I guess I'll just have to wait."

"You might want to wait in your room, Harry. That face is going to scare the hell out of the norms."

Leanna tried to grin at him, but that part of her face was missing and she just looked ghoulish instead. "Just fuck off, Ben."

Jonah and Leanna ended up in the infirmary together while Orkin debriefed them. Jonah and Orkin wore comm sets so they could communicate with Leanna. The two space suits were write-offs from the shrapnel damage, and the medic had to cut the foamed suit from Jonah's arm. "Your arm isn't too bad. You get to keep it." He turned to Leanna and stared at her face. "You, on the other hand, might think about another download. The best you could hope for is ugly, instead of disgusting. Patch jobs never look as convincing as the original blank."

Once they finished the debrief, Orkin looked as bitter as Space Corps coffee. "Based on Scooter's report, we assumed that Euphrates tried to kill you and we sent an officer to bring Max Fern in for questioning, but apparently you already dealt with him."

"Yeah. We're pretty sure he's dead." Jonah said. "Although I'd be happier if I'd seen his body. So how about the rest of Euphrates management? Any arrests for the theft? Or the sabotage on our own runabout?"

Orkin shrugged. "Unfortunately, no. Scooter's speculation on the use of mining bots to degrade the gas storage and fusion reactor are just that; speculation. If we had recordings of their intership comm traffic, it might be another matter. Or if we had Fern here to grill. But we don't. Euphrates is also telling us that the nanites they captured from Golden Belt have eaten their way out of confinement and vanished, so they can't give us another sample. It's complete bullshit, but we have…what?" His communicator beeped with a high-priority message.

"Go ahead," he said.

"Sorry to interrupt sir, but we just received a message from the Claims Office that Euphrates has announced that they located the missing third of the asteroid, and is claiming the 300,000 credit reward. Figured you'd want to know."

Captain Orkin shook his head and frowned. "They know the game is up and they're trying to make the best of it. Turning their attempted theft into a finder's fee." He glanced sourly between Jonah and Leanna. "So what's so friggin' special about this dark matter? If they can't touch it, what do they expect to do with it?"

"It's a wild card, Captain," Jonah said. "If it's got its own chemistry, then whoever figures out the dark periodic table is going to have a leg up on everyone else. Their density measurements from the gradiometer could tell them if the dark matter is a solid, liquid, or gas. Irregular density will point to a solid mass. A perfect sphere suggests a liquid or gas."

Orkin held up his hand, "Yeah, thanks, that's enough."

"And it'll change how we think the Sun works. And the Earth's core dynamics."

Orkin sighed and rolled his eyes. "And how is that?"

"If the Earth's core is carrying a substantial amount of dark matter in it, then the actual normal-matter core could be much less dense than we think it is. We think we have an iron core, but maybe it's something a lot lighter."

"Lava has a lot of iron in it."

"Lava is largely silicon and oxygen, believe it or not," Jonah said.

"Really?" He looked unconvinced. "So, he who gets there first can take advantage of the knowledge gained?"

"If they can figure out how to interact with the stuff using something besides gravity, they'll make a killing."

"Then why give up the mother lode for 300,000 credits? Why don't they try to hide the dark matter?" Orkin asked.

"We already know it's there and there's no way they can move it fast enough to hide it. But I wouldn't be surprised if they figure out how to grab a chunk before they turn it over to Space Rock. Once this gets out, everyone will be sending ships out into deep space with gradiometers to troll for DM clouds or Kuiper asteroids with DM cores. It'll start a new gold rush. But for now, a kilogram of that stuff is going to be worth a CEO's ransom. And Space Rock is going to own some millions of kilograms, once Euphrates turns it over to them. But it'll be in their best interest to sell off parts of their claim, once they realize their monopoly can't last."

"Dear bloody red Sol," Orkin muttered. "This job was supposed to be easier than this." He looked over at Leanna. "Office Carroll, you haven't been saying much."

Leanna wobbled slightly, sitting on the exam table. "I don't feel good."

"That's no surprise. You've taken a lot of damage."

Jonah stood next to the exam table and put a hand on the side of her face, looking into her one good eye. "Thanks for saving my ass out there. Let's see what Dr Stevenson can do for you. You just relax. There should be plenty of blanks Earth-side. They can get you set up for transfer."

"I'll see you down there," she said, taking his hand. He squeezed it and let go.

Captain Orkin left the room. Jonah sat down in the exam room.

"You don't have to stay," Leanna said.

"I'll stay," he said.

Stevenson said, "Okay, let's see what we have to work with, here." He swung a camera over Leanna's damaged head and brought the image up on a large screen, zooming in on various details. "Your nervous system should have shut down all the pain sensors in the damaged area. Are you in much pain?"

"No, there's not much p…p…puh…" Her body jerked convulsively, slamming her head into the overhead camera, then became rigid.

"What's going on?" Jonah demanded.

Stevenson hurriedly fastened restraints along the edge of the table, aided by his nurse. He quickly surveyed her body. "Feedback from the damaged areas to her mind shouldn't be able to affect the rest of her body; there must be something going on with the brain core."

It took the doctor a couple of minutes to access the brain core in the armored chest while Jonah waited anxiously. Repositioning the camera above her chest, Stevenson maximised the magnification, scanning through depth layers, then stopped and gasped. "Nanites!" On the monitor, Jonah could see winding traces, like worm holes, twisting through the layers of her brain, mining the rare elements that made up the data highways of the crystalline matrix. The tiny blue-black monsters were chewing through Leanna's essence, getting closer to the central core, following the richest and thickest veins of metal. The doctor called out to the ship's AI, "Andrea, give me a priority link to Orkin."

It took only seconds. "Orkin here, Stevenson, what's up?"

"Captain, I need an emergency transfer to another blank stat. Officer Carroll has mining nanites eating away at her brain. If Golden Belt could shut them off…"

"Golden Belt is ten light-minutes away. How much time does she have?"

Stevenson glanced over at Leanna's body. "She? Uh…maybe minutes before major permanent damage. The nurse is hooking up the body for mind transfer right now."

"Sol's balls," Orkin cursed.

"If there's a blank on Earth that's ready for a transfer—" Stevenson began.

"They don't keep hot blanks Earthside. Or the Moon," Orkin said. "And there's no time for a round-trip verification. Someone had to be ready to catch the ball without knowing that it's been tossed their way." The comm was quiet for a few seconds, then Orkin continued. "Rochelle's World, however, in the Kuiper Belt, always keep a blank open. I'll have to notify them. We won't be able to get a response since they're seven light-hours away, but once they receive my message, they should be able to prep to receive the transfer in less than a minute. I'll notify them now. Get ready to transmit the template on my go."

Stevenson trailed trunk cables across the room and plugged them into the body moments before Orkin's message came through, "Go!"

He stood and inspected the setup as the nurse stepped back from the table, verifying that all the connections were in place, then turned to the control panel, assured that the coordinates were preset for the Space Corps station at Rochelle's world, and tapped the transmit icon.

Jonah stood close behind Stevenson. "What the hell just happened?" Jonah asked, his voice rough.

Stevenson opened his mouth and closed it.

Jonah approached the body and looked into its dead eyes.

"I'm sorry, Detective. When your ship exploded, some of the activated miner nanites must have gotten into his suit."

Or more likely planted in their suits to begin with, Jonah thought, on the unlikely chance that they might escape the explosion. He glanced at the suit that the medic had cut off him, a crumpled heap on the floor. "My suit's probably contaminated, too, then."

"We sent a message to Golden Belt. They'll send the deactivation codes for these nanites."

Jonah returned his gaze to Leanna. "She was transferred to Rochelle's World?"

Stevenson nodded. "In seven hours, they'll receive Orkin's request for the emergency transfer. A minute after that, the data beam for Harry's mind will arrive there and be downloaded into a new blank."

Jonah stared grimly at the empty receptacle before him, then thumped a closed fist against the blank's hard chest. "Bloody hell."

• • •

"I don't understand why Earth doesn't have blanks prepped for receiving minds," Jonah said. He was bedraggled, emotionally wrung out.

Captain Orkin stared glumly at the haze of stars in the digital viewport. He was one of the only people on the ship that knew that Harry had been Leanna, and that Jonah and Leanna had more in common than just work. "I'm sorry, Jonah. There was an incident about ten years ago where a convict managed to get his brain scanned and transmitted to five prepped blanks on Earth. All five of them became copies of the murderer and three got loose."

"Right, right. I remember that now," Jonah said. "So that resulted in a no-active blanks policy, then?"

"Not a policy, it's a law. They don't allow hot blanks at all on Earth."

Jonah shook his head and clasped his hands together, squeezing them until the knuckles turned white. "And Rochelle? Why the open blank there, then?"

"They need people. And for cops, the transfer is not only free, but they give you a 5000 credit bonus for transferring out. Cops are—" He hesitated.

"Not safe there?" Jonah said.

"Yeah, you could put it that way. Attrition is high. The lack of any real sunlight makes people crazy after a while, I think. A dark ice-ball planet is no place to live. You going after her?"

Jonah rubbed his face, thinking. He could go back to Earth and take up where he left off. Or go into the deep black of the Sol-forsaken dark planets to chase after a twice-dead woman with likely brain damage, in Sol-only knew what sort of an artificial body. Did he love her enough to chase after an echo of her? Whatever she was now? Would she even remember him?

"She could get retransmitted back to Earth," Jonah suggested. "If I go back to my old job, I..." His voiced faded when he saw the agonised look on Orkin's face.

Orkin folded his hands together and took a deep breath, letting it out slowly. "About that," he said. "While you were up here, just after Leanna died from the Europan virus, Congress passed a law quarantining everyone who's currently off-Earth. That, unfortunately, includes you, until the quarantine is lifted. It could take months."

Or years, Jonah thought. He ground his jaws, certain that Captain Albright, Leanna's father, had known the bill was in the works.

"There's a job for you here in the Belt, if you want to stay on," Orkin continued, "but Rochelle's World is recruiting, too."

Jonah looked around at the steel walls, sparsely decorated with scenes from Earth, thin reminders of what life could be, and felt trapped. The Captain's desk was aluminum processed from asteroids. On his desk was a large, dark-blue crystal of some mineral, dug out of rock. No wood, no open windows with warm summer breezes, no sunlight or trees, just work, wrapped up inside a plastic suit or a metal coffin. Could Rochelle be any worse?

"That's a four-month trip, isn't it?"

The Captain nodded. "One-gee acceleration for a day, coast for four months, and decelerate for a day. It's an expensive trip."

"And Rochelle pays for that?"

"Generally, the Space Corps would pay, but I think we can finagle a trip out of one of Space Rock's ships in a luxury berth. You saved them a ton of money and they're grateful. And their ships are a hell of a lot nicer than ours."

"Hmm." Jonah stood up. "Guess I better get packing, then." He stopped at the door of the small office and looked back at Orkin. "It was good working with you, Captain. If you get a chance, next time you talk to that son-of-a-bitch Albright, tell him his daughter is still alive."

Orkin smiled sadly. "I'll see what I can do."

• • •

Jonah sent a message to his brother on Earth to deal with his belongings in his apartment. He felt like he was casting off a mooring line to Earth, setting himself adrift.

He had to wait a week for the ship scheduled to travel to Rochelle. During that time, he pondered on whether Max Fern could have planned all this as some sort of petty revenge against Leanna and him. The idea seems ludicrous, since Max would have been a fool to bring the two of them up to work on a case that implicated him. And yet, Max had known that Harry was Leanna. He was certainly aware of her download and how it went. Could Albright have been involved, too? It was remotely possible; he blamed Jonah for his daughter's illness, and possibly her death. He banished Jonah to an off-Earth position, and maybe the coincidence of Leanna's ex-boyfriend Max being there was only that; a coincidence. But then, if Max had been keeping tabs on Leanna, then he knew she was sick, and he could have learned that she wanted to download, and orchestrated the entire download screw-up.

Could Max have arranged for his transfer to the asteroid belt through Albright? It was possible. After all, the report of the asteroid mass theft had already been filed, and a detective was bound to show up, so it was just a matter of putting a bug in the right ear to send him up here, and here he was. Quarantined from Earth due to the vague threat of unknown off-world diseases.

He stared up at the steel ceiling of his small cabin, lying on his stiff bed. Was it a coincidence that there was a blank handy at Rochelle, or had Max planned that, too? Would he have guessed that Jonah would head that way himself, blocked from returning to Earth? Could he have known about the pending quarantine? And did it matter now? Max was dead.

Tired of speculation, he finally sat up and ordered a stout from the food dispenser. What good was speculation without some facts to back it up? It was easy to make coincidence look like a conspiracy. He'd seen that too much as a cop, though that didn't mean it wasn't true.

In a perfect universe, it should have taken only fourteen hours for a message to come back from Rochelle's World that Leanna's transmission had been successful. If there hadn't been a blank ready to receive her, Leanna's electromagnetic essence would have continued further and further, the tight beam of her mind diverging into a thin field of meaningless photons, too broad to be captured or interpreted by any dark world beyond Rochelle. Practically, the round-trip message would take at least sixteen hours, since the revived blank would have to be thoroughly checked out.

Jonah waited. When the message arrived, Comm patched the signal directly to his room.

"Jonah?" The voice, at least, sounded like the Leanna he knew.

He said, "I'm here," before he remembered that she was seven light-hours hours away. All he could do was listen to her message.

"Jonah, I'm alive, again, I think. You're not going to believe this, but they screwed up again."

Jonah's face darkened as he sucked in a breath between clenched teeth.

"There was a female blank all ready, but they had an unexpected transfer like fifteen minutes before mine arrived. Then they had no blank at all, and, uh…"

He squeezed his eyes shut tight, hoping to keep reality out.

"…they put me in a ship's brain. The existing ship brain requested a transfer to the blank shortly before Orkin's message got here, and they let it download, so the ship brain was the only space available, and they put me there. I'm a fucking space ship. But they swear that they've started to grow another blank, and it should be ready in a month. By the time you get here, I'll be me again. Please come. Please tell me you're coming."

Leanna kept talking. Something about her weapons and sensors, but he'd stopped listening. He leaned his forehead against the cool steel wall of the cabin and wished that Max Fern were still alive so he could kill him again.

THE END

Meet Tom Jolly

Tom Jolly's short SF and fantasy stories have appeared in Analog, Daily Science Fiction, Something Wicked, Compelling SF, Amazing Stories, and elsewhere. He also designs board and card games, such as Wiz-War, Drakon, Cavetroll, Got It!, Cryo, and Manhattan Project: Energy Empire (co-designed with Luke Laurie). When he isn't doing either of those, he's making obnoxious puzzle designs, which he encourages those with woodcrafting skills to produce (over 40 to date). His latest book is *Unnatural Remedies*, a sequel to his book, *An Unusual Practice*.

He retired as an astronautical and electrical engineer in 2015 after working at Lockheed-Martin for 27 years on launch support for the Titan program, and satellite transportation for the Payload Transportation Systems group. His first launch in February of 1986 (a Titan 34D) blew up.

He lives in Port Orchard, WA, with his wife of 40+ years.

You can find more of his short fiction at **https://sites.google.com/view/tomjolly/stories-and-articles**

Not Tomb Enough to Hide the Dead
By Lee Allred

"Filth capital of the world," the man in the window seat muttered as he looked out at the city lights rushing up to meet the plane in the dark of midnight.

Nathan Fairchild nodded, more to work his jaw muscles to pop his ears as the plane descended than in agreement. It wasn't the mountains of drug needles and human feces littering San Francisco's sidewalks or the smash-and-grab flash mobs of shoplifters he hated, it was the ancient evils hidden deep in the bowels of the city. The unholy evils Fairchild was forced to slave for, bound to for the rest of his immortal days.

"Pity it just doesn't slide right into the sea," Window Seat said. The plump little man smelling of Old Spice and a half-spilled Bloody Mary just wouldn't shut up about societal collapse. Not like the Midwest, the man bragged. Godfearing citizens and neighbours who looked after kids in the neighbourhoods. Apple pie and Norman Rockwell and knowing what's what. If it wasn't for these consarned business trips, he'd never leave Iowa, and that's a fact.

The plane's retracted landing gear thumped free. A squeal of tires and a very sleepy flight attendant welcomed Fairchild to San Francisco.

While Window Seat and the rest of the passengers were still struggling with overhead luggage an empty-handed Nath Fairchild exited the plane. He'd abandoned his gear back in Oregon. When the Judge tells you to drop your investigation and get back to the Rookery immediately, crash basis, you don't stop to pack.

Fairchild allowed himself a grim smile. The Judge was going to choke on what Fairchild had found up there in Omsberg. And the Judge had a nasty habit of shooting the messenger. The grin faded as he walked through the gate into the near-deserted concourse.

They were waiting for him at the gate.

Two hatchet men he'd never seen before and he bet the Judge hadn't either.

They weren't Rookery men. Tall, thin, and almost ethereal. Tailored Italian suits. And eyes ancient as the everlasting hills.

Bloodborns, both of them. The aristocrats of the vampire world. Part of Ruthven's mob, the Viennese *Krähenhorst*. Brutal psychopaths who ruled Europe's lesser rookeries and thought they ruled America's as well.

The Viennese didn't employ adjuncts like Fairchild — humans who'd resisted the Bite but had picked up some vampiric powers in the process – as troubleshooters, investigators, and feral-slayers, Stakeholders in vampire parlance. No, the *Krähenhorst* their Wild Hunts. And when there wasn't a feral to be hunted down and slaughtered for sport, Ruthven's bloodborns hunted down random baseborns, the subjacent class of vampire composed of former humans turned by the Bite.

Adjuncts like Fairchild the *Krähenhorst* merely slew out of hand. Nothing must taint the Blood. Humans they saw as nothing but feed cattle, less than offal.

Fairchild idly wondered just how they managed to slip past security. The technique, was all. Not like the three-hundred-pound wonders of the TSA were up to stopping purebloods.

"You will come with us," the blonder of the two rasped.

"But first wait here," the other said in an even heavier Austrian accent. His tongue flicked over half-hidden incisors. "It was a long journey from Vienna."

The other passengers from the red eye were beginning to spill out of the gate. The two vampires followed the first man headed into the nearby lavatory, Window Seat as it happened.

They emerged from the men's room a short while later, licking their chops.

All the remorse of a housecat with a budgerigar in its mouth.

"Nothing like cornfed Iowa beef to slake one's hunger," the

blonder one smirked.

"'No. Don't. I've a wife and kids,'" the other pantomimed, hissing in amusement.

Fairchild slowly let out a breath. "It's going to be a real pleasure teaching you two table manners."

The blonder one tensed, shifting weight on his feet. "Big talk from someone the Blood rejected."

The darker one placed a restraining hand on Blondie's arm. "Business before pleasure. That is, if Ruthven leaves us anything to play with." He gestured towards the exit way leading to curbside. "Shall we?"

• • •

Little had changed in the Judge's Inner Sanctum since last time Fairchild had been there. Located in the deepest recesses of the Rookery nest in the Tenderloin district. Dark-paneled and decorated with Depression-era furnishings right down to a candlestick telephone. The huge office was dominated as usual by an eight-foot-wide desk, but unlike all the other times Fairchild had stood before that desk, it wasn't the Judge who sat behind it.

Skeleton-thin with skin like petrified leather, the most ancient of all ancient vampires Lord Ruthven reposed in his commandeered high-backed throne of imported Montalban leather and gliding castor wheels. Claw-like fingers lay preternaturally still as upon the glossily waxed desktop.

Ruthven's reptant, slitted eyes flicked towards where a very battered and bruised Judge hung crucified against the wall, tension steel spikes – the very tools Fairchild used as Stakeholder – pinioned his wrists and feet. The bruises faded as the Judge's bloodborn metabolism began its accelerated healing.

Two of Ruthven's goons flanked the hanging Judge. Each held in his hand a ten-pound sledge. At a nod from Ruthven, the two began whaling on the half-conscious Judge, battering him with the hammers and smashing bone to powder. They continued beating him until the Judge's skin began to smoke with heat, then abruptly stopped.

"He could of course extricate himself from the wall," Ruthven croaked in a voice as desiccated as a sepulcher, slithering and susurrant. His breath stank of ichor and grave mold.

Facial skin cracked as Ruthven's mouth pulled up at the corners in a rictal smile. "Alas, the constant healing – involuntary on his part—keeps him right on the brink. The additional effort needed to pull himself free would result in self-immolation."

Vampires weren't the arcane creatures of popular legend. Their speed and strength were due to a strictly-physical phenomenon – super-charged oxygenation of vampiric blood. Their abilities came at a cost: heat. Exertion at top levels caused vampires to rapidly overheat. The least additional amount of heat – internal or external – caused an overheated vampire to spontaneously combust. Folklore had it wrong; vampires could venture out in daylight. They just preferred operating at night when the added warmth of the sun wouldn't immolate a vampire in flight-or-fight mode.

A vampire's almost-instant healing also derived from the same oxygenation process jumpstarting cellular repair. The Judge would burn to cinders if he tried flexing his wrists and feet free of the steel spikes.

Ruthven eyes flicked back toward Fairchild. "Don't mistake my sparing this bungler for the present as mercy," Ruthven said, sibilating like a cobra. "Nor as some desire to maintain the power structure of this nest of racial mongrels and baseborn curs."

The Judge cursed through broken teeth. It earned him another hammer blow.

"I simply find that I need this dangling piece offal," Ruthven continued, "to corroborate portions of your report." Again, the skeletal smile. "After that, we shall see."

"I couldn't care less either way," Fairchild said.

"Yes, your intransigence and lack of fealty is known even in Austria," Ruthven said. "That is why I have him –" he made the slightest of head tilts at the Judge " —to tell me when you are lying. His expertise, you see." He nodded at Fairchild's two minders. "And I have *them* because your sympathies for cattle is also known. Should I discover that you have used what you found at Omsberg in some misguided notion to save livestock from the Bite, Hans and Dieter will rend you to pieces. *Their* expertise, you see."

Ruthven leaned forward, resting his elbow upon the surface of the desk and tenting his fingers together. The inch-long fingernails, sharp as daggers and white as petrified ivory, clacked like the Devil's castanets.

"Omsberg," Ruthven demanded. "Your investigation there. You will start at the beginning and leave out nothing."

•••

I'd been wolfing down a greasy burger at a truck stop outside of Boise when my phone rang. Dispatch with a new assignment. A new feral, making its way down the Pacific Coast from British Columbia. Latest reports put it northern Oregon somewhere.

Nobody knew why vampires suddenly went feral, losing all capacity for rational thought, becoming little more than frenzied killing machines. So far, no common factor had been discovered. Neither age nor bloodline seemingly mattered. Croft, head of Dispatch, liked to think it was a vampire's atrophied conscience finally catching up to them, but then Croft was a romantic even for a baseborn.

Regardless, ferals had to be dealt with. The first rule of the vampire world, perhaps its only rule, was Don't Foul One's Nest. Vampiric existence depended on secrecy. Judicious feedings. The occasional killings spread out. A feral's wanton rampage endangered all that.

That is why the Rookery employed Stakeholders like Fairchild. To dispatch ferals and clean up the resultant mess.

I caught the first flight out to Portland and picked up a full kit and a vehicle at the depot there. Generic black SUV with a gross of various GS government licenses plates.

By this time Dispatch had two items of bad news for me. First, the feral had gone to ground. Yamhill County, Croft thought. Ferals may not be rational but they had animal cunning. They could sense pursuit. Fight or flight.

Second, the feral wasn't one of ours. The Rookery assigned a specific hunting ground to each of its vampires. All our British Columbian vampires were accounted for. This one was a tourist

– a German from the Viennese *Krähenhorst*. Even worse, a blood-born.

I could think of a few choice words to say.

"I've already said them myself," Croft said over the phone. "I've notified the Judge, of course."

And the Judge would notify Vienna as fast as he could dial the number.

He'd want to micromanage this one personally. And he'd naturally twist it in his mind as some sort of diabolical plot by his main rival Croft and his cabal to usurp him. Vampire in-fighting is like that. The Judge had already been driven from power once during the 1910s. He'd amused himself and avoided pursuit playacting at being a human, one Judge Joseph Force Crater, for a couple decades or so until he managed to regain his throne atop the Rookery on August 6, 1930. Since then, the Judge had kept a paranoic iron grip on his domain.

"Send me everything you have on Yamhill and surrounding counties." I told Croft. "Then I'm breaking contact."

The less I had to do with Croft and Dispatch right now the better for both of us.

I transferred Croft's files to my laptop and spread out my paper map of Oregon. Yamhill County was west-southwest of Portland just outside practical commuting distance. McMinnville held the most people, thus the most meals, but there was also the casino town of Grand Ronde with hordes of transient tourists in RVs. The feral Horst Wulff could be anywhere. Newburg, Sheridan – there was a federal prison there, tasty sardines in a can. He could strike nearby Lincoln City on the coast or Tillamook or Polk County or double back to Portland and wouldn't that just be an unholy mess?

I pulled up the Rookery map of hunting grounds and compared it with my paper map. The hunting grounds of rural Oregon west of the Cascades were a desirable sinecure, divvied out as political plums. Summers mildly hot and humid, but the winters – cold, rainy, and drizzling overcast – were perfect for hunting. After politicians had euthanized the logging industry, rural Oregon's economy had tails-pinned. Towns and outlying hamlets were chockablock with abandoned buildings taken over by meth labs and weed runners. Corpses nobody would care about. Easy pickings.

Vampires might be immortal, but they didn't all maintain youthful vigor as they aged. It was not uncommon for them to grow feeble, crabbed, decrepit, shuffling about like octogenarians. Greybeards who'd in the past been loyal allies to Croft were the sort assigned plum territories like Yamhill. Easy pickings were about the only prey these greybeards could feed upon.

Easy pickings for greybeards would be an effortless paradise for a feral.

About that time, Judge Crater called. I had my phone piped through the car speakers as I drove. I let him rant how he was in charge now and that I'd better not call Croft for anything, anything, do you hear me! – which was beyond stupid as any new information Croft might have he'd have to learn from Croft and Dispatch anyway. But that's paranoia for you.

When he paused for breath, I asked how he wanted me to proceed. "Skrag the bloodborn or wait for Vienna to show up?" The *Krähenhorst* would excrete an entire brickyard if us yokels harmed one of their precious purebloods, feral or not.

"One less *Krähenhorst* ponce in the world is a thing of beauty," he growled. "But take care of it before they get there. I'm sure Ruthven already sending a small army over in private jets. If you can't, pack up, come home. Let them handle it."

Vampires never willingly ceded authority over their territory. Ruthven must have the Judge totally cowed.

"I should have time. Looking at kill pattern vectors, I 've narrowed things down to either the town of Yamhill or maybe Oms County." Oms County was unassigned territory, flagged with a classified marking on the Rookery map.

"Never you mind about Oms County," the Judge barked, just a shade too quickly. "You concentrate on Yamhill."

"I'm pulling into the outskirts now," I said and broke off the phone call.

Outskirts was putting it a bit strongly. Yamhill held about a thousand people. A grain silo, a gas station, a red brick downtown of all of maybe one block, a school. The only notable person Yamhill had ever contained until Horst Wulff had been the children's author Beverly Clearly. She had grown up here.

It wasn't quite dawn. The feral, if he were here, would just about be heading back to his temporary lair before daylight hit. I cruised around the edges and backroads looking for empty, abandoned buildings.

A half-collapsed wooden farm house set deep in grove of leafy oak trees looked promising.

I parked a way away and strapped on my equipment. Tactical vest with tension steel stakes. Road flares in my cargo pockets. Knitted watch cap covering a Kevlar skull cap helmet. Fingerless gloves.

I approached the tumbled down shack from downwind, nice and slow and easy. Caught a whiff of the feral inside. Heard it snuffle and grunt, shuffle around inside as the eastern sky hinted of dawn'.

Suddenly an explosion of catamount screams and thrashing bodies. The weathered grey wood planks of the shack shattered and flew in all directions.

Had *Krähenhorst* gotten here first?

Two writhing, wrestling bodies slammed through the last wall standing, splintering it into flinders. One body was definitely the feral. The other was some female vamp.

The two were going all out, scratching, clawing, biting. The stronger the vampire, the quicker they combust. The feral was already starting to overheat. I could smell the burning flesh and see the smoke. The girl — I pegged her as a baseborn — was still not yet at the brink but that wouldn't matter. If the feral went up like a Roman candle, she would too, locked in a clinch as she was.

The two of them landed hard on the ground, but they both sprang to their feet and began clawing at close quarters again. The feral was just this side of catching fire.

I tensed and made a leap of twenty feet, making a flying kick.

Adjuncts don't oxygenate on the level of a true vampire, we're weaker and slower than them—even baseborns—but that also means we don't overheat as fast or as easily. Half the ferals I've ever sanctioned I had done so by outlasting them in a fight until they combusted.

So caught up in their battle with each other, neither vampire noticed my leap. My foot caught the girl mid-torso and sent her cartwheeling ten feet or so. I'd kicked her rather than the feral because if I'd hit him, it would have surely pushed him right over the combustion threshold., burning her, too.

The feral, mindless as an animal, just stood there for a split second, blinking at the sudden and unexpected disappearance of his opponent.

That was all the opening I would ever get. And all I ever needed.

With my right hand, I drove the steel stake into the vampire's chest. I just missed his heart but that didn't matter. With my other hand, I flicked the ignition cap of the road flare as I shoved the sparking flare into the fist-wide body cavity I'd just carved. I leapt back next to the girl and watched as the feral burst into a flaming inferno. Overkill, maybe but you don't take chances with a feral.

I watched the flames. The Judge was right. It was a thing of beauty.

One less vampire in the world.

One less to enslave me.

I turned to question the girl only to catch a roundhouse kick to the head that dropped me like a stone. I thought I heard her say *you fool, you've ruined everything* or words to that effect as she sprinted away at vampiric speed.

Groggily, I got to my feet and followed after, but she was already well up the road. She piled into a waiting car. Late model something-or-other. I was too dazed to get a good look. Someone else, a man it looked like, sat at the driving wheel. As soon as she dived in, the car peeled out and sped away. I was too out of it to follow.

Behind me, the dry-as-tinder remains of the farm shack had caught fire, lighting a fiery beacon in the night sky every fire truck and police in town was siren-screaming towards.

I had just enough time to drive away myself before they arrived.

• • •

Lord Ruthven's eyes narrowed. "Crater made no mention of any girl."

Fairchild snorted. "I don't blame him. It would have pointed you straight to Omsberg as it did me. I reported the girl to him, though. An unassigned baseborn where there shouldn't have been any attacking a *Krähenhorster*? I would been a fool not to report that."

Ruthven glanced over at Crater. The battered Judge managed a weak nod.

The vampire lord turned back to Fairchild. "May develop later that you are indeed a fool, but it appears in this particular moment at least you tell the truth. Continue."

• • •

I had a pretty fair idea of where to head next: south on Route 47 to McMinnville, cut west to Lincoln City on the coast, then up 101 to Oms County and Omsberg.

The girl didn't belong to any of the nearby assigned hunting grounds. Those superannuated vampires could barely manage to feed; none of them had the strength for Turning. That left Oms County.

Oms County was an anomaly, ten square miles of coastal headlands wedged between Lincoln and Tillamook. Back a hundred-and-fifty years ago while Oregon was still creating new counties, a state senator named Oms carved himself out his own vest pocket fiefdom. Seems he'd struck silver and wanted total control of the area.

Well, the silver vein played out about a week or two after he got the county ratified. Oms turned timber magnate and ran cut-rate paper mills out of Omsberg. His descendants carry on in the same tradition. After lumbering died, the Oms family turned the county into a haven for cut-rate retirement homes and assisted living centers of last resort. Third-world doctors and illegal alien attendants and dubious generic medicines. As county-commissioners-for-life runs, the Oms clan runs legal interference to kept them running.

Patients die by the cartload, of course, but of planned neglect, not the Bite.

That's the first thing I found when I started number crunching the data. Someone from Dispatch or a trained Stakeholder like me can roughly suss out from public figures the number of Bite deaths in an area. Oms County didn't show any.

Not one.

Impossible.

I didn't need the Judge ordering me away from the area to know that all that nonsense about it being an "unassigned" hunting ground was just that. Nonsense. That classified market all but guaranteed it *was* assigned territory.

Past-their-prime loyal members of your faction isn't the only ones Rookery masters give sinecures to. Sometimes it's cheaper and easier to buy out your rivals.

A bloodborn named Mitchell Royden, Croft's predecessor in Dispatch. had been a brilliant scientist, what I guess you'd call a biochemist, who knew more about vampire physiology than any living or undead soul. He was big in the cabal that had briefly ousted Crater and when Crater came back, he gave Royden the chop. I'd always heard that the Judge had let Royden pack up for New Zealand, but I'd bet my life – in fact I was doing just that – that Royden had relocated to Omsberg under a new identity and a classified marker had been slapped on the whole deal.

Royden got to live, Crater got to keep somebody with a lot of potentially useful knowledge on tap and under his thumb.

I don't know how Royden tied into the girl or the lack of Bite deaths in Olms County, but if somebody on their own accord was sending out baseborn hit squads to kill ferals, I needed to know about it and the Judge needed to know about too.

I was going to have to throw away the manual with this investigation, though. I couldn't call up Dispatch, I couldn't let the Judge know I was poking around in Omsberg, and I was under severe time constraints. I had just hours before the Viennese arrived (whether they'd land in San Francisco to see Crater or head directly to Portland and Yamhill, I couldn't guess). I had even less time before Crater twigged to the fact that I was in Omsberg.

I made my first stop at the County morgue. GS license plates and an ID card fresh off the printer attested to the fact that I was a federal National Institute of Health official, but I probably could have just walked in off the street and asked my questions. The county coroner was a garrulous old coot happy enough to talk to somebody who wasn't a corpse that he talked my ears off.

I did a spot inspection of random cadavers on hand, citing some flummery about a new NIH, but none of them showed any marks of feeding, let alone Bite deaths.

The dead were segregated into two piles as it were. The morgue was equipped with a refrigerated cabinet with three dozen slab drawers. These were for either locals or nursing home corpses whose families could afford to ship the deceased back home. The rest of the dead were simply wrapped in white sheets and stacked like cordwood in a large adjoining warehouse.

"Poverty row," the coroner told me. Those dead whose family couldn't or wouldn't afford transshipment or even a burial.

"What happens to them?" I asked.

"Oh, Joe comes along and carries them off. Joe Stokes, that is. He runs Mercy Crematorium. State pays him five bucks a body, and I guess there's some charity or something that pays his operating expenses. Angels of Last Resort."

I asked the coroner which of all the nursing homes in town he'd send his sainted mother to if he had to. The Elysium chain, he gathered. Who ran it, I asked, and he told me the name of one of the Olms scions. Seemed all the nephews ran one of the chains. The Elysium was for paying customers who *could* pay.

I made the corporate offices of the Elysium. Arturo Olms was a mincing fussbudget who wasn't very keen on having a NIH fed show up on his doorstep. The Olms family had enough pull in Salem to keep State inspectors at bay. Feds were another matter.

Setups like Omsberg usually kept one outsider firm around to serve as a patsy in case things went south. It didn't take Arturo any prodding at all to point me to it.

"Really," he sniffed. If it's improprieties you're looking for you really should be looking at the Superior. Shockingly bad. I've heard tales that would curl your hair."

"And who runs that," I asked.

"A non-profit called Force Majeure," he said, pulling out from his desk drawer a dossier folder he probably had printed up by the gross.

I thanked him and asked about mortuaries in town. Only two, I was told. One was Olms Mortuary. The other was our good friend Mercy Crematorium.

I made a brief stop at the Olms place and met an overly somber version of Arturo with the same Olms nose and chin. I asked how many stiffs a week he usually handled and who supplied his embalming fluid.

Then I booked a room at the Ocean Breezes motel directly across a side street from Mercy Crematorium. Rock bottom rates. I had the place to myself. I guess nobody likes the thought of sleeping next door to crematorium smoke.

"Better than it used to be," the owner-proprietor told me. "Old Joe used to smoke us out on a daily basis. Then he put some new scrubbers in or something. Can hardly tell its burning anymore."

To tell the truth, my motel room could have used a little smoke. The smell of mold damp from the wet ocean air permeated the carpet and bedclothes. At least the towels were clean.

I laid one out on top of the bed's quilted comforter and sat on it with my laptop and phone. Called around, looked up a few things on government websites, not that I really needed to.

It was pretty obvious Joe Stokes owned all those non-profits. He was paying himself to burn the bodies he hauled away from his own rest home.

Only he wasn't burning any bodies.

Or feeding on living humans.

The two were somehow related.

Maybe he had succeeded where millennia of other vampires had failed in finding a way to subsist off of the blood of corpses.

• • •

"But you don't believe that any more than I did," Fairchild told Ruthven. "You didn't fly six thousand miles because you were worried Mitchell Royden – alias Joe Stokes – had found a substitute diet plan."

The ancient vampire glared.

"You're worried Royden cracked the problem from the other end. Instead of altering what vampires feed on, Royden had found a way to eliminate the need to feed altogether."

"By reversing the Bite, changing vampires into *humans*?" Ruthven said, spitting that last word in disgust.

Fairchild smiled. "You don't like the idea?"

Ruthven dug his claws deep into the polished wood of the desktop. "Because it's not a curse, you fool!" he said, fangs bared. "Because bloodborns were never human to begin with."

"And you're worried it could wipe out your kind altogether."

As if on cue, the battered Judge Crater mumbled from swollen lips. "Thhuh gurrl."

"Yes, the girl!" Ruthven agreed. "Royden had already 'cured' himself, presumably in laboratory conditions. Then he sent his baseborn flunky out to test his weaponised version out to test it on a feral. *'You fool, you've ruined everything'* – by immolating their test subject."

Fairchild's bitter laugh caught Ruthven by surprise. "I only saved you the trouble of killing him yourself. Him and Royden and the girl, the feral."

The ancient vampire clutched and unclutched his talon-like fingers like some great bird of prey. "And you. And Croft and anyone else you've passed Royden's formula on to. But I shan't kill you until after you've finished making your report."

• • •

I peeked out the motel room window at the Crematorium. I'd pieced together as much as I was going to without seeing for myself what lay in Royden's little house of horrors.

The Judge would be calling any minute now and order him out of the area. I needed to act now, if I was going to.

I packed up, throwing my gear in the back of my ride, everything but the gear I had strapped to my vest.

I paused, then added two items to my load out. A body cam – the Judge would believe what he wanted to believe unless I could back up my side of events with something more than mere words.

I also strapped on a gun belt. Bringing a gun to a feral fight is usually worse than useless, but I wasn't fighting ferals this time. My gun didn't look like much more of an up-sized pepperbox derringer than anything, but the four-barrel contraption had its uses.

The front of the rambling two-story crematorium faced the town's busy main drag – Highway 101 in all its four-laned glory. The back of the structure, including the garage door for the hearse, bordered Fleet Street, the same street as my motel.

I felt like a sitting duck crossing Fleet Street in broad daylight, tac vest on and a gun strapped to my thigh.

Seagulls screamed overhead. I could smell the tang of the ocean air and salt water taffy from a nearby souvenir shop. Fifty yards up the street was a tourist in a Hawaiian shirt and I'm dressed like Rambo.

The crematorium grounds hadn't been landscaped. Gravel crunched under Fairchild's feet as he sprinted to a side door next to the garage. The weather-beaten wooden door looked like it dated back to the 1920s. Flimsy and rusted. I didn't bother kicking the door in, I just palm-thrust the knob right through the punked wood. I was inside before the metal knob could hit the indoor carpet.

An ungodly smell hit me immediately – the foulest stench I'd ever encountered in my life. Look I've hunted ferals in the nightmare trenches of the First World War, crawled around in the muck of No Man's Land through a sea of half-rotted corpses. But I've never encountered anything as strong or as sick-making as this.

The smell was coming from a cellar door down a narrow hallway lined in peeling wallpaper. Rags had been stuffed in the door jam to try to keep out the odor. Reluctantly, I opened the cellar door. The dirty rags, stiff with accumulated filth, fell to the floor in a heap.

A low-wattage bulb lit the top of the twisting staircase. I descended into what proved to be the abattoir of Hell.

A large basement – at least forty feet square – lay at the bottom. It was nothing but a dug-out pit filled with mud and water and hundreds of rotting human corpses – floating on the surface and sunken in the mire.

Not regular corpses, but flensed corpses. Deboned, with only the skin and meat and body fat and soft organs tossed into the hellish bog.

I stood there on the tiled rim of that pit as my mind reeled and my stomach threatened to heave.

Adipocere, my gibbering mind screamed. Royden was harvesting corpse-wax. Bog butter. Putrefied body fat. Whatever Royden's process was must call for adipocere – staggering amounts of it, an amount his steady intake of the unwanted dead of Omsberg readily supplied.

The almost tangibly foul air must have dulled my other senses. I didn't sense her until she flung herself at me in attack.

She was new to being a vampire, unused to her new abilities. That's all that saved me. That and dozen decades of experience.

I spun away from her leap, body-checking her as she arced past me. She landed heavily on the lip of the sludge pit.

I had my gun out before she could get to her feet.

A single pull of the trigger fired all four barrels.

Four gyrojet shells rocketed towards her, shells tipped with white phosphorous. Willie Pete.

The burning tips embedded themselves deep in her guts. Meant to set ablaze even an unoxygenated vampire at dead rest baseline temperature, they instantly pushed her over the threshold, oxygenated as he was from her attack.

She burst into vampiric combustion. Her burning corpse toppled into the water muck of the bog pit but even that didn't quench the burning phosphorous.

Coughing from the poisonous smoke, I staggered back up the stairs.

I found Royden in his lab. He must have heard me coming for I received a hurled glass jar to the face the moment I opened the door.

I brushed away shattered glass from my face. Retorts and chemical jars and papers with pencil scrawls covered a long wooden table. I didn't stop to look at any of that.

Royden had already ducked out a side door.

I followed after him, scattering chemical flasks and scientific equipment in my wake as I leapt over the table.

The side door led to the street outside. Highway 101.

Royden was already halfway across, running straight through the busy traffic. He got as far as the middle of the street before a tire-squealing SUV plowed into him. With Royden affixed to the grill, the southbound SUV swerved and T-boned a northbound dump truck.

I caught one glimpse of his smashed form, impaled perfectly through the heart with a flange of chromed metal, before some spark set the puddling gasoline ablaze, consuming the body entirely.

· · ·

Fairchild extracted a camera memory chip from his pocket and tossed it at Ruthven. "It's all there. It confirms I held no conversations with either Royden or the girl, removed any notes from Royden's lab, or even glanced at them. I know no more about Royden's formula than your Eurotrash goons here. I don't even know, can't even confirm, if there ever was some reversal formula. I can't even be sure if the Holmes I fought was human or vampire.

"You can waste your time watching the chip, waste your time killing me. Or you can get yourself to Omsberg and raid Royden's lab before the cops do. It may take them some time to identify Royden's body or realise he's missing."

Fairchild shrugged. "In any case, nothing I know could help Croft recreate a Bite reversal technique that may not even exist. Not that I would tell him anyway. Not a technique that requires a basement full of corpse wax for a single dose. The secret is safer with me than it is with you."

The Judge moaned.

Fairchild hooked a finger at his battered boss. "And you're going to need Crater, too, to sweep the Omsberg mess under the carpet. And keep Croft from nosing about, much as it pains me to take *his* side of things."

Ruthven stared at him in silence, then gave a single, jerky nod. He rose ghostlike from the chair. The two thugs who'd been torturing Judge Crater, flanked him like trained Dobermans.

"I'm posting Hans and Dieter outside this office. They'll hold you incommunicado until I satisfy myself about the contents of Royden's laboratory."

The ancient vampire and his escorts swirled out of the room.

Fairchild began pulling steel stakes out of the wall, freeing the Judge.

He hefted a bloody stake in each hand as the Judge rubbed his rapidly healing wounds. No thanks from the Judge, of course. If anything, needing Fairchild's help in getting free only angered him all the more.

"And what are you planning to do with those?" the Judge asked in his weakened state, as if he expected Fairchild to strike..

Fairchild smiled. He titled his head towards the door where Hans and Dieter stood guard on the other side. "There was an unauthorised feeding at the airport tonight by a couple vampires outside their own territory," Fairchild said. "I promised to teach somebody some table manners."

The Judge, murder in his eyes, picked up the other two steel stakes. "Allow me to join you."

Meet Lee Allred

Lee Allred has had his hands in dozens of professional publication credits, including such venues as *Asimov's*, *Pulphouse Magazine*, and numerous anthologies. He's also scripted comic books for DC Comics (Batman '66), Marvel (Fantastic Four) and IDW Comics (Dick Tracy).

His novella "For the Strength of the Hills" was named a Sidewise Award for Alternate History finalist. A great love of history and historical detail infuses all of Lee's work, whether he's writing steampunk, vampire tales, alternate history, or military SF.

Lee served three rotations in Iraq as part of Operation Iraqi Freedom for the United States Air Force. After retiring as a Master Sergeant, Lee settled down to a writing life hidden away in his Fortress of Leeitude hollow mountain redoubt. Discover more at **https://www.leeallred.com**

Men Of Glass
By William Burton McCormick

I refuse to sit near the barroom mirror, Irwin. I told you on the phone where to meet. Didn't you take me seriously? Reflections unnerve me. Look at us in the glass. Three dimensions rendered in two. Backwards. It's God's sleight of hand, I tell you. How can you trust an illusion? I won't. Don't laugh, Irwin. We all have our demons. You throw salt over your shoulders at every meal and hook a rabbit's foot on your keychain. Isn't your wife a devotee of astrology? So, what if I won't let myself gawk into the looking glass, anymore? You never know what you'll find there. Listen…this speakeasy has private nooks away from the bar. Go to the table behind the stairs where we can avoid our reflections. Let the mirror accost the other drunks, they don't care. Bring the beers, my man, I haven't much time.

Good. These are better seats anyway, Irwin. Away from the band music where men can talk. I called you here about Rory Seward. Yes, the mobster. Finn McMathan's underboss. Rory owns this joint and a dozen others throughout Massachusetts and Rhode Island. Now he's gone. I read your article theorising he's in the North End, a prisoner of Joe Lombardo's boys. I'm afraid that's not right. The other papers speculate Havana, Chicago or back to Ireland, but they're wrong too. The police, I suspect, have no clue. Neither does the mob. Nor the glory hound prohibition agents like Fenster Martin and his "Wrecking Crew", who are more interested in busting open beer casks for photo ops than facing down men like Rory or Finn. Yes, I'm certain of what I say. I was there when Rory left. I know where he went even if I don't understand why. And if you hear me out, and keep an open mind, you'll know too, Irwin. As a freelancer, it could be good copy for you. You'll have to omit my name. And have the nerve to print the facts. I don't really know who else to tell. Can't trust the bartender or the wife. I showed the evidence resting in my pocket to a priest. He recommended I check myself into a madhouse. But I will go mad if—

Here's the cigarette girl, Irwin. Take a packet of Old Gold. She's a good girl. Looks like someone I know. A likeness. I hate that word.

Thanks, honey.

Wait a minute, Irwin…yes, she's gone. Let me take a puff. All right…I bet you're wondering how a Harvard man like me, got involved with riffraff like Rory Seward and the mob? I have vices, Irwin, hidden from you and society, ones harmless to anyone but myself. Rory gave me a pass when the costs of those ill habits – physical, reputational, and legal – came due. I knew I owed Rory, and guessed that when he called in his favour, it'd be something a financial man like me could do for him. After all, my skills kept men solvent in '29 when others were jumping out windows. I expected the favor might be something similar: money laundering or cookin' books. Maybe, letting him use my property upstate for…whatever. Rory has many curious habits himself. With a name like Rory Seward, and birthplace of Cork, you'd expect him to be a Catholic, but he's something like the opposite. No, I don't mean Protestant.

Anyway, the request was nothing financial. Nothing expected. And the results, well…Let me have another puff on that cigarette to settle the tremor in these hands… Don't give me that patronising look, Irwin. Hear me out. I got the phone call a week ago, past ten pm on Wednesday. I was to come immediately and alone to an address in Lowell. That's all Rory said then. His voice was desperate, more broken and pleading than threatening. Nothing like the usual firebrand. Still, I didn't dare refuse. We all knew Rory's reputation. Only Finn is more feared and not by much.

The drive was tortuous. Throughout, I kept wondering if Rory meant me harm, we all know what happens when men are "sent for". But his agonised voice…I kept thinking if it was a trap, wouldn't he play it calm? Or insistent? Not panicked, not shattered…

My destination turned out to be a foreboding, dark tenement on the wrong side of the Merrimack River. Without a functioning streetlamp for blocks, I parked in the blackness of an alleyway. To my surprise, I found two expensive-looking cars gleaming under my headlamps, their metallic masses clogging that inky lane. A cherry red Buick Roadster, a new model unconnected to anyone I knew, and a silver 1930 Pierce-Arrow Model A, well-known as one of the vehicles Rory favored. Both automobiles impressed me as hiding from the world. My own Ford joined their secluded number.

The tenement entrance was open to the summer air and I climbed five floors of abandoned landings, shuffling through refuse and past silent, peeling doors. Not a human in sight. On the top level, I navigated a dark hall by flashlight until I found a door different than the others. New paint covered the panel, a lattice of iron bars reinforced the barrier, and four key bolts ensured even the best locksmith or lockpicker would have a slow and difficult entrance. On the door frame someone had scribbled in blue ink: "Do what thou wilt."

There was no bell, so I knocked between gaps in the iron. Light appeared in a peephole so small, I'd thought it only a speck in the paint. The bolts turned one by one.

The door opened a crack. A bleary eye and unshaven cheek were all I could see. But the voice I knew well.

"Are you alone, Driscoll?" asked Rory, a little calmer than he'd been on the phone.

"I am."

"Gimme the torch."

I slid the flashlight between the bars. He turned it around, using the beam to examine me, and the hallway behind. As he did, the door opened wider, and I got a better look at the man. He was wearing trousers and an undershirt, both stained with sweat. Normally exceedingly handsome – you've seen him in this speakeasy, right? Rory's the spitting image of a redheaded Rudolph Valentino but that night his face was drawn in a ghastly pallor with shadows beneath his eyes and beads of perspiration over his brow. One arm was bandaged with a torn bedsheet.

"Come on," he said, releasing the iron lattice around the door to let me in. "Better you don't ask questions."

I stepped inside, onto a floor awash in blood. My God, man... The smell alone was enough to make me dizzy. The sights repulsed, visions out of nightmares. Here and there, soaked towels and strips of bed sheet lay coiled like bloated snakes about the floor, where attempts had been made to absorb the blood. The source of the gore was a woman, mummified in a sheet, laying on the naked mattress of an iron bedframe. The wrapped head wore the thickest, darkest stain on the left side, where more balled towels and a pillow had been set in an effort to dam the wound. A crimson trail over the mattress told the path the life-blood took in seeking the floor.

I swooned and stuck a hand towards the wall to maintain balance. Instead, my palm struck something solid, cold and wrapped in its own sheet, leaning there. It was an enormous, framed picture, as high as a man and half again as long, covered completely. Its subject as anonymous as the dead woman on the bed.

But I thought only of her. And my own safety.

"Who is under that sheet...? How...?"

"I told you no questions, Driscoll," growled Rory, pulling me from the covered object to stand on my own. "We take the girl in your car. First."

"Wh...wh...where?" I stammered.

"I'll show you. And I'm drivin'."

He motioned for me to pick up the body. We hoisted it from the bed, Rory at her shoulders, me lifting the legs and took the sheeted corpse out into the hall. There Rory set the woman down, and despite the exposure of an open passage, took the time to wipe the blood from our shoes with a rag he produced from his trouser pocket. When clean, he tossed the rag into his room, shut the door and its iron grill, and locked all bolts with four separate keys on a ring – and you'll appreciate this, Irwin– which also had a rabbit's foot affixed along with more exotic talismans.

We needed the luck those totems brought. I was terrified we'd encounter some straggler from this dead tenement. Floor by floor we descended in the dark, the corpse strung between us, but we encountered no one. Not in the building, or the street, or alley. When we set her in my trunk, well, I can't call it relief, Irwin, as I was more frightened than I had ever been in my life, but there was a brief, relative calming with the body hidden from sight. A reprieve that allowed me to think for the first time since entering that blood-soaked room.

And I asked myself, why Rory chose me to assist in getting rid of a victim? Your own articles, Irwin, mention how efficiently the Irish mob deals in disposing of corpses. Rory must have numerous underlings better suited for this work than I. Even in his panic after he apparently killed the poor woman, why would I – an Ivy League banker – be the one to summon as a co-conspirator to hide the dead? Why in Heaven's name, Irwin, did he pick – or pick on – me?

This horrible question weighed on my mind nearly as much as the corpse in the trunk, while Rory drove us in a winding route east out of Lowell through Andover, past Lake Cochiche-wick and beyond into the little hamlets of northeastern Massachusetts. There was some traffic on the road despite the hour. In Georgetown, a police patrol pulled up next to us at a corner. Rory nodded politely to the officers, but it must have unnerved him. Two miles outside Rowley, he pulled over and bought a coat off a Hooverville bum. The jacket reeked, stench filling the whole car, but it covered his bandaged arm and the bloodstains he'd accrued on his undershirt and trousers.

I looked down at the crimson on my own clothes. No such disguise for me.

We passed south through Ipswich and were in the region of Essex Bay when Rory turned onto a dilapidated side road. We followed this pot-holed highway for some miles without a car in sight, until we came at last to a ruined town locked between the sea and salt marshes on the landward side.

"'Twas a bootlegging town," said Rory, as we drove through abandoned streets and past lamp-less windows, "until Fenster Martin and the government men raided her in '28. Dynamited the brewery, locked away the workers, and run off everyone else to shantytowns, the bastards. Still, this place has uses for men o' spirit." He made a sharp turn onto a rickety bridge, and I gasped feeling the structure sway under the weight and inertia of our car. By God, Irwin, I half-hoped we'd plunge through into the inlet below and terminate this nightmarish journey the only way it could. Yet, somehow the bridge held, and we exited on the other side to the usual forsaken road.

Ahead were the creeping salt marshes, on their margins a black-stone refinery with a central chimneystack stretching seventy feet or more up into the dark night. Rory pulled up to the ruined gates, turned off my car and sat quietly.

"What are we doing?" I asked after a time.

"Waitin'," he said. "Saw mist on the bay. Let's see if it drifts inland." He motioned with his thumb towards the trunk. "Better cover for gettin' rid of 'er."

"Cover? I thought this town was abandoned."

"Mostly abandoned, I reckon." He fiddled with the rearview and side mirrors, turning their panes away, angling them to see if anyone approached the car from behind. Or so I believed then.

Now, I'm not so certain.

We sat in silence, listening to strange croaking from the marshes. At last, towards three a.m. by the car clock, the sea fog spread its smoky tendrils through the town and out over the refinery grounds. I watched as the upper reaches of that chimney tower faded into the mist.

"We're goin' up that smokestack, Driscoll. Let's open the trunk."

I prayed it was a sick joke, Irwin. But God does not listen to murderers' accomplices. Those prayers went unanswered. Soon, we had that wrapped body out of the car and were carrying it though the labyrinthian interior of the refinery, climbing the dusty stairs to the roof and standing at the base of that towering chimneystack, all the while surrounded by invasive fog that made every step a gamble.

"Put 'er over your shoulder, Driscoll. I'll follow with the torch to make sure your footin' is secure. When you reach the top, throw 'er in."

I glanced at the "ladder" affixed to that chimney. The rungs were nothing more than iron staples in the concrete skin, missing in places, and even accounting for the roof's elevation, still stretched up into fog and night for some fifty feet above my head.

I found the courage to say "No."

Rory floored me with a brutal punch. Split my lip in two places. Look, see the scabs? I put Sarah's makeup on it so no one would ask me about the marks. Little good it did. I wish I could say it was merely shock that set me off my feet. That blow rattled my brain like no other, like nothing since that stallion kicked me as a child up in New Hampshire, the injury that made me what I am today, dependent on men like Rory.

By the time I rose, Rory had drawn a pistol from his trouser pocket.

"Up you go on that smokestack ladder, Driscoll! Me, Smith & Wesson all out vote you. Three-to-one. You Ivory League boys love democracy, don't you?"

I considered forcing him to shoot me. A quicker route to my inevitable destruction. But I'm a coward, Irwin. Never went to the Great War as you did, sold my place to a pauper then, unable to take a fatal stand now. Instead, I lugged the mummified woman onto my shoulder, set a foot on the first iron-staple rung, gripped two trembling hands on another rung at face level and climbed up into the swirling mists.

Rory kept the flashlight on me from the ground for the first fifteen feet or so, then pocketed his pistol and followed my climb at a distance, keeping the beam just ahead of me to aid my ascent.

No mountaineer ever had a more torturous climb, Irwin. Not above those dead marshes and the deader town, through fog and darkness, with a corpse on my shoulder and an armed gangster threatening me at every step. Once, a rusted rung came loose in my hand, and I nearly toppled backwards to my doom. It took all my will and strength to right myself and balance my precious cargo on my shoulder. A few feet higher, another rung half-dislodged, and as I climbed over it, the freed end hooked the corpse's covering. My tugging attempts to dislodge it, pulled the sheet from the woman's head and torso. She was nude beneath that cloth. The left side of her face was nothing but an unrecognisable bloody mass, but the right was clean, Irwin. Beautiful. Almost angelic in the flashlight beam. I knew her instantly.

Dymphna McMathan.

Wife of Finn McMathan.

Finn McMathan, Rory's boss. The Boss of Bosses.

And I knew then why Rory came to me, why he dared not contact any man in the mob, no matter how lowly. That he needed a *person non grata* in their criminal world to assist. But I was in it now, deep as any man, part of the conspiracy. If we were found out, what do you think Finn McMathan will do to me? No, don't answer that…Give me another puff of tobacco.

Do you remember the cigarette girl, Irwin? The likeness? She is Dymphna's younger sister. The family must be searching for Dymphna now, never knowing that a man who had a hand in fixing her grave is sitting right here. Perverse to smoke the Old Gold the sister sold us, but I need the fix…and a minute…. or two…Look at her over by the piano. Dymphna's double… I prefer my doppelgangers animate and living. Yes, I can say that with confidence. Animated. Not frozen. Like a corpse. Or a painting. Stop staring at her, Irwin. Yes, I know I said to look… I should continue while she's across the room. I don't think I could tell of…the disposal…if she approaches again even with the jazz music…

Let us resume.

When the body was exposed, Rory sped up the ladder, tore the sheet off the rung, and shoved the bundled end into the back of my trousers. Together, we reset the corpse onto my shoulder, while he assured me: "You're almost there, Driscoll. You can be a rich man or a dead man, dependin' on how you handle these next minutes. Up!"

Up I went. What choice did I have? I climbed under a mental fog thicker than the mists about me. At last, I reached the very top, standing on a rickety final rung, leaning over a dark and plunging flue, as if gazing into the maw of some sky-swallowing gargantuan worm. From this cavernous opening rose a stench like an exhumed grave. My stomach retched and eyes watered at the putrid smell. It was obvious even under my duress that other bodies were recently deposited here. Somewhere below in the darkness was a manmade bottleneck, a clogging of corpses, to keep the dead from dropping into disused furnaces where they might be discovered. The enemies of Rory Seward entombed forever in the chimney flue of an abandoned refinery in an abandoned town off a lonely bay. No investigator would dare climb these rungs and if decades hence some wrecking ball toppled this chimney there'd be little evidence left to prove anything.

I felt sickened, nearly vomiting. I slid Dymphna's body out of the sheet and into that chimney-grave, watched as the white skin and bloody face tumbled into darkness, heard a soggy impact somewhere below. A swarm of yellow flies rose up the flue to buzz about my head and bite my bleeding lips. I balled up the sheet and cast it in, then looked down to Rory, his beam shining up from just below. In the foggy glare, I could not read his expression.

All he said was "Grand. Love under will."

I believe the drive back to Lowell was by a more southerly route than we had come. I don't know. I was too stunned by my experiences to observe much of anything. All I can say for certain is no word passed between us until we parked my car again in the tenement alley. Then Rory turned to me and spoke in a slow, measured voice:

"I mean to rub out Finn soon, Driscoll. If you're smart, stay quiet and do what I say, you'll be my money ace, laundrin' for us, takin' a piece of everythin', richer than Beelzebub in his gilded palace. If you ain't smart, you'll be dead. You, Sarah, your son, even your mama up in Hampshire, we'll dump you alive all down that chimney. Let the flies have you. An' don't think you can hide. Remember what I know on you." And he listed my vices in detail. No, I won't give them to you, Irwin. Consider those omissions the price of this story. When Rory finished accounting my sins, he said: "Now, here's what we do. While I get rid of Dymphna's roadster, you're going across state lines. Some of those Pawtucket and Providence dealerships open at seven o'clock to get the 'before work' customers. You're gonna buy a van in your name. Then you're gonna buy two of the thickest mattresses you can find. Be back in Lowell before noon. I'll meet you in the apartment."

I did exactly that, Irwin. There was no thought of escape. My only detour was to stop by the house, replace my bloodied clothes with fresh attire, shave, and kiss my family while they slept. Sarah awoke. I explained a client was on suicide watch after bad investments. There'd been more drops in the market, it sounded plausible. I told her I had completed one shift but wanted-ed to go back and assist my colleague for a few hours. The man was desperate, I said, and needed the fraternity of well-wishers.

I don't think she believed me. I'm never a convincing liar. Sur-prised our marriage has lasted.

I was back at that tenement with the van by eleven o'clock that morning. Somehow the building looked worse in the light. Darkness camouflages many kinds of degradation, Irwin. The roadster was missing from the alley though Rory's Point Ar-row was present, noticeably muddier than it had been the night before.

I climbed the tenement stairs, found the apartment door, rapped between the bars. The peep hole opened, the bolts turned, the iron lattice unlocked, and Rory bid me enter. The change in man and room were equally dramatic. Rory was now dressed in a silk Italian suit, hair combed, face calm, handsome as Valentino's best day. The bedroom floor was spotless. The bloody mattress removed. All that remained from last night's horrors was the empty iron bedframe and the large, covered pic-ture against the wall.

Rory nodded towards the latter. "We're moving this. You get the van and mattresses?"

I responded affirmatively and we were soon lugging that cov-ered object down the stairs. It was impossibly heavy for a paint-ing, and though he usually called it "an heirloom" or a "picture" at least once Rory referred to the item we carried as a "mirror." He certainly acted as if it were breakable, overly cautious at every corner, and wincing when we scraped it against a hallway wall. I recall my deductions at the time, Irwin. If it was a mirror, I thought then, its glass was protected by more than just the sheet about it. An old canvas or photographic print had been added as additional padding for I could just see a still image of someone or something through the thinness of the sheet, though I could not make out what it was. Perhaps, it was a surrealist painting, for there seemed to be the trace of what looked like many limbs askew and a body or bodies at the oddest angle. On the back, through a gap in the sheets, I caught sight of a stamped auctioneer's price of two British Pounds. On this same side was also an inscription in Gaelic printed in thick, dark script and easily read through the sheet: *"Taigh Both Fhleisginn."* If only my grandfather were alive to translate, Irwin. I'm ashamed to say I knew not a word.

I know them now.

Enlightened by these clues, I deduced it a fairly common mirror or painting given its low price, sold perhaps at some British or Irish estate auction desperate to clear away inventory. Likely, it was stolen by Rory or his men when brought to this side of the Atlantic by a victimised traveller or merchant. I assumed Rory didn't wish risking any mobster connecting him to the apartment where Dymphna died and thus continued using me as an accomplice. I felt satisfied with my detective skills at the time, Irwin, but one thing puzzled me. If it was only worth two British pounds, why bother moving it all? Why not just lug it into the bin outside the tenement?

Be careful of assumptions, Irwin. They can lead you down tragic paths.

When we reached my newly purchased van, we slipped our burden between the mattresses. Rory produced a roll of cord from his jacket pocket and proceeded to bind the mattresses tightly about the sheeted frame. The effort caused him visible pain and I wondered about the extent of his arm injury from the night before.

We drove the loaded van to a warehouse in Peabody. An elderly guard helped us carry it inside. Rory motioned towards a wall at the back.

"Does he…?" asked the guard, clearly half-deaf and shouting at Rory in full volume while nodding towards me.

"Aye, he knows," replied Rory. "Knows more than a man ever should."

We set our cargo down and Rory and the guard moved aside what proved to be a false rear wall. Behind were countless kegs of whiskey and beer and an ample supply of packing lumber. Using tools we found there, we crated that framed item, mattresses and all, and placed it securely in a corner, hidden behind rows of rum barrels. Then Rory and the guard set the camouflaging wall back into position and we left the warehouse at a quarter past two in the afternoon.

I prayed my penance was served and the favors balanced but Rory insisted we have a drink at his Back Bay brownstone. I demurred, but he told me I'd lost the vote again to him, Smith and Wesson. We took the van.

In his lavish living room, decorated with rather degenerate and disgusting artwork on darkly paneled walls, Rory relayed a strange tale to me over glasses of sour.

"I'll tell you what it's all about, Driscoll," said he. "Seein' as you been waiting and can't repeat it to no one, it doesn't matter if you believe me or think I'm crazy as the proverbial loon. But it's the truth. And I'll only say it once. So, listen close…I was makin' love to the boss's wife when the mirror up an' busted. But not the way mirrors usually bust.

"Ha. I can see you don't know what to make of that, Driscoll. Let me back up a wee bit. Dymphna and I started our affair while Finn was in the stir. Fancy flings in ritzy hotels and Cape Ann inns. All was as it should be 'tween a man and woman until Finn gets out last March, and we had to go on the sly. One whisper and we was dead, but neither of us wanted to stop. A violation of 'love under will' from the Good Book. No, not your 'good book', Driscoll.

"Wantin' a private place for meeting Dymphna, I found an old tenement scheduled for destruction among the falterin' Mile o' Mills housing slums. Got the demolition pushed back 'til September, givin' us plenty o' time for trysts. The place was well outta Finn's sights, he's no rackets that side o' the Merrimack. I fixed up a room, chased off the hobos with my pistol and tapped into the 'phone line, so I could call out but no one would call in. Don't know who lived in that room before us, Driscoll, but there was a massive mirror, face resting 'gainst the wall. Yeah, the one we moved today. Didn't know where it came from or why it was left. Only clue was an inscription on the back in Gaelic. Scottish

Gaelic, not even Irish. 'Taigh Both Fhleisginn' That mean any-thing to you, Driscoll? You lose your Gaelic roots in America, you Harvard pansy? It means 'Boleskine House'. You heard of that sinister place on the shores of Loch Ness? Where the magi-cian Aleister Crowley lived? Where in his twelve-mirrored-ora-tory room that necromancer bound the dozen Kings and Dukes of Hell, one for each mirror, but fled in terror without sendin' em back. They still reside there, near twenty years later, haunting the Highlands and the dark depths of that loch. When Crowley retreated about '13, Boleskine went to seed, and the décor sold to pay his debts. On that mirror's back was written the auction price '2 £', you seen it yourself Driscoll, I saw you. A pittance for a piece of this size and quality, but fair trade if you knew where it came and maybe what comes bound along with it. An emi-grant might afford that price, think himself winnin' the bargain and take it with 'em to America. These tenements are full of Scottish workers nowadays. A ship came direct from Inverness not three years ago. I know 'cause we shook 'em down on the pier. Who knows? This mirror might 'ave been in that ship's hold while we were breakin' jaws on the deck above.

"Anyhow, whoever brought it, they left that lookin' glass for me to find. No Irishman fears anything Scottish. Dymphna and I thought it a lark. We turned that mirror around so we could watch ourselves makin' love on the bed. Best sex we ever had. Wanton. Bestial. Lust without thought. Went on ten hours that first night until our sexes were worn and bleedin', limbs spent and couldn't be raised.

"Things turned strange after that, Driscoll.

"That bestial lust wouldn't ebb. Our twice-a-week affair be-came nightly couplings into the wee hours. Even when we knew Finn was looking fer Dymphna, even when I'd a tip that Fen-ster Martin would raid three Boston speakeasies that night, we cared only for rutting before that mirror. We no longer pleased ourselves. We performed for it. Appeased the reflection. Or something behind that reflection. We weren't ourselves no more. Sometimes, Driscoll, I swear I was on the other side of that glass looking out. And it wasn't always Dymphna I was makin' love to. She thought the same sometimes. These escapades weren't enough after the first month. The mirror needed more. We lured in outsiders one-by-one, two-by-two to pleasure ourselves and our carnal doubles. Outsiders who aren't around no more, who never survived the nights. Sometimes the acts killed 'em, sometimes my knife, Dymphna was devilishly clever with a rope trick, but no one lived to tell Finn. We made sure of it. Their bodies clog that refinery chimneystack. Dymphna carried the torch while I dumped 'em in one at a time. Like you and I did last night. You smelled those old corpses, didn't you, Driscoll? When the flies came for you.

"For nearly five months those sensual rites went on before the glass, that mirror absorbing every sight and motion. Carnal. Animal. Murderous. Demonic.

"Until last night it stopped, Driscoll. We'd just finished three hours of it and were laying among the twisted sheets, sexes bleedin', lamp turned off, drinking brandy from a snifter, and wondering who'd we bait in tonight for our mirror's appeasement. Your name was raised, Driscoll. Yours and Sarah's. Would you have joined? Dymphna coveted you. No answer? No need, those days ain't comin' back.

"I'd just mentioned a fiendish way o' catchin' your wife when Dymphna gasped 'The mirror!'

"In the darkness, I could see little but the faintest outlines of two figures on that glass. I thought them prowlers for half a' second, since we lay prone on the bed and these were mostly upright. Yet, several heart beats passed, and they remained unmoving, steady as any sculpture. I slid forward to the edge of the mattress and turned on the nightstand lamp. The naked bulb illuminated the mirror's face, but there was no glare, nothing reflected now. The image was still as a painting and vivid as the finest photograph. Preserved before us were the likenesses of me and Dymphna in the act of lovemaking, our entangled bodies exposed, faces clear and visible as any portrait. A sensual position we'd submitted to only moments before.

"How can a mirror stop, Driscoll? How can it freeze like an old photographic plate? I couldn't believe my eyes. The erotic spell we'd been under dissolved. Our minds free again. The words in my ear: *'Do what thou wilt.'*

"Dymphna started screamin' hysterics. 'Finn will know! Finn will know! Get rid of it, Rory!'

"'He'll know, nothin'." I got off the bed, went over and touched the glass. It was flush, warm as human flesh, not cold as glass is. 'How can this be?' I muttered. 'Aiwass deceives!'

'Finn will murder us!' repeated Dymphna from the bed. "Destroy it!" For five months she'd been blinded by desire, uncaring of her husband's wrath. Now she trembled, a babe in the sheets.

"'*Do what thou wilt,*' echoed in my mind. Again and again.

"Finn won't lay a finger on you, Darlin'," I said, and went to my clothes, found my knife. "I'll cut it away." I scraped one pass at my own image but slipped somehow, opening a deep gash in my arm at the spot where I'd struck my frozen reflection.

"I grunted in pain, and too late warned Dymphna as she cast the snifter at the mirror. It struck her double in the temple. A wound erupted on Dymphna's head. As blood flowed from the living woman, glass fell from the mirrored likeness, the rupture expanding across the whole left side of Dymphna's face. She shrieked like a banshee and collapsed on the mattress. I dammed the wound with pillows and bed sheets, but her blood flowed through my fingers, Driscoll. And freed of spectral lust, for the first time in months I felt human emotions, love an' loss.

"*Do what thou wilt.*

"In seconds, she was dead.

"Inside the blood pools on mattress and floor were contoured pieces of floating glass. Like wee fragments of clear sculpture. Not from the mirror but as if Dymphna's face had turned to glass before breaking.

"I gazed at the identical hole in the mirror. Felt the stiffness on edges of the gash in my arm. Like me flesh crystalized. Impossible? I broke off an arm hair, thin, smooth, and clear. Snapped off a chunk of crystal flesh half-an inch long.

"I went a little mad then.

"When my mania stopped, I knew enough not to call me boys. They'd betray me to Finn or hold it over me forever. Or call me a warlock and turn me over to the despicable Church. I couldn't have any o' that. So, I called you Driscoll, an outsider who owed me favors.

"Now your fate's locked in mine, Driscoll. Made o' glass too in a way and, frankly, I don't care if you believe. Tomorrow, you're gonna take money from your bank and pay off that van, get your proper plates so no coppers harass us when we go cross country. I own a mine in West Virginia. Don't pay much. I'm shuttin' her down. We're gonna put that mirror into the belly of the Earth, five hundred feet down, seal those mine doors virgin tight and nobody's gonna disturb it ever again. I'll transfer the deed to you, so it won't come up on any government list as mine. You're the caretaker from now 'til doomsday! Startin' tomorrow, I'm gonna tell my men to come gunnin' for you, if anything *unnatural* ever happens to me, Driscoll. Excepting that unholy event, you're a rich man now. I'll repay your efforts and silence. Wealthier than your fool Cambridge chums."

I thought him mad, Irwin. Soon, I'd rescind that opinion.

It was four o'clock by then, and you know what happened in Peabody because you reported it. Took the photograph of Fenster Martin in front of that opened barrel yourself, Irwin. Rory's telephone rang and though I was sitting across a table, the guard on the other end was shouting with such hysterical volume I could hear his words.

The prohibition agents were raiding the warehouse.

The "Wrecking Crew" was through the false wall.

Government zealots swinging railroad hammers and lumber axes, opening barrels, ripping into kegs, flooding the room with lost spirits.

Fenster Martin now past the rum barrels, a fifty-pound hammer in his hands…nothing safe.

I saw the first crack then.

The second, a third. Rory's face expressionless as he went. Flat, two-dimensional…

And now do you wonder why I hate mirrors? For the love of God, Irwin! The man shattered right in front of me!

Give me the cigarette…where are you going, Irwin?

I'm not another mad heroin fiend!

A hat n' tails addict from Newbury Street?

It's the truth, I swear by almighty God!

Come back, Irwin! We were friends! Just like the priest…

I beseech you…Look at the shard in my pocket!

Meet William Burton McCormick

William Burton McCormick is an Edgar, Thriller, Shamus, Derringer, Sliver Falchion and Claymore awards finalist whose fiction regularly appears in *Ellery Queen's Mystery Magazine, Alfred Hitchcock's Mystery Magazine, The Saturday Evening Post, Black Mask, Mystery Weekly* and elsewhere.

He is a graduate of Brown University, earned an MA in Novel Writing from the University of Manchester and was elected a Hawthornden Writing Fellow in Scotland. He is a member of Mystery Writers of America, the Crime Writers Association, International Thriller Writers and the Short Mystery Fiction Society. His historical novel of the Baltic Republics, *LENIN'S HAREM*, was the first work of fiction added to the permanent library at the Latvian War Museum in Rīga.

A native of Nevada, William has lived in seven countries including Latvia, Russia, the United Kingdom and Ukraine for writing purposes. Find more on William Burton McCormick at **https://www.williamburtonmccormick.com/**

Afterword

My first contribution to an Inklings anthology was a murder mystery called Upgrade to Murder. It took an Agatha Christie style mystery and set it on a space station, adding my own sci fi spin to the proceedings. That was in our third anthology, *Tales from the Universe*.

Since then, the Inklings books have visited places far beyond this universe, to bring tales from alternate earths. Tales of wonder, magic and destiny. And tales from pirates' coves and deep underground.

Inklings Press started as a hobby project for a group of friends wanting to publish their own stories. It has become an award-winning publisher who still encourages new and upcoming writers, publishing them alongside some real names in the industry.

I'm very proud of my role at Inklings, both as contributing author, and one of our submissions editors. In more recent years I became de facto project manager for the books. I have learned a lot working with the team, and my novels (available now!) are only possible because of the things I learned here.

I'm proud of all the new writers we've given space to over the years. I truly believe we have introduced some real talent to a new audience. Thank you to every author who submitted to us. To every author who accepted my occasionally weird and pedantic developmental notes. And to every author who trusted us to get their stories out there. You are all pretty amazing people.

The Tales of Mystery duology will be my last Inklings Press work, at least as project manager. I want to thank Ricardo, Brent and Stephen for welcoming me to the team, and tolerating me sending them messages to chase up edits and covers and stories.

You can find my story, "The Mystery of the Angry Knife", in this book's sister anthology, *Dead for a Spell*. It is, in an effort to square the circle, an Agatha Christie style mystery, adding my own fantasy spin to the proceedings.

All that remains is for me to say one final thank you. To you. Thanks for reading. You're pretty amazing people too.

Cheers,
Rob Edwards
Finland, March 2024.

How to contact Inklings Press
Twitter: @InklingsPress
Facebook: Facebook.com/InklingsPress
Visit our website: www.inklingspress.com
Email: theinklingspress@gmail.com